NIGHT OF THE LETTER

(Former title—Darling Clementine)

The moon shone on Brigit's face. She had been awake. She had scarcely slept at all. The house was silent. There was nothing to keep her wakeful. Yet she remained intensely wakeful, and deep inside her a cold fear was stirring. And it was not now fear about her physical condition, but another fear, unnamed and unexplainable, like a ghostly finger on her shoulder . . .

'Nothing will happen while I'm away,' Fergus had said.

Also by the same author

The Marriage Chest
Sleep in the Woods
Samantha
Whistle for the Crows
Bella
Cat's Prey
The Voice of the Dolls
Never Call it Loving
Winterwood
Bird in the Chimney
The Vines of Yarrabee
Siege in the Sun
Afternoon for Lizards
The Shadow Wife
Waiting for Willa
Melbury Square
The Deadly Travellers
The Sleeping Bride

and available in Coronet Books

Night of the Letter

(Former title—Darling Clementine)

Dorothy Eden

CORONET BOOKS
Hodder Paperbacks Ltd., London

First published 1955
Penguin Books edition 1959
Coronet edition 1968
Second impression 1969
Third impression 1972

Printed in Great Britain
for Coronet Books, Hodder Paperbacks Ltd.,
St. Paul's House, Warwick Lane, London, E.C.4
by Richard Clay (The Chaucer Press), Ltd.,
Bungay, Suffolk.

ISBN 0 340 02925 0

ONE

In that forlorn time between late night and early morning Brigit awoke. She could see the illuminated face of her bedside clock with its faint glow-worm light. It said a quarter past three.

Three hours till daylight. Now she would not sleep again. Three hours in which to think. She turned her head restlessly and moonlight caught her in the eyes. The great white staring moon was hanging in the branches of the mulberry tree outside the window.

The tree was dead. Although its trunk had been stiffened with cement to stop its splitting and falling all but one of its branches had withered and died, and now it stood there against the sky, crooked and witchlike, hugging the moon in its bony arms.

Couldn't they have put her in a room with a view of a living green tree? Brigit wondered in sudden lonely anger. Or if she must have this room because it was large and sunny couldn't they have thought to cut that lunatic tree down and left her only the uncomplicated sky? She knew that Captain Phillip Templar had planted the tree two hundred and fifty years ago, with the thought of cultivating silkworms as a hobby—he needed a hobby from his buccaneering on the high seas, a nice peaceful hobby that did harm to no one but the mulberry leaves—and that the tree had subsequently become as much an heirloom as the gold plate and the Chinese ivories and the family portraits. Because of this, even dead, the tree would stand there, marring the view, curiously evil in its twisted death, as if it had caught some of the evil of the Templar family.

No, no, that was a sick unbalanced thought. The family was not evil now. That particular type of badness had died with Captain Phillip. From generation to generation they had grown more respectable. They had amassed money and respectability in equal quantities. Finally, great-grandfather Andrew had been decorated by Queen Victoria and with that royal gesture the family had arrived. All its inherited vice and cruelty now ran deeply and was glimpsed only by the sharp-eyed or the unfortunate.

Even Fergus agreed that her family was highly respectable. He said he adored Uncle Saunders with his quaint elderly jokes, and that Aunt Annabel was a poppet. And of course Guy, being Brigit's brother, was above reproach.

But Brigit knew what Fergus really thought. He despised them all, Uncle Saunders for his miserliness, Aunt Annabel because she was a silly old lady who let her husband bully her, and Guy because he was weak. How then could he love her, she whose veins were full of Templar blood?

Especially now . . .

Brigit flung her head away from the cruelly staring moon. A stab of pain went through her. Life—was it life? She moved her legs and watched intently the moon-blanched coverlet of the bed. The two mounds that were her feet stayed motionless. Tears filled her eyes. She was so sure that she had moved. But they said one still felt one's legs even when they had been amputated. Hers, useless as they were, at least remained attached to her body. Her physical condition was improving. With that back to normal this curious paralysis would leave her. It was merely a matter of shock to the nerve centres. Such a thing sometimes took time to mend. The important thing was not to worry.

No one else was worrying. Fergus certainly wasn't. Neither were the children. They were as happy as sandboys with Prissie, who was a treasure. Aunt Annabel and Uncle Saunders were not worrying either. They liked company, even if it was a sick woman and a couple of children. The house had been gloomy lately with only Aunt Annabel's everlasting cats. And Nurse Ellen was not worrying. She was expecting daily that Brigit, like the young man in the Bible, would take up her bed and walk. It was almost a game with her.

'And how many tootsies will wiggle this morning? Not one of them? Well, we'll have to try playing "This little pig went to market". Never mind, ducky, wait till tomorrow.'

Brigit didn't really mind being called ducky and talked to like a child. It was only for such a short time. They all kept telling her so.

'Darling, darling Brigit, I love your silly legs.' That was the memory of Fergus's voice in her ears. 'I always knew they had a will of their own and one day they would say they were having a rest. Which is not surprising, the way you've run them up and downstairs and over hill and dale. Let them have their rest. We won't fuss about them.' And then Fergus's kiss first gently dried the tears in her eyes and then lingered on her mouth. 'Nor the baby either,' he whispered.

But remembering that made the tears come back. Not because Fergus was being so heart-breakingly kind and sweet, but because the old nagging doubts were in her mind. He hadn't really wanted the baby, he hadn't really wanted Nicky and Sarah, but when they had come he had been as sweet about them as he was now about her silly useless legs.

Perhaps it was a good thing about the baby. Because she, too, secretly hadn't wanted it...

Brigit moved her head again restlessly. The pillow had got clotted into uncomfortable bumps beneath her neck. She tried to straighten it, but her efforts only made it worse. The clock, with its glow-worm light, showed only half past three. The night and that moon caught like a blazing moth in the spider-web of the tree were going on for ever. For ever ... For ever ... The clock with its small busy tick was laughing at her, gaily tripping over itself with laughter.

'You'll lie there for ever ... you'll never walk again ...'

With the moon and the dead tree and the blanched sky watching her ... She would gradually rot away until she was as thin and dry and twisted as the mulberry boughs that once had borne delicious fruit. Fruit for Fergus, who loved to hold her, burying his face in her shoulder, stroking her with a hand that trembled...

'You'll never walk again . . .'

That wasn't the tick of the clock, or her own mind seeming to speak aloud. Those words were actually being spoken in a hoarse secret voice that came from the direction of the fireplace.

Brigit turned her head sharply. There was a curious sibilant noise in the room. Someone was breathing deeply and heavily.

'You'll never walk . . .'

Frantically, on the half-finished sentence, Brigit felt for the bell on the night table and rang it. She kept her finger on it long after the clangor had filled the room.

A bundly shape in the corner moved and sprang to life. A light went on. Nurse Ellen, blinking and full of alarm, rushed to the bedside.

'I fell asleep. What's the matter, Mrs Gaye? Are you feeling sick?'

Brigit, breathless and weak, sank back in the pillows. The sibilant noise had been Nurse Ellen snoring. She had forgotten that Nurse Ellen sat up with her. Fergus had insisted on that although the need for a night nurse was past. Perhaps because he thought she would be lonely for his arms. Oh God, she was. So lonely . . .

Still, she mustn't get neurotic, too, waking Nurse Ellen up because the poor girl snored.

But the voice, the cruel insistent words . . .

'Nurse, look in the passage quickly. I heard something.'

'Of course you did. This house is full of sounds. I never heard such a noisy house in my life.' Nurse Ellen went to the door and peered out. 'No one here,' she said. She switched on a light. 'Unless it's one of Mrs Hatchett's ghosts, and that wouldn't make a noise, or so I'm told, ghosts losing their speaking faculties with their clothes. What was it you heard, dear?'

'A—sort of voice,' Brigit said, half ashamedly.

'I think you were having a bad dream, ducky. What about a nice cup of tea to put you off to sleep again. Oh, there it is, the thing you heard.'

Brigit's head shot up.

'One of those damn cats,' Nurse Ellen said cheerfully. 'Begging your pardon, Mrs Gaye. You probably heard it miauling. One thing I can't stand in the dead of night is a cat miauling. Well, there are all sorts of places, aren't there? But I must say I've never been in one with cats and ghosts quite so plentiful.'

'And voices,' thought Brigit silently. But she said no more. What she had heard had not been one of Aunt Annabel's cats.

But had she heard anything? Had it not been just in her own mind? Her subconscious growing voluble, speaking the fear that her tongue dared not.

'You'll never walk again . . .'

Oh, Nicky, oh, Sarah, oh, Fergus, Fergus, darling . . .

'No wonder you woke up,' said Nurse Ellen, 'with that piece of gold plate staring you in the face.'

Gold plate . . . That was what Captain Phillip Templar had brought home from the Spanish main . . .

It was almost the first thing Fergus had noticed when she had brought him to the house in Montpelier Square. He had whispered, 'Do you actually eat off it?' and she had begun to giggle, so that she could scarcely perform the introductions with decorum.

From the first Fergus and her family had disliked one another, she knew that. Although Fergus was sweet to Aunt Annabel, who was being deliberately vague and slightly idiot as only Aunt Annabel could be, polite to Uncle Saunders, who plainly showed his disapproval of Brigit's choice and made loud challenging comments about the manner in which Brigit was accustomed to being kept, and even creditably decent to Guy who at that time was going through a revolting stage of insolent superiority, he had had difficulty at first in concealing his dismay at the prospect of her family.

'Now why, with all that money of their own,' he had said afterwards, 'should they expect you to marry money?' Fergus himself was the son of a hard-working, honest, highly intelligent but poor country solicitor. His family could boast of little but their integrity, their sense of humour, and their appreciation of pleasant things. It was not the sort of background that would impress a Templar, and when Brigit, meeting Fergus at an Air Force ball, began to grow more than a little interested in him, Uncle Saunders had made no secret of his disapproval and disappointment.

Brigit had tried to answer Fergus's question honestly and fairly.

'They have been used to it for so long. They've got into the habit of thinking it's one of the major virtues.'

'It isn't, you know.'

'I do know. And I haven't got any, darling. Guy and I have been completely dependent on Uncle Saunders since our parents were killed in an air crash. My mother was disinherited when she married.'

Fergus had suddenly looked hopeful.

'I hope the same will happen to you.'

'Oh, so do I. I hate the Templar money. It was stolen to begin with, and it's gone on being amassed in horrid ways.'

'Has it got blood on it?' Fergus inquired interestedly.

'Yes, it has! Fergus, I hate my family. It's an awful thing to say, but even my mother never got over being disinherited. She was bitter and arrogant and made life quite impossible for Daddy. Sometimes she wouldn't speak for days. We were all afraid of her. Oh, darling, I'm so glad you haven't got any money.'

'Enough for a cottage in the country and a new dress for my wife every Christmas.'

Brigit was crying a little for happiness.

'Fergus, are you sure you still want to marry me, now you've met my family?'

'Curse of the Templars and all,' he said cheerfully. 'Try to stop me.'

Later, much later, when the elaborate wedding was over, the cottage, picturesque and charming, had materialized, also a daily help, a dog, and a cat, Brigit said to Fergus:

'Great-great-great-great-grandfather Phillip murdered and plundered for his wealth. He was a pirate, so that it made it more or less lawful. Great-great-great-grandfather

Thomas was a slave trader and enjoyed it. Great-great-grandfather Silas was more respectable. He merely starved his employees and killed his wife by subtle cruelty. Great-grandfather Andrew was decorated by Queen Victoria for his contribution to industry. He was the most notorious exploiter of child labour in England. Grandfather Ernest was a spendthrift and a bad loser. He cheated at cards and had so many shameful affairs with women that he became a social outcast. Even he couldn't quite run through the family fortune, but he was very glad to have the opportunity of disinheriting my mother when she married my father. It saved him a marriage settlement. During all my childhood I listened to her hating him and planning to get even with him. I was frightened of my mother. She was so bitter and unforgiving. Can you imagine that, Fergus? Being frightened of one's own mother?'

It was late at night and they were in the pleasant bedroom with its sloping timbered ceiling and daffodil printed chintzes. Moonlight was shining softly on the window and an owl was calling with a drowsy country sound.

Fergus's arm tightened round Brigit.

'And what, may I ask, is this song of hate in aid of?'

'Fergus, we're going to have a baby.'

The bleakness of her voice must have startled him, for his arm went tighter still, hurting her, and not taking time to express surprise and pleasure at her news he said almost angrily:

'It will be our baby, won't it?'

'Fergus—I have the Templar blood, the blood of robbers and murderers and child exploiters and misers and——'

His fingers on her lips stopped her desolate recital. He switched on the bedside light and then flung back the blankets and looked at her gravely and appraisingly.

'You're clean and sweet and lovely,' he said. 'You make me think of apple blossom, or a rose just before it opens, tender and full of fragrance. I want to hold you and smell you and stroke you and listen to you laughing, and have you for ever.'

All the familiar laughter was gone from his eyes. They

were full of gravity and tenderness such as she hadn't before been aware of.

'It will be our baby,' he said. 'The start of a new line, a new dynasty if you like, but ours, the Gaye dynasty.'

He kissed her long and deeply. Then the laughter was dancing in his eyes again and he was saying:

'Just forget that blood-and-thunder stuff, will you? I'm sorry to be so lacking in melodrama, but honestly your ancestors were probably painted larger than life. Uncle Saunders is absolutely harmless—I think he stores nuts for the winter like a squirrel. Anyway, our baby will probably have wings. And did I say,' he went on, leaping up, 'how clever we are, anyway! This calls for a celebration.'

So they sipped champagne in the pale moonlight and then Brigit, dissolving in laughter, made Fergus hide the bottle so that Mrs Smythe, the daily help, wouldn't find it in the bedroom in the morning. And the owl went on calling, and a plane on a night flight droned overhead, and Brigit thought of Fergus leaving early in the morning because he, too, flew planes, and now her arms tightened round him and Nicky was forgotten ... Nicky who was born seven months later without wings, but fair and sweet and innocent and even more like Fergus than Brigit had dared to hope.

She almost lost her apprehension before Sarah's birth three years later. How could she keep it when Fergus reduced her terrible ancestors to mere comic opera villains by thumbing his nose at all the portraits on the stairs in the big house in Montpelier Square, and treating Aunt Annabel and Uncle Saunders in a careless friendly way as if they were a stuffy but harmless old couple. Guy, the budding stockbroker, who looked as if he might have the Templar cold, almost inhuman ruthlessness, Fergus looked on as a slightly irritating and silly younger brother.

When Sarah, too, was fair, sweet, and innocent it looked as if the dominating Templar characteristics might really have been subdued at last.

The third baby, Brigit had almost looked forward to with a timorous pleasure.

But that was so short a time ago. It might have been a dream from which she would still awake.

She had been so happy that day. It was her birthday and they were having a party. It had to start without Fergus who was at present a pilot on the London to Rome flight, and would not be home until late in the afternoon. But everyone else was there, Aunt Annabel and Uncle Saunders, Guy down early from the city, and some small friends of Nicky's and Sarah's.

Watching the children tumbling on the lawn Brigit thought the garden had never looked more delightful. The peaches were ripening along the high brick wall, the roses had made a wonderful show and were going to linger late into the autumn, the heavy scent of carnations filled the warm air. Soon there would be another baby to sleep under the umbrella of the weeping elm. She would tell Fergus tonight. He would be pleased. She knew he would. He would say, 'Long live the Gaye dynasty!' and then hold her in his arms and she would try not to fall asleep the whole night long, because it would be so delicious curled up in Fergus's arms listening to the owls, and watching the friendly moon.

The thought made her so happy that she even smiled with complete affection at Uncle Saunders who was making no secret of his boredom at a day in the country, and obviously itched to get back to town to his mysterious lists of figures and his stock-market reports. She even ignored Guy's too frequent trips into the house from which he emerged slightly flushed, and smelling a little more each time of whisky.

Guy was drinking too much and his eyes had an evasive look. He didn't talk to her about anything that mattered, but Guy always had been secretive. He had used to hide his toys so no one else could play with them. Since her marriage to Fergus, Brigit had been able to look on Guy's idiosyncrasies as slightly comic, and not to be interpreted as major diseases, as she had once thought them. A good wife, Fergus had said easily, was all the boy needed.

Brigit wondered if it was her six years away from the

house in Montpelier Square that made her relatives seem to her a little more queer each time she saw them. Aunt Annabel, for instance, had lately become wrapped up in a society dedicated to the welfare of animals and was filling the house with cats. She was beginning to look rather like an untidy Persian herself, Brigit thought, with her mass of coarse smoke-grey hair that defied pins, her peculiarly coloured pale-green eyes, and her habit of wearing a somewhat draggled fur cape draped crookedly over her shoulders. Once she had been a beauty. What had Uncle Saunders, with his immense preoccupation with money, done to her to make her this dowdy vague obsessed person, old before her time?

'Brigit dear,' she was saying now, 'you really work too hard. Fergus should get you more help.'

'We can't really afford it,' Brigit answered cheerfully.

'Then you must ask Saunders for money. Goodness knows he has plenty. Though really he has been behaving in the oddest way lately. He hides the housekeeping money. Each week I have to look for it.'

'Hides it!'

'It's just his idea of a little joke. One has to be amused, of course. It's only fair. And besides he does show ingenuity. One week he will choose an easy place, and the next it will be so difficult that Mrs Hatchett and I have to spend the entire morning searching.'

'And what happens if you can't find it?' Brigit asked, fascinated.

'That's the game, of course. Then I forfeit it.'

'You mean he doesn't give it to you that week?'

'No, I have to make do,' Aunt Annabel said serenely. 'Saunders said we had to cut down expenses and this is his way of doing it. He always liked little jokes, you know.'

Brigit looked at the grey head and high red forehead of Uncle Saunders behind *The Times*. She remembered when she was a child that Uncle Saunders had had odd skittish occasions that she had found obscurely frightening, but she had thought that he must long ago have outgrown them.

'Don't you find it awfully irritating?'

'Actually I do,' Aunt Annabel confided, in a whisper, giving a quick nervous glance towards her husband. 'But I have to pretend I enjoy it as much as he does, otherwise I doubt if he'd give me any money at all. And really, I find it awfully hard as it is to run that big house with only Mrs Hatchett and Lorna.' She clasped her hands in her lap. 'It's just his peculiar sense of humour. I remember one night on our honeymoon there was a frog in the bed. He swore he knew nothing about it, but he must have, of course.'

'Aunt Annabel! That wasn't a joke!'

'Well, no. I sometimes wondered if it was meant to be something more subtle.' Again her eyes flicked towards her husband. 'It's a pity we never had children. I think he always blamed me.'

But coldness, or whatever cruel suggestion Uncle Saunders had been making, had nothing to do with not having children, Brigit thought, suddenly filled with pity for the aunt who had given her a home and mothered her in a detached ineffectual way. She had always been too preoccupied with her committees and social occasions to bother much about two orphaned children. But perhaps she had been seeking her way of escape, too. Of recent years she had given up her social life because Uncle Saunders, with his growing miserliness, had said it cost too much, and now her refuge was animals. One didn't need to wear model gowns to impress a stray cat, she said mildly.

She really looked much sweeter as an untidy old cat, Brigit decided, than as a wealthy philanthropist opening a hospital.

Guy broke into her thoughts.

'What did Fergus give you for your birthday?' he asked. Guy was good-looking in a thin rather boneless way. He had the black Templar brows, prominent cheek-bones, and a beautiful sensuous mouth. His chin was perhaps a little indefinite, and there was something in his eyes, an evasiveness, a coldness, that disturbed Brigit. Because she was older than he and had always mothered him, Brigit felt a deep bond between herself and her brother. But sometimes she felt that she didn't know him at all. This fact disturbed her and made her feel curiously guilty, as if she had failed him in some way. If she had not failed him he would surely have been less secretive.

'Fergus hasn't give me anything yet,' she said lightly, in answer to Guy's question. 'After all, I haven't seen him today. He'll be here soon.' All her happiness, forgotten for a moment in her vague uneasiness about Guy, came flooding back. She laughed at herself for her girlish silliness. Why should she be so excited because Fergus, whom she had seen only yesterday, would shortly climb out of his shabby red sports car at the gate, and come striding in to join the party. Was it natural to be so much in love with one's husband after six years of marriage?

Natural or not, Brigit told herself, it was the most utterly lovely thing in the world. She wanted to hold for ever this sunny day with the flowers blooming and the children's voices and the shadow like a shawl under the weeping elm where the new baby would sleep, and the sense of delicious anticipation that filled her. Soon Fergus would be here . . .

'I'm sorry I couldn't give you a larger present, my dear,' Uncle Saunders boomed from behind *The Times*.

'But, Uncle, you gave me a hundred pounds. That's a tremendous present.' It was, too, to her. She was going to put it in the bank for the new baby.

'Only a trifle,' said Uncle Saunders. 'But money's difficult now. I have to be careful. Your aunt knows that.'

Aunt Annabel gave a deep purring chuckle.

'So ingenious, dear. In the coffee pot this morning. It was the Sèvres set. We might never have found it, but Mrs Hatchett was careless enough to break the pot we normally use, and we had to use the Sèvres. And there was the housekeeping money. Such a joke!'

Uncle Saunders scowled, as if he were disappointed, then reluctantly gave his great bark of laughter because he always laughed at his own jokes. Would he truly have taken back the money and made Aunt Annabel scrape through the week on almost nothing? Brigit had a fantastic vision of him sitting up late at night in a dark room in the basement with a bag of sovereigns, a sprawling Nero counting and gloating. Was he perhaps a little mad?

Aunt Annabel had forgotten the subject of money, and was back on her present obsession, her cats.

'No one really likes them except me,' she confided, 'so I have to give them extra affection. I've taken the furniture out of the studio so they can use it to scamper about as much as they please. We have a committee meeting once a month.'

'You and the cats?' Brigit said bewilderedly.

'No, dear, the society members and I. We report all the animals we have helped to save during the month, and really you'd be surprised——'

Brigit had an absurd vision of alley cats crouching primly over Moody and Sankey hymn books, and longed for Fergus with whom to share the joke. Fortunately Nicky, tugging at her skirt, saved her from laughing outright at Aunt Annabel's amiable nonsense.

'Mummy, when will daddy be home?'

'Soon, darling.'

'Mummy, will you like his present better than mine and Sarah's?'

Nicky's and Sarah's gift, carefully chosen in the village with the assistance of Mrs Smythe, had been a gilt brooch set with tiny blue stones in the shape of forget-me-nots. Brigit was wearing it now.

'I shouldn't think so, darling. It would have to be very beautiful if I did.'

'You're still crazy about Fergus, aren't you?' came Guy's drawling voice. 'What are you going to do if he falls in love with another woman?'

'Give him his freedom, I expect,' Brigit answered lightheartedly. She was completely unable to take his question seriously.

'Mummy, mummy!' Nicky shouted. 'Here's daddy now!'

'Daddy coming!' echoed baby Sarah, making her slow sure progress on her fat legs towards the gate.

The other children, six of them of varying ages, followed, and when the dusty red car drew up and Fergus leaped out, he was surrounded with children. So that at first Brigit thought he was unaccompanied.

It was only when he had cleared the children, like lapping waves about him, away, that Brigit saw the small dark girl standing beside him.

She was a complete stranger.

Fergus took her hand and brought her towards Brigit. She came meekly, like a child.

'My birthday present for you, darling,' he said gaily. 'This is Prissie.'

TWO

HER name was Priscilla Hawke. It was not until later that Brigit saw that she was much more than a child. Her hair, which was dark and straight, she wore cut short, with a brief fringe that shortened the height of her forehead, and balanced her face. It was a small face, quite colourless, and slightly hollow-cheeked. The dark brows over the wide eager eyes were slanted slightly, giving the girl an elfin look. Her figure was elfin, too. She looked like a twelve-year-old until one perceived the maturity in her face. That only leapt out at odd moments, rather disturbingly. Most of the time Prissie was smiling in that eager-little-girl manner that Fergus clearly found enchanting.

'She's an air hostess turned mother's help,' Fergus explained. 'She wants a job with a pleasant family, so I've brought her down to see you.'

Fergus, towering over the girl, was obviously very pleased with himself. Brigit's first qualm of distrust (was it distrust?) vanished, and she smiled welcomingly at Prissie.

'But how sweet of you to want to come to us. Are you sure you want to be a mother's help after flying? I thought being an air hostess was such a glamorous job.'

Prissie wrinkled her miniature nose. 'Not so glamorous, if you get air-sick when it's bumpy. I thought I'd get over that, but I haven't. And really what I love most is children. Which are yours, Mrs Gaye?'

Brigit called to Nicky.

'Come here, darling. Bring Sarah.' As Nicky came, dragging the unwilling Sarah who had decided to swing on the gate, Prissie went down on her knees to them. 'These two? These little blonds? But how adorable!' She ruffled their heads and smiled engagingly at them. Sarah, plump and placid, gave her a wide friendly smile in return. Nicky, shyer and more wary, drew back a little, staring.

'Say hullo to Prissie, Nick,' said Fergus. 'She may be looking after you from now on.'

'I know millions of stories,' said Prissie. 'Simply millions.'

Nicky stared, considering.

Brigit thought to herself that she was the same as her small son—considering. Who was this dark-haired dark-eyed girl who had been presented like a whirlwind to them? Why had Fergus decided to bring her here without one word to her first? And anyway could they afford her—nice as it would be to have a pleasant person in the house, with Fergus away so much and a new baby coming.

Fergus didn't know yet about the baby... So it wasn't that that had made him decide Brigit needed help.

'I'll take over the children right away, Mrs Gaye,' the girl was saying. 'You have your husband just home.' Her hands were drawing the children away. She was giving that wide irresistible smile.

'But you!' Brigit protested. 'You've just arrived. You'll want to wash and see your room——'

Which was Prissie's room? Why had she suddenly said so surely that there was actually a room for her?

Fergus's arm was round her waist. 'Prissie will be all right. She's used to finding her way about. I haven't spoken to your family, nor you.' His eyes rested on her. He bent his head to kiss her and his lips lingered. 'Happy birthday, my darling.'

There were too many people watching, Brigit thought. But she didn't care. Fergus was her husband and she had been waiting all day for him. She returned his kiss warmly, then turned to take him over to Aunt Annabel and Uncle Saunders.

Aunt Annabel promptly said, 'Who's that child you brought, Fergus? Is she one of the neighbour's children?'

Brigit looked towards the dark-haired girl who already had the children in an absorbed group about her.

'She's not a child, Aunt Annabel. She's what you said I needed, a mother's help. Fergus has given me a surprise.'

Uncle Saunders's head was turned and he was watching Prissie with interest. When he turned back his pale eyes had the protuberant sly suggestive look that attractive young women always aroused in him.

'Can you afford this, Fergus? Servants cost the devil of a lot these days.'

'Yes, darling, I've just been telling Aunt Annabel we couldn't afford any more help,' said Brigit.

'Brigit is alone too much,' Fergus answered. 'I've meant to do this for a long time. If Brigit likes Prissie, certainly we can afford it. But if she'd rather,' his mischievous smile flashed out, 'she can have some diamond ear-rings.'

Guy's eyes followed Prissie and rested on her with interest.

'But why this girl, Fergus?' Was his voice more pointed than it need have been? Was he suggesting that Fergus need not have selected such an oddly attractive girl? But where Uncle Saunders was openly joyously bawdy, Guy made those not quite pleasant remarks with underlying meanings. It was just a habit he had, Brigit told herself, a defence against the world which had always frightened him a little. As an older sister she knew a great deal more about her brother than he suspected.

'Yes, why so suddenly?' Aunt Annabel inquired. 'Shouldn't Brigit have interviewed her in the usual way? This is so out of order. And she looks far too young.'

'Why should one run one's life like a committee meeting?' Fergus asked good-naturedly. 'Brigit and I always like the same people. Anyway, it was to be a surprise. Prissie understands that she's here on approval. She's quite happy about the idea.'

He looked baffled for a moment and Fergus baffled was endearingly young himself. He had thought this would be such a unique and wonderful present. She couldn't disappoint him even if she was, obscurely, not quite happy about Prissie's so sudden advent. She put her hand in his.

'Prissie is my birthday present, Aunt Annabel. I think she's going to be a priceless one. Think of all the spare time I will have at last. I can really do things with the garden. Oh, and——' She stopped suddenly, remembering that the baby was still a secret. It would be so wonderful to have help now that there was going to be a new baby. Fergus must have had an intuition. Suddenly she couldn't wait any longer to tell him. She tugged at his hand.

'Darling, come inside and help me with drinks.'

'Guy will help,' said Aunt Annabel. 'I want Fergus to talk to me. He never has time. Always rushing off to catch a plane. And he might know what to do for fur falling out.'

'Fur!' Fergus echoed.

'Cat's fur, dear. My latest find, that poor sweet marmalade——'

Brigit firmly pulled her husband away.

'I want Fergus, Aunt Annabel. He mixes a better martini than Guy.'

'Can they afford martinis as well as mother's helps?' Uncle Saunders's voice boomed after them as they went hand in hand across the lawn.

'Mummy, Prissie is teaching us a new game,' Nicky shouted.

So he was being friendly with Prissie, Brigit thought. That was a good thing, because Nicky could be difficult. There had been a baby-sitter with whom he had behaved very badly. It would have been a pity if he had behaved badly with Prissie because one could see at once that she was going to be an absolute treasure.

'Well,' said Fergus in the hall. He knew she wanted to tell him something. His thick fair eyebrows were raised, his eyes quizzical.

Brigit said breathlessly, 'Darling, we're going to have another baby,' and then went into his arms and cried.

His hands stroked her hair. 'Biddy, that's wonderful. But why the tears?'

'B-because it's my b-birthday, and I'm only t-twenty-eight. By the time I'm sixty—I won't be able to b-bear it—I get happier every year——'

'So do I,' said Fergus simply, and kissed her, not lightly in deference to the people watching, but deeply and completely. There was sunlight in the hall, and a smell of potpourri. A massed bowl of dahlias that she had grown herself stood on the table beside her. The house was beautiful, and her own, and she was so happy it was true that she could scarcely bear it.

A slight sound made her stir in Fergus's arms. She turned her head and saw Prissie in the doorway, hesitating as if she had just come—or as if she had watched for long enough . . .

Had she been watching? And should one mind?

Without giving herself time to ponder Brigit moved decisively out of Fergus's arms.

'Prissie! Do come in! I'm being an awfully bad hostess. You'd think Fergus and I had been separated for years. We're always crazy like this, I'm afraid.'

Prissie's lashes hid her eyes.

'I'm sorry. I just wondered if I could help with anything.'

'You can, but not until you've had tea. Come and I'll show you your room. We'll have a talk later on.' Suddenly, because she had a sensitive impression that Prissie felt shut out and lonely, and because she was always kind, she went on impulsively, 'We are being a little extra foolish today because I've just been telling my husband that we're going to have another baby. I hope that that won't frighten you away.'

Fergus grinned broadly at the girl in the doorway.

'Of course it won't frighten her away. She likes babies, otherwise she wouldn't be here. Isn't that so, Prissie?'

The girl lifted her heavy lashes and looked straight at them. Her gaze was wide and full of that attractive eagerness.

'It seems like fate I came, doesn't it?'

Later Fergus told Brigit the story of how he had come to bring Prissie home. She had been flying with him for a month, he said, but he had not realized before yesterday the strain each trip was on her. They had encountered storms half an hour out of Rome, and just before circling to land the plane had been struck by lightning. There had been no damage done, but everyone had got a fright and one or two of the passengers had been panicky. Prissie had done her job efficiently, and it was not until they had landed and everyone had disembarked that she had collapsed. Fergus had found her white and trembling and virtually unable to leave the plane unassisted.

She had been very ashamed of herself, and confessed that she had never been able to get over her tendency to be both air-sick and scared to death. She was afraid she would lose her job if anyone found out. Anyway, she didn't care much. She had stuck to the job because the aunt who had brought her up was so proud of her and liked to boast about her and show her off when she came home in uniform, but what she really wanted was a quiet place in the country, perhaps looking after children. She adored children, and looking after air-sick adults didn't really compensate. She had made a face, wrinkling her absurd nose, and in that moment Fergus had known that she belonged to them. She was Nicky's and Sarah's, and Brigit's and the new baby's—only he hadn't known about the new baby then . . .

'And yours?' Brigit asked, smiling teasingly.

'And mine,' Fergus agreed. 'She's a cute little thing, and she's going to be invaluable in assisting with the Gaye dynasty.'

'Anyone who assists with that,' said Brigit, 'will be welcome in this house. But seriously, she is sweet. Even Aunt Annabel thinks so. Just think, a thunderstorm and out of it a soft little thing like Prissie. It must really be fate.'

THREE

BEFORE Prissie unpacked the single bag she had brought she took out a writing pad and began quickly to write a letter.

> I got the job, so I won't be home for a few days. If I stay here it means I'll be stuck in the country but I'll arrange about week-ends. They like me, so I'll soon be able to ask favours. The house isn't my idea of comfort, those low doorways where you're always cracking your head, and stairs like corkscrews. The family's town house is the one I want to see. Later, perhaps. Or not perhaps. You know me. But her family! They're shockers. Not her herself, she's like any other girl, as you would expect. Crazy about her husband, but you can hardly blame her considering what he looks like. By the way, don't write to me here. I'll let you know in a few days whether I intend to stay or not——

Someone was coming up the stairs. Prissie hastily slipped the letter inside her writing pad and closed it.

When Brigit came into the room she was taking clothes out of her suitcase and shaking them out. She turned with her glowing smile and said, 'Did you want me for something, madam?'

'Prissie, don't call me madam. If you stay here we must be friends.' Brigit didn't know why she suddenly had the impulse to speak in that manner, except that Prissie looked so small and somehow defenceless. Not very much bigger than Nicky. Was that how Fergus thought of her—as someone to be protected?

'But, tell me, are you sure you want to stay here? It's very quiet. Fergus is away a great deal and there's only me and the children. After your interesting life——'

'Interesting!' Prissie broke in. 'When I could never get over being scared. I can tell you, this will be heaven.'

Brigit sat on the low bedside chair. This was her second guest-room but she was quite glad for Prissie to have it.

The girl seemed to fit in here, with her quick grace and her neatness. Almost as if the rose-patterned chintz and the warm red rugs had been chosen for her.

For a single moment Brigit had a queer feeling of timelessness, as if, when she had furnished this room, she had known Prissie would occupy it, as if Prissie had always been in her mind . . . But why?

It must be her condition, she told herself, shaking herself out of her momentarily fey mood. For the first two or three months of pregnancy she was always in this dreamy otherworldish state.

'Have you given notice?'

'Yes, I did when I got back today. I was due for leave, anyway, so I just said I wouldn't be back.' She sat on the floor in front of Brigit and sighed. 'Oh, if you knew how happy I feel!'

Brigit smiled involuntarily. 'Do you like your room?'

'It's heaven. These lovely chintzes. And silk sheets, really silk. I looked,' she said naïvely.

'Oh, those were a wedding present. When they're worn out there won't be any more.'

'Why not?' Prissie asked, fingering the monogram on the corner of the sheet.

'Because my husband and I can't afford luxuries like that.'

'But your family——'

Brigit eyed her coolly.

'What do you know about my family?'

'Oh, everyone's heard of the Templars.'

'Yes. Unfortunately.' Brigit looked at the girl again, and decided that she had spoken innocently. She changed the subject.

'What will your aunt say about your changing jobs like this?'

Prissie's eyes flickered slightly.

'She'll be disappointed, but she'll get over it. She was worried about me losing weight, anyway.'

'Where does your aunt live?'

'In Putney.'

'Then you'd like week-ends off now and then to go and see her.'

Prissie looked up eagerly.

'Oh, Mrs Gaye, that would be wonderful.'

Brigit looked again at the small attractive person sitting on the floor in that attitude of grace. Everything Prissie did would be graceful. She was small-boned and supple. Her head was poised exquisitely on a delicate little neck. Her hands were thin-fingered and almost miniature size. Her face, without animation, would be plain, but one couldn't imagine it unanimated. It was so mobile and alive.

She could make anyone do anything, Brigit thought slowly. Just as she had made Fergus bring her here. But why had she done that? Why choose them? Had it been because Fergus happened to be on the spot, or had she other motives? Why did she have this sudden desire to be a mother's help? Brigit thought more soberly. Certainly she might love children, but soon enough she could have them of her own. All men must find her attractive.

'Tell me about yourself, Prissie,' she said.

Prissie looked up with her appealing wide-eyed candour. 'There isn't much to tell. I'm an orphan. I never knew my father and my mother died when I was very small. Aunt Maud brought me up. She did her best for me, but she only had the money she earned as a nurse. Ever since I was a kid I had to earn enough to pay for my education. Aunt Maud wouldn't have worried about it, but I was crazy to get a good education. I used to go hop-picking in the holidays and mind babies after school, and when I was a bit older I got holiday jobs in guest houses, washing dishes and waiting on tables. Aunt Maud thought I was mad. She wanted me to get a nice respectable job in a shop, selling buttons or trimming hats or something, when I was fourteen, but I wouldn't. I *had* to learn things.' The glowing eyes fixed on Brigit gave her the most extraordinary feeling that she was hearing her own story, that she had been that thin energetic child, pushing baby carriages, waiting on tables, plunging her childish arms into sinks full of dirty dishes.

Not having time for any youthful fun ... The girl should have been an actress.

'And you did learn things?' she asked.

Prissie's quick grin that gave her face its elfin quality flashed out.

'Oh, yes. I learned things. Even Aunt Maud had to admit that.' She began to finger a slender gold chain and locket round her neck. 'When I got the job with the air-line Aunt Maud was as proud as a peacock. She thought the whole thing was due to her. Poor old darling, after all she had given me a home and fed me and been terribly kind. I was glad she was proud of me.'

Brigit felt her eyes stinging with sudden tears. It was *she* who had pleased an old lady by making good ... What an extraordinary way this girl had of projecting her personality on to one.

'Of course I had to be decently educated,' Prissie went on, speaking half to herself. 'I owed it to my parents.' Then she sprang up in a nervous way as if afraid she had been talking too much.

'Please,' she said, 'show me the children's things and what I am to do for them.'

'You must call me Brigit,' Brigit said, almost as if compelled to do so. 'You're not here as a servant. We'll be friends. After all, I'm an orphan, too, although I can remember my parents.' She thought fleetingly of her mother, and the hard unhappy reflection that perhaps Prissie was lucky not to have any memories of her mother passed through her mind.

'You're so sweet to me,' Prissie was whispering. Her eyes were bright, as if with tears, and Brigit, moved by the girl's emotion, said lightly:

'Not at all. You're my birthday present, remember? Come and I'll show you the nursery. By the way, you seem to have got round Nicky. He can be rather difficult at times.'

'He's not sure yet,' said Prissie. 'Why is he so nervous?'

'I don't know. He always has been.' (Had it been her prenatal fears that had made Nicky such a nervous and sensitive baby? Sarah, about whom she had worried much less, was so much more placid.)

'But, Prissie, tell me,' she said abruptly, 'when you made such efforts to get a good education why should you be content to do a job that any girl can do?'

'Because I've found it's what I wanted after all.' Prissie gave her eager smile. 'Silly of me, isn't it? Probably I'm crazy about children because I was such a lonely child myself.'

'I was, too,' Brigit said involuntarily.

The two stood regarding one another. Then Prissie said softly, almost significantly, 'Well, there we are.'

In their bedroom that night Fergus said:

'Well, how do you like Prissie now you're better acquainted?'

Brigit said enthusiastically. 'She's the most extraordinary person. I believe, if she wanted to, she could twist anyone round her little finger. Even Uncle Saunders was impressed. She looks such a child, but she isn't really. She must be almost as old as I am. It seems strange that someone so attractive hasn't married. But I think she's been very mixed up and she feels as if she's had to fight the whole world. She'll be wonderful company for me and the children. Sarah, of course, adores her already. Sarah takes everyone on trust, just like you do. Nicky is more like me.'

'Don't you take my birthday present to you on trust? Don't you think it was one of my happier inspirations? Or would you rather have had the diamond ear-rings?'

Brigit found herself hesitating. She was going to say something incoherent about the peculiar effect Prissie had on her. Then she saw Fergus's happy confident look and could not bear to spoil his pleasure in his unique gift.

'She's sweet,' she said warmly. But she didn't want to talk any more about Prissie. The day, since five o'clock, had become Prissie's, and it was hers, because it was her birthday. She was not a thin orphan child compelled to fight her way through the world, as Prissie had seemed to will her to believe, but Brigit Gaye, with two handsome children and a very handsome husband. It was silly to have to remind herself of that.

But she was remembering, all at once, how Nicky had fought back embarrassed tears as Prissie had bathed him. Nicky was shy and sensitive. Fergus had said he would have to be broken of it. Fergus was right, of course.

But Brigit was chilly, all at once. Inexplicably she was shivering. She laughed. 'Someone walking over my grave. It's cold. Let's go to bed.'

She knew the familiar enchantment would come back on her as soon as she lay in Fergus's arms. So it did, for a little while. His arms were so warm and loving, and he began talking nonsense into her ear, in a whisper, as he did only when he was completely happy.

But when the light was out the enchantment, as frail as a ghost, dependent on a mood, an atmosphere, left her. The moonlight was the colour of daggers, a shadow hung menacingly.

'What's the matter, darling?'

Fergus, much too perceptive about her moods, was instantly aware of her distress.

But was it distress, this cool thing that invaded her?

'Nothing,' she said, burying her face in his shoulder. 'Nothing at all.'

For how could she tell him that it seemed, for a moment, as if Prissie had stood at the foot of the bed watching them, Prissie whose gallant lonely life had been a struggle for the things she had not yet attained, a husband, children, deep and adoring love ... There was no reason at all that Prissie should give Brigit a guilt complex, but how could she flaunt this last of her many precious possessions in the face of this wistful hungry-eyed girl?

Yet was Prissie so wistful or so hungry for love? Brigit, walking into the nursery in the morning, heard the end of a story.

'So that's how I have royal blood. The evidence is all in here.' Prissie was touching the heavy gold locket that lay between her small breasts. Her large eyes were shining with pride and excitement. It seemed impossible that Nicky should not be drawn into her fantasy. Yet he remained stubbornly sceptical and logical.

'If your grandfather was a prince why aren't you a princess?'

'Well, you see——' Prissie hadn't noticed Brigit. She sat back on the low stool, her skirt spread about her, her hands clasped, and the pink of excitement colouring her cheeks prettily. 'You had a grandfather who was a pirate but that doesn't make you one. And I think you had one who was a millionaire. Let's hope that does make you one.' She grinned infectiously.

'Then where are all your jewels?' Nicky demanded.

Prissie looked crestfallen.

'I'm afraid I haven't any. Only this locket that holds a secret. Although my grandfather was a prince my grandmother was only a poor dancer—like this.' She stood up and spun round, slender arms spread wide, like a figure on a musical box. 'And she was very proud. She didn't tell anyone she had a prince for a lover, so her children were just dancers instead of princesses.'

'Was your mother a dancer?' Nicky inquired, with his precocious intelligence.

Prissie hesitated. She said, 'Yes,' then 'No,' with curious defiance. After that again she said, 'Well, yes, I expect so. No one told me,' and before Nicky could cross-examine her further Sarah began to revolve slowly, imitating Prissie, her plump little body suddenly all unexpected grace. 'Me dance,' she said in her high eager voice.

Brigit decided it was time to indicate her presence.

'I think we must have Sarah given lessons in ballet when she's a little older,' she said briskly. 'She's got a surprising aptitude. Prissie, what is this extraordinary story you've been telling the children?'

'Prissie's a princess,' Nicky said. 'She's got it in her locket.'

Prissie's fingers closed over her locket. Her eyes were innocent and sparkling, but her fingers seemed to be guarding a secret.

'Oh, I was romancing a little. Not—not altogether. But

there isn't any proof, you see, and anyway where would proof get one?'

'That depends what the proof is about,' Brigit said practically.

'It isn't anything, really. Just a family legend. I always thought it was fun to believe it.'

Brigit could understand that. The lonely imaginative child whose aunt wanted her to sell haberdashery must, of course, have taken refuge in dreams. To imagine oneself the granddaughter of a prince and a ballet dancer was perhaps satisfying enough. Prissie was not ordinary. It could even have been true. Anyway, it fascinated Nicky, who was almost, but still not quite, capitulating to Prissie's charm.

And it amused and interested Fergus when Brigit recounted the tale to him.

'You're all having your legs pulled,' he said. 'I told you the girl was a charmer. I wonder what she has got in that locket? A picture of a boy friend, I expect.'

Nicky's apparent capitulation took place the second night of Prissie's stay. He had one of the nightmares to which he was frequently subject. Brigit heard his sudden cry and knew in the silence that followed that he was hiding his head beneath the blankets, rigid, trying to overcome his fears. She always went to him, though lately Fergus had begun to protest, saying that Nicky was getting too big to be babied. He wasn't meaning to be unkind, Brigit knew, but because she suspected he disliked Nicky's nervousness more than he admitted (did he think Nicky took after Guy, with his neurotic tendencies?) she usually tried to go to the child without waking Fergus.

Her elaborate caution not to make a noise on this occasion caused her to be a little slow, and when she reached Nicky's room the light was on and he was not alone. Prissie was in the bed with him, and had her arms folded tightly round him. His tousled fair head was on her breast, but somehow she did not look maternal. Rather she looked like another child herself, in her white nightdress with a blue ribbon drawn primly round the neck, and her dark hair hanging long and straight on either side of her face. They looked like a couple of babes in the wood, Brigit thought, with curious wryness. There were even tears on Prissie's cheeks to keep company with Nicky's.

'He had a nightmare,' she explained huskily to Brigit.

'Yes, I heard him. He often has one.'

Nicky, hearing his mother's voice, struggled eagerly away from Prissie.

'Mummy,' he cried, holding out his arms in a baby fashion that Fergus would have deplored. After all, he was not quite six years old, still young enough to be a little of a baby in the dark. But Brigit, in fairness to Fergus's injunctions, refrained from putting her arms round him.

She patted him on the head.

'It's all right now, isn't it, old man?'

'Yes. They went when Prissie came.'

'What went, dearest?'

'The things. Like black paper. Fluttering.' Suddenly, because his mother was not responding to his demand for reassurance, he hid his head in Prissie's breast again, holding her tightly.

So he was capitulating to Prissie at last, Brigit reflected. That was a very good thing. Nicky was impossible to manage unless he trusted one. All the same, Prissie must be told not to pamper him. And really she looked so much a child herself, it was absurd.

'I cried, too,' she said simply. 'It just seemed so awful, the dark night and being all alone and afraid.'

'We're not afraid now,' said Nicky in drowsy content.

'Thank you for going to him,' Brigit said. She was angry with herself for her voice being a little stiff. Yet she couldn't help going on. 'My husband says Nicky must get over these things.'

Nicky stirred, with returning apprehension.

'He's only a baby,' Prissie murmured, and Brigit saw Nicky relax again.

'Well, make him lie down and get back to your own bed,' she said crisply. 'If he cries again I'll go to him.'

Nicky didn't cry again. If he had she was fairly certain that Prissie would have disobeyed her and gone to him. If she could shed tears in sympathy with a child she would not be able to lie in her own bed and listen to him cry. It was wonderful that she was so tender-hearted. It meant that one could leave the children with her any time and know that they would be most carefully looked after. The funny little thing really was a treasure.

She did not see Prissie early the next morning completing the letter begun two days ago.

> Sorry I haven't finished this before, but I wanted to be sure about what I was doing before I wrote. I've definitely decided to stay. She and the kids like me, the boy wasn't so sure at first, but he's all right now and everything's fine. The kids are cute. Don't be cross with me about this. It's something I have to do just the way I had to get an education when I was a kid. Something I couldn't see driving me, although now of course we know why. You might say it's fate.
>
> I'll be up as often as I can and I'll send things. You'll manage, I know. It might not be for long. Or it might be something I've started and can't stop. No, I don't mean that, or if I do you're in it with me.
>
> You should see the children's clothes and things. She says they've only got his salary, but there's plenty comes from the Family. I've got to stay, see?

FOUR

But that was all a month ago, another age, another world. Where had those lovely days of early autumn, those happy hopeful days, gone? Had they ever really existed, Brigit wondered. Sometimes she thought now that the beginning of reality had been that morning when she had had the accident. The interval of six years with Fergus before that had been a happy dream. She was a Templar with a heritage of bloodshed and cruelty. What right had she to be happy? The accident had been a reminder that she could not escape her inheritance. She had had a six-year reprieve, that was all.

It had all happened in the most unnecessary way. Aunt Annabel had been staying for the week-end, and Uncle Saunders had driven down with Guy to take her back to London. Unexpectedly they had decided to stay to lunch, and Brigit had got fussed because there was not enough food in the house. Prissie had offered to take the children for a walk into the village to shop, and while they were gone Uncle Saunders had begun one of his loud and inquisitive questionnaires as to how she and Fergus spent their time and money. He was in one of his pin-pricking moods, and Brigit, who was having one of her rare mornings when the baby was making her feel sick, had little patience with him. Also Fergus was due home shortly, after a week's absence, and she had been planning to have him alone, not with the Templar family, which he hated anyway, round his neck. When Uncle Saunders transferred his cross-examination to Aunt Annabel, and when Aunt Annabel, who had been nervous and jumpy lately, suddenly burst into tears, Brigit found herself turning on him indignantly.

'You're nothing but a bully,' she said. 'Surely it doesn't matter how much Aunt Annabel's new club is costing her. You can afford it. She doesn't spend much these days, goodness knows.'

She gave a significant glance towards Aunt Annabel's shabby appearance, and Uncle Saunders said in his booming voice, 'I won't have my house filled with all the lame and diseased cats in the neighbourhood, that's all. So long as she's this friend to the friendless thing she'll have the place overrun with animals.'

'It doesn't cost me anything,' Aunt Annabel snuffled. 'Actually I get money. I collect subscriptions.'

Uncle Saunders gave his loud derisive laugh. 'Keep it then, why don't you? What a golden opportunity. None of your loony friends will expect to know what's happened to their money. Or better still,' he leaned forward eagerly, his pale blue eyes protruding, 'give it to me to invest. I'll show you a handsome profit.'

'Saunders!' Aunt Annabel protested.

'Dammit, where does being honest get you? If old Phillip had been honest where would the Templar family have been today? You wouldn't have been living in a West End house, you can stake your life on that. Of course one has to dispense with bloodshed nowadays. Only a little mild foolery like embezzlement or misappropriation of funds,' he finished waggishly.

'Saunders, you're joking.'

'My dear, I never joke.'

'No, all Uncle Saunders's games are serious,' said Guy in his drawling disillusioned voice. 'After all, Aunt Annabel, if you don't find the housekeeping money that's so much more to buy shares with. So it's not really a game, is it?'

Uncle Saunders roared with laughter.

'That's it, boy. You have the right approach. The Templar approach, eh? And there's that girl of Fergus's coming. She's too small for my taste. What about you Guy?'

Prissie was crossing the lawn with her shopping basket. She moved with a light step, her black hair blown back from her face. She looked very thin and slight, but full of vitality and happiness. Her red skirt billowed about her like a full-blown poppy. In the month she had been with them she hadn't put on any weight, nor had she lost her tenseness. Indeed, she had a look of inner excitement as if she were burning up inside, but that, Brigit realized, was natural to her and a part of her fascination. Frequently she stopped and hung over things in the house, stroking the polished stair railing, picking up a good piece of china, such as the Royal Worcester plate with its small perfect country scene, like a delicate bubble in its circle of rich crimson and gold, smoothing the silk sheets on the beds and looking all the time as if she were a child with her first Christmas tree. It was satisfying to observe the pleasure she derived from her surroundings. In its turn it made Brigit herself doubly appreciate them, and she was also satisfied now about the genuineness of Prissie's desire to leave the airline.

Guy, Brigit noticed, made no answer to Uncle Saunders, but his eyes were fixed on Prissie and his face had lost a little of its sullenness. She tried to concentrate on Guy's interest in Prissie, and to think how nice it would be if Guy found happiness as she had done. In that way she could control her anger against Uncle Saunders.

'Uncle Saunders, I'd rather you didn't refer to Prissie as that girl of Fergus's.'

Uncle Saunders looked at her in genuine surprise.

'Why, my dear, he brought her here, didn't he? Must have been attracted by her. Because I'm quite sure your budget doesn't run to companion helps, or whatever you call these people? Does it, my dear? No matter what Fergus says about diamond ear-rings being the alternative, I shouldn't be surprised if the ear-rings were necessary, eventually.' His prominent eyes were unbearably waggish, his full lips smiling suggestively.

'Saunders, that's abominable,' protested Aunt Annabel.

'And I think a little far-fetched,' suggested Guy, his eyes defensively on his sister.

Brigit had stiffened and could not relax. This time she could not tolerate her family. When Uncle Saunders, actually seeing that he had gone too far, lumbered over and patted her on the arm, saying, 'Sorry, my dear. Only joking, you know. The girl is damned attractive, you must admit that, if you like 'em small,' she could only draw away rigidly, fighting her anger. After all, if she gave way to anger and shouted she was no better than they were. Oh, why did her family have such a devastating effect on her?

'Come along, Biddy. Men will be men, eh?'

It was no use. She didn't shout, but she gave way to a low controlled anger.

'Oh, I hate you with your filthy mind! But how can I expect you to have anything else? You're a Templar! I suppose I have one myself without knowing. I suppose Nicky and Sarah have one. And now, heaven forgive me, I'm bringing another Templar into the world.' Uncle Saunders's large red face, Guy's supercilious one, Aunt Annabel's kind shapeless bewildered one seemed to float before her in a mist. She was aware, suddenly, of Prissie, the innocent cause of the quarrel, looking in the doorway, and her face, too, pale and cool, swam like a water lily. The uncontrollable tide of her anger swept over her.

'Oh, I hope my baby will never be born!' she cried, and rushed out of the room.

The one thought in her mind was to get to Fergus. Only his arms about her and his sane voice in her ears would rid her of this loathsome feeling of decadence that her family gave her. He would say, 'Don't be silly, my sweet. You're out of sorts, that's all. Uncle Saunders is only a noisy pompous ass, puffed up by too much money—I expect he eats bank notes, and probably sharpens his teeth on sovereigns—and Aunt Annabel is a gentle old tabby. Guy will be all right when he marries a nice girl. Perhaps he'll marry Prissie. She would be just right for him, plenty of sense and shrewdness in that little head of hers. No one is completely evil, darling. They all have some saving grace, even the Templars...'

That was what Fergus would say. Brigit almost smiled to herself in a tense overwrought way as she crossed the lawn towards the stables. But she had to hear him saying it quickly. He would be on his way home now. She would ride to meet him, so that they could come the rest of the way alone, unintruded on by either children, elderly relations, or companion helps. She hadn't ridden since she had known the baby was coming, but if she took quiet old Polly and rode very gently she would be all right. They might even have lunch at the Mitre on the way, and to hell with the family...

Afterwards she could remember only the scarf on the stick poking at her suddenly from the thick hawthorn hedge, and Polly rearing sideways in fright...

The brilliant colour of it fluttered before her eyes for days afterwards. It was the colour of pain, she thought. She only wept when she was told that it was Fergus who had found her, and that she had been unconscious and unable to hear all the reassuring things he had been going to say to her. So she never did hear from his own lips that Uncle Saunders was a pompous ass, and no one to be afraid of, and that Prissie had been provided purely for her and the children's comfort and pleasure, and that any other thought regarding her had never entered his mind.

The opportunity to ask him those things and to hear his reassurances had gone for ever. For she lay in hospital with an injured spine, and it looked as if Fergus, young and full of vitality, had an invalid wife for the rest of his life.

There was the baby, too, that now would never be born. Over and over again Brigit heard her last spoken words, like doom, inside her head, 'I hope my baby will never be born,' and the slow tears trickled down her cheeks until the sister lost patience with her and said:

'You must cheer up, Mrs Gaye. You'll soon be walking again, and if I had a husband as good-looking as yours I'm darned if I'd be crying.

'And those adorable children,' she went on, as she saw a tremulous smile coming to Brigit's face. 'And that nice little girl who brings them in. You're so lucky, knowing they're well looked after.'

Brigit did remember the children at her bedside one day, Sarah poking inquisitively into her bedside locker, Nicky holding back, white and strained and obviously trying not to cry. And Prissie smiling gently, whispering, 'There's nothing to worry about at all. The children are fine. All you have to do is get well.' Prissie with her elfin face, and glowing eyes that could will you to think anything she chose. Or was that imagination, too?

And had anyone told Fergus of those last angry words she had spoken before she had left the house? She had to know that.

She remembered Fergus at her bedside. She had wanted to lift her hands and stroke his worried face. But she couldn't. Her arms were lead, her mind full of misery.

'Fergus! You know about the baby?' Her voice seemed far-off and remote, as if it were not a thing of any importance.

'Yes, of course, darling. But you mustn't worry about it. There's plenty of time to have more.'

'But there's not! There's not! I can't walk.'

It was Fergus now, stroking her face, leaning over her with his eyes full of gentleness.

'You will soon. Don't be so impatient.'

'Impatient! How long is it now?'

'Only a fortnight.'

'But I can't move my legs,' she cried desolately.

'Darling, you will. It's something to do with the nerves.'

She clutched his hand.

'Did they tell you what I said about not wanting the baby?'

'Darling, anyone could say a thing like that under stress. And I admit Uncle Saunders does cause a state of stress if you take him seriously.'

'They always were murderers,' Brigit muttered.

Fergus bent closer. 'What did you say, sweet?'

'Murderers! My family.'

Then there came his hearty outburst of laughter, and all at once the miasma of misery cleared, and she felt the tears running down her cheeks.

'Fergus, don't you mind that I killed the baby?'

'Complete nonsense, my sweet stupid!'

She clung to his hand. 'Darling, I didn't mean to. It was that stick with the scarf on it poking at me.' Suddenly she was saying, '*Who did that?*'

'No one did it. It was a handkerchief caught in the hawthorn hedge. We found it afterwards. We told you, don't you remember? A red and white spotted handkerchief like tramps use. I didn't know you could still buy them.'

'It waved in front of me. Suddenly. It was on a stick,' Brigit insisted.

'Yes, darling. I suppose the wind was blowing it.'

'No. Someone was waving it. I know. I have nightmares about it. Sister will tell you.'

Fergus said uncomfortably, 'I think you ought to rest.'

'I don't want to rest! I want to know who didn't want us to have the new baby!' Her voice had risen, and the sister was approaching. She looked significantly at Fergus.

'Now, Mrs Gaye. Time for your rest.'

'But I can't rest until I find out the truth.'

'Well, you'll do better about that when you've had a sleep.'

Fergus was kissing her and then moving away. Brigit reached towards him despairingly. Then her hand fell to the coverlet. Could it be that he hadn't wanted the baby either? Could it be that? Was he perhaps even glad that she had lost it?

The prick of the needle administered by the sister was merciful.

But she was not in that state verging on hysteria all the time. The day Fergus told her that she would have to go to the family's house in Montpelier Square she was quite calm and rational.

She said, 'Is that what you want?'

'It's the only practical thing, darling. You'll have to stay in London for treatment, and you don't want to stay in a hospital indefinitely. Besides, to be quite honest, we can't afford it. There's the big house in Montpelier Square, and they're delighted to have you. The children and Prissie have settled in very well. Truly, it's the most sensible thing. And it won't be for long.'

Brigit's eyes beseeched him. He smiled with his familiar loving gentleness. (But it wasn't gentleness she wanted, it was the old flashing look of equality and passion, and his mouth hard on hers. Had that gone for ever?)

'The doctor says any day you'll find you can move your legs again. There isn't anything organic, as he has told you. It's purely nervous. So just rest, and no worrying or tension. Understand?'

He stroked her hair. She whispered, 'Fergus!'

'Yes, darling?'

'Am I still—nice to look at?'

'Don't be an idiot, darling. Here, wait till I get a mirror.'

It seemed to her that she had grown very thin and pale. She was all eyes and mouth, her eyebrows were dark half-moons against the paleness of her skin, her lips colourless.

'Oh, Fergus! My lipstick, please. Why didn't you tell me what I looked like?'

'I shall only kiss it off.'

'Not with sister watching.'

'Sister will give me her blessing.'

It was so strange to be smiling again, to be feeling almost light-hearted. Perhaps because leaving hospital was the first step towards being well. She wouldn't let herself think of how she disliked the big house in Montpelier Square. As Fergus said, to go there was the sensible thing to do. And it would not be for long. She was determined to overcome this peculiar paralysis and be well as soon as possible.

'Tell me about the children and Prissie,' she said. 'What do they do all day? And isn't it a blessing we have Prissie. What on earth would we have done without her?'

She could see that Fergus was pleased with her, whether for agreeing without a fuss to go to Montpelier Square or for approving of Prissie, she didn't know which. But it didn't matter. As long as he was pleased, and no longer looking strained and worried. It had been a bad time for him, too. She had to remember that.

'Oh, Prissie's completely organized,' Fergus said. 'She's turned the top floor into a temporary nursery and bedrooms. The children don't worry anyone up there, though really they make much less noise than Uncle Saunders. Prissie, actually, is delighted with the move, because now she can visit her aunt in Putney. She seems very fond of her. Really, she gets on extraordinarily well with everyone. Aunt Annabel was afraid Mrs Hatchett would be disturbed about this sort of invasion, but Prissie manages her, too. She's rather a witch in her own way.'

'I know,' said Brigit rather briefly. Then, regretting her brevity she said with amusement, 'She must be a witch if she can manage Mrs Hatchett. Has she still this thing about ghosts?'

Fergus laughed. 'There are more cats than ghosts in the house at present. Uncle Saunders is getting extremely touchy. The whole place is rather a circus, with the accent on comedy. You'll enjoy it.'

In spite of her determination to be light-hearted, the shadow of the house in Montpelier Square slipped over her. Suddenly she was reaching for Fergus's hand.

'Darling, you'll be there?'

'As much as I possibly can. Silly child. What are you worrying about? They've prepared the best bedroom for you, and your nurse is called Ellen and she's a blonde.'

'My nurse?' The fear was inside her again, a living thing, choking her. 'Fergus—am I that ill?'

'Well, my darling, who's going to wash you and feed you? Certainly not Aunt Annabel. She would be giving you cat's meat by mistake. And someone has to talk to you in the night when I'm away.'

Brigit watched him speechlessly. So he knew about her nightmares, when she awoke crying because someone was waving a red scarf on a stick at her, trying to make her have an accident. Or to kill her . . .

'Can't have Mrs Hatchett's ghosts frightening you,' he said lightly.

'Ghosts?'

'Actually I believe there's only one. A little man in a brown coat who stands at the foot of her bed and says nothing. She's rather attached to him. She's convinced that one night he will speak to her, and she can't wait for the revelation.'

Brigit began helplessly to chuckle. Then she realized that this was what Fergus had meant her to do, and it was all she could do to keep on laughing for him. *Oh, Fergus, if I can't ever walk again, oh, darling, what shall I do?*

FIVE

PRISSIE loved the big house. She liked to come in and stand silently in the hall looking up at the wide curving staircase, at the high carved ceiling and panelled walls, and then, if the children could be induced to loiter, she liked to climb the stairs very slowly, looking at the portraits, one by one. She never tired of the portraits. She searched their features over and over; the long-nosed hawk-eyed Phillip, pirate of the Caribbean, the parsimonious Silas, and the fat blue-eyed loose-lipped Ernest. The women, too, absorbed her; most of all she was fascinated by Brigit's mother who, at eighteen, had been beautiful, dark-eyed, white-skinned and with the lovely sensual mouth that Guy had inherited. In fact, it was Guy who was the first to notice Prissie's interest in the portraits.

He said, 'They're a fine lot, aren't they?' in his habitually mocking voice.

'If you hadn't any at all of your own,' Prissie flashed, 'you would realize how wonderful they are.'

His eyes showed interest. 'But you have ancestors.'

'Oh, yes, indeed,' said Prissie proudly, fingering the locket round her neck.

Guy watched her inquisitively. 'What is it that you have in there? Why don't you show me?'

'No, I can't.' Prissie moved away. 'But the day will come,' she said mysteriously over her shoulder.

Guy took her arm. 'You funny little thing, why don't you show me now? You can trust me.'

'Trust you! Do you think it's something I'm ashamed of?'

Guy laughed at her indignation. She was very pretty and so extraordinarily alive. She could almost make one believe in her world of fantasy. Royal blood, indeed! Brigit had told him about that. Her grandfather had more likely been an ambitious but poverty-stricken actor. But one had to admire the girl for the façade she put up. Funny she hadn't married. Too ambitious, probably. That could explain her desire to get into one of the homes of the wealthy. Wealthy! Guy twisted his lips wryly. He looked at Prissie again, and suddenly wanted to kiss her.

'You're too romantic,' he said.

She smiled at him, and was all warmth and friendliness again.

'I guess I am. Brigit would think so if she knew how I admire these portraits.'

'Biddy doesn't like their history.'

'But at least they had big splendid vices, not mean little ones. After all, you might as well be hanged for a sheep as a lamb.'

'None of them was hanged, unfortunately.'

'Oh, you're as bad as your sister. Why should you be so cynical. You have everything. You're even good-looking.' Her dark eyes twinkled. 'Which is more than one can say for your Uncle Saunders, or your grandfather——'

Guy looked into her warm persuasive eyes.

'You're a funny little thing. Uncle Saunders couldn't think what Fergus saw in you——'

'Fergus!'

'Brigit and Fergus, I mean. But I can see. You're not pretty, and yet looking at you is like watching a flower suddenly begin to open—a morning glory, I think.'

Prissie gave her soft peal of laughter and looked up at the portraits.

'Which one of these was a poet?'

'Great-uncle Ernest, I should think. He was the one who liked falling in love. Will you have dinner with me one night?'

'Why——' Prissie hesitated. 'I'll have to see. The children——'

'Brigit's nurse arrives today. She'll listen for the children. We'll go somewhere gay. Wear your prettiest dress.'

The prospect of going out with Guy gave Prissie satisfaction rather than pleasure. Pleasure she derived more from the house and its furnishings. The chandelier in the dining-room, a shining shower of crystal, pierced her to the heart with a queer delight. When no one was about she would touch the china, Royal Worcester, Sèvres, Meissen, with caressing fingers. There was a Dresden shepherd and shepherdess that seemed to have come out of one of her childhood dreams. As for the gold plate, it made her think of cathedrals, the rich trappings of bishops, and incense, and an indescribable feeling of almost erotic pleasure went through her. There was a tiny gold angel with outspread wings, like a fat thrush, that she adored. She used to show it to Nicky and Sarah, as an excuse for handling it herself, but Nicky said he would rather have real feathers and Sarah was not even interested.

It was all such waste, she thought indignantly. Here was a house full of treasures which no one appreciated. Brigit loathed and was even frightened of them, the silly thing. Aunt Annabel acted as if they didn't exist. Guy gave them his cynical glances, and Uncle Saunders remarked occasionally that all that money shouldn't be tied up in works of art. Lorna, the maid, dusted them and complained about the work they caused. But no one loved them. Except Prissie herself, and already she did in the most overpowering way. She wanted to stay in the house in Montpelier Square for a long long time...

Of course the cats were a bit off, and Mrs Hatchett hadn't been particularly friendly at first. Prissie had had to use all her tact and charm to become friends, and felt that she had achieved a major triumph when Mrs Hatchett unbent. The maid Lorna presented no problem. She had her round her finger in no time at all. Aunt Annabel, if one were prepared to be sympathetic about her cats, was harmless, and Uncle Saunders all bark and no bite. As for Fergus, he always had been sweet. (Had Guy been serious when he had made that remark about Fergus liking her?)

It hadn't seemed fair that one girl like Brigit should have so much. But she hadn't so much now, poor thing. Indeed very little at all...

There was no sense in being unhappy because of someone else's misfortune. Prissie intended to make the most of her stay in the Montpelier Square house. There was no need to write so many letters, either. But she still enjoyed writing them for the sheer pleasure of putting her thoughts on paper and gloating over them. And because some things she found easier to explain by writing.

So she wrote:

'I unpacked old toys from cupboards today. There are

enough for a royal family. I will let Nicky and Sarah play with only one thing each day. Sarah usually chooses a doll, but Nicky is never sure what he wants. I think he is rather a sissy child. His father wants him broken of nervousness, but how can I do this until he has confidence in me? He is very like his mother. She isn't sure of me either. Silly of her. But she pretends she is because Fergus likes me, and he's as innocent as a lamb. Really, he is. Brigit is coming home tomorrow and the nurse arrives today. Aunt Annabel (I call the family by these names because that will make it easier for you to know who I am talking about) says I'm to go to Harrods and buy the children new clothes suitable for London. She says they're shabby and countrified, but the quality of their clothes, Sarah's frilled petticoats, Nicky's coat with the fur collar—I wouldn't say they were shabby. Why should there be different standards for different children? Oh, and Guy wants to take me to dinner. I think this is a good idea because I will get to know him better. I think he may be important. I know you will agree. But I'll have to get a new dress. I'll need about ten pounds——'

In the next room, where Nicky and Sarah were playing, Sarah suddenly began to scream. Prissie finished writing hastily:

'I will see you on Thursday—that is going to be my day off—but sooner if possible. Don't try to ring me up here.'

She folded the letter, tucked it in her bodice, and went into the nursery.

Nicky had an umbrella and stuck on the end of it a torn flag. He was waving this in Sarah's face aggressively.

Prissie exclaimed, 'Nicky!'

As if he had been actually slapped, Nicky dropped the umbrella. He turned a frightened but defiant face to Prissie.

'Nicky, why are you doing that?' Prissie asked more gently.

'It's what happened when Polly was frightened and Mummy fell off.'

'How do you know?' Prissie asked swiftly. 'You didn't see.'

Nicky's eyes fell. 'Y-yes——'

'Nicky, you couldn't have. You were with me and Aunt Annabel and Uncle Saunders at the house. No one saw what happened.'

'N-no——'

Prissie moved the umbrella away and knelt beside him.

'Nicky darling, you mustn't believe nasty things like that. They're bad for you.'

The gentleness of Prissie's voice and her arm about him made Nicky's sensitive lips begin to quiver.

'Mummy said——'

'Mummy's sick, darling. She imagines things. She has nightmares like you do. You know those nasty old nightmares of yours are never true. And you know, too, that you didn't see a scarf on a stick. It was a handkerchief caught on a branch. Daddy found it.'

'Yes,' Nicky muttered.

'Then you're a naughty boy to frighten Sarah like that, and to tell lies. But never mind, it was just a game, wasn't it?'

Prissie drew the child to her and kissed him warmly on his forehead. He was such a funny little scrap, a mass of quivering nerves.

'Look, I've got a surprise for you. I found it this morning.'

''Prise,' said Sarah eagerly, her tears vanished, her fat little hands extended expectantly.

'Oh, you! You're the greedy one!' said Prissie good-humouredly. 'This is a surprise for Nicky because he's older than you and he'll understand it more.' She went to the toy cupboard and opened it, saying over her shoulder, 'But you'll have to be very careful of her, Nicky, because she's very old, and I should think quite valuable. Look!'

She held in her hands a doll, about twelve inches high, made of wood, and dressed as an old woman wearing a wide peaked hat, and a tight-waisted full-skirted black dress. In her hands there was a miniature tray on which were strings of coloured beads, reels of cotton, pins and needles. Her face was pallid, she had a long sharp nose and beady eyes. Her expression, meant to be a smile, had become with the fading of the paint on her lips a curiously malevolent grimace.

'There! Isn't she cute,' said Prissie gaily. 'She's a pedlar woman. Look at her wares for sale. What would you like to buy? A pretty string of beads for your little sister?'

Sarah stretched out her hands. 'Me! Me!'

'No, not you, greedy. You're too little to appreciate a doll like this. Although Nicky's a boy he'll like her. She's a friendly soul. She sings, like this...' In a high sweet voice Prissie began to sing, *'Oh, my darling, oh my darling, oh, my darling Clementine* ... I know, that's what we'll call her. Clementine. There, Nicky, don't you like Clementine? She'll be your friend and play with you. But you mustn't tell lies, like seeing things you haven't seen at all. Clementine always knows when you are lying.'

'Yes,' whispered Nicky.

'Well, take her in your arms.'

But at that Nicky stepped back, his face stiff with distaste. 'No, no!'

Prissie looked at him in surprise.

'Why, you funny little creature,' she laughed. 'I do believe you're frightened of her. She isn't as magic as all that.'

SIX

At home there had been a pear tree outside her bedroom window. At this time of year it was garlanded with small fat lime-green pears, and its bark was like a lizard skin. It had character and friendliness. Here, the mulberry tree with its dead limbs had an almost malignant significance. It was like herself, useless. Oh, why had they put her here where she had to lie and look at the mulberry tree all day?

That thought had come to Brigit the moment she had

been carried into the large airy room that had been prepared for her. But with a great effort she concealed her dismay and tried to be bright and cheerful for Aunt Annabel's sake.

Aunt Annabel had obviously gone to a lot of trouble with the room, and when Brigit was settled in bed she stood hugging an enormous silver-grey persian cat and beaming at Brigit. With her fly-away grey hair, her fur collar, and her plump crumpled face, one could scarcely tell where the cat ended and Aunt Annabel began.

'There, dear, you'll be comfortable here, won't you? This used to be the master bedroom before we did the alterations upstairs. That was before your time, of course. You'll be the only one sleeping on this floor, which will make it nice and quiet for you. And it's also only one flight of stairs from the kitchen so your meals won't get too cold on the way. Oh, and if you hear any scampering over your head it's only my cats. I've emptied the old studio just above you and it's entirely theirs. They have great fun in it, the blessings.' She tucked her chin into the grey persian's fur, and her eyes looked out soulfully over his head. She was growing a little queer, Brigit thought, but harmlessly queer. And it was pleasant for the cats.

'How many cats have you at present, Aunt Annabel?'

'Only six, dear. The two black and whites I found homes for yesterday. Nice clean places with kind people.'

(As if they were children being adopted, Brigit thought, fascinated.)

'But I quite expect to have another tonight. I caught sight of the most wretched tabby in the park yesterday. I couldn't lure it to me then, but I shall go back today. It looked quite starved, poor pet.' She gave Brigit her wide vague smile. 'I call them my displaced people.'

'That one doesn't look very displaced,' Brigit commented.

Aunt Annabel snuggled against the cat in her arms.

'This is Renoir. He's so fat—you know those fat nudes in the Pitti Palace in Florence—not that this Renoir looks nude. He's my own treasure. He merely tolerates the waifs and strays. By the way, dear, I've given you the Spanish bed. They say Phillip had it brought from Madrid for his bride, and that it belonged to a Spanish infanta. Anyway, it's very comfortable and it does go with this room. I had rather an argument with that nurse'—Aunt Annabel looked round furtively to see if the nurse were within hearing—'who said it was much too large and inconvenient to nurse a patient in. But I said you were a Templar and sleep in the Templar bed you should. And, darling, you look absolutely ravishing lying there. If Phillip were to see you I'm sure he'd get you the bed of the Spanish queen herself.'

'It's not a bed I want,' Brigit cried in anguish. 'It's my own two feet!'

'I know, darling, I know. All in good time. Here's nurse coming, and presently Prissie will want to bring the children in. I think she has them in the park at present, they've been so happy and good. And then you must rest before Fergus arrives this evening.'

Fergus hurrying home to an invalid wife, to a pampered useless person lying decoratively in an antique Spanish bed . . . Brigit bit her lip and turned her head on the pillow.

'Thank you, Aunt Annabel. You're so sweet to me. And all those lovely flowers. Who sent them?'

'Why, Fergus of course, dear. Who else? You're a very lucky girl.'

Nurse Ellen took up the same refrain when she came in. She was a plump healthy-looking girl with a pleasant face and thick blond hair twisted into neat coils beneath her cap. She looked as if she would stand no nonsense. Brigit liked her at once. So far she was the only thing she liked about the Montpelier Square house. Again, she had Fergus to thank for seeing that she had a pleasant nurse. Dear kind Fergus with his invalid wife.

'You are a lucky girl, too,' said Nurse Ellen briskly. 'I only saw your husband once, but I'd work my fingers to the bone for him. And I wouldn't do that for many men, I can tell you.'

Again Brigit made an effort to look bright and interested. 'Don't you like men, nurse?'

Nurse Ellen set down the tray of tea.

'Not some of them,' she said shortly. 'There's more hypocrisy goes with a pair of trousers—well, maybe there are exceptions. And your husband's one.' She smiled, and her rather pudgy face was very kind. 'You'll have to get well quickly for him.'

Again a sense of panic, as of time flying by and leaving her forgotten, invaded Brigit.

'Nurse—have you had any other cases like mine?'

'Well—yes. A year ago I had a crippled lady. But she wasn't half as lucky as you. She didn't have a royal bed—who do you think is going to call on you, ducky, King Henry the Eighth?'—her pale-blue eyes were full of roguishness—'nor did she have a room this size, nor that florist's shop, nor lingerie like yours, either.'

Brigit wanted to say that she hated this bed with its slender twisted posts and its carved headboard, and that she knew she would never get well in it. She wanted to tell the nurse that she would willingly have had the other woman's poverty. But there was a more vital question.

'Did she—walk again?'

'Well, no. She might have, but she died first, so we never did find out whether she'd ever have walked. Sweet little thing she was. Oh, I shall like being here.'

'Shall you?' said Brigit faintly.

'Oh yes. I adore luxury. That girl you've got looking after the children does, too. I see her touching things.'

Brigit suddenly remembered Prissie's thin light fingers moving caressingly over the silk sheets. Now were they moving with the same sensual pleasure over the treasures in this house? Why, she wondered, should she dislike the thought? She had reason to hate the Templar possessions, but Prissie hadn't. To Prissie they were objects of beauty. Let her touch them if she wished.

'Prissie's a treasure,' she said firmly.

'Yes, I could see that. She's like a mother with the children. Didn't I tell you how lucky you are? Now come, have this nice cup of tea while it's hot.'

The tea was hot, but its flavour was spoilt. Why should

she mind Prissie temporarily behaving like a mother to Nicky and Sarah? Nurse Ellen was right, she was so fortunate to have Prissie. It was only that she kept thinking of Prissie's slim mobile legs while her own remained as stiff and immovable as the bedposts. She resolutely blinked back tears.

'Don't you think Prissie's a nice girl, nurse?'

'Sure. Everyone's nice in this house. Your uncle's a wizard with his jokes with the housekeeping money, your brother has the nicest manners, but he needs building up. Vitamin B, I'd say. And the housekeeper with this thing she's got about ghosts. Says this little man in a brown coat comes into her bedroom every night. Indecent, I call it. I'd soon ask him what his game was, ghost or no ghost. Drink your tea, ducky.'

Brigit obediently took another sip.

'When will the children be back from the park?'

'Prissie said she'd keep them out of your way until you got settled and rested. I think she said she'd take them to the bus stop to meet your husband. That's if he comes by bus, of course.'

'He always does. From Victoria. It only takes ten minutes. The four o'clock train. He never missed it if he could help it. I remember——' Brigit's voice faded away. What did it matter, what did it *matter*, she asked herself fiercely, if it was Prissie at the bus stop this time? At least it would be someone for Fergus. He had always found someone there in the past...

'What do you remember, ducky?' Nurse Ellen's voice was unexpectedly gentle. Brigit dashed away her tears.

'Only that I always used to meet Fergus there. Oh, that's years ago, before we were married. He's probably forgotten.'

'Well, if he's due at four you've got to have some rest first,' said Nurse Ellen briskly. 'So just settle down to that. I'll wake you in plenty of time to titivate.'

'Thank you, nurse.' Brigit smiled. 'I think I'm going to like you.'

'And so you should. After all, your husband chose me.'

Fergus had chosen Prissie, too. Had he an instinct about

the kind of women she would like?

The move from the hospital had been exhausting, and Brigit did fall asleep. But her sleep was light, and punctuated with little soft runs and thumps and pounces as Aunt Annabel's cats frolicked in the studio overhead. She wasn't yet used to the different bed, and she had a dream that it was Prissie lying there, indolent and graceful, her dark hair spread on the pillow, her sparkling eyes and piquant face so much more suited to the Spanish infanta's bed than she with her English fairness. She herself was down at the corner, standing in the misty dusk, waiting for Fergus's bus. The two pictures were clear in her mind, Prissie luxuriantly in the big bed, herself stamping her feet softly and impatiently in the chilly wind, her cheeks whipped pink with cold and anticipation. That was how it should be, she thought, in the detached way of a dream, and awoke suddenly to the sound of Uncle Saunders shouting, and children's footsteps running up the stairs.

'Yes, we got her home in good shape,' Uncle Saunders was booming, obviously unaware that his voice carried all over the house. 'And there she is lying like a princess. It was my wife's idea about the Spanish bed. Something about surroundings and influences. I never did understand this psychiatry, or whatever it is. But I guess if one's got to lie in bed for months it might as well be an ornamental bed.'

Someone said something to him, and he said irritatedly, with no lowering of his voice, 'I'm not shouting. This is my normal voice. Couldn't hear me in the next room. Anyway, I didn't say anything.'

The protesting voice, obviously Aunt Annabel's, made another remark, and Uncle Saunders answered testily, 'Well, it's true, isn't it. No one can say definitely she'll ever walk again. Even the doctor can't, though personally I've no faith in doctors. Lots of quacks. Annabel, either the children or those cats of yours have been at my clippings. No, I don't know either what cats or children would want with Stock Exchange clippings, but the fact remains, they've disappeared.'

The booming voice died away. Quick footsteps

approached her door. Brigit, lying frozen in the big bed, could think only of the opening lines of a poem she had once read called 'Pavanne for a Dead Infanta . . .' It was no way to greet Fergus, Fergus who wanted a smiling and optimistic wife, quite sure that she would be running to meet him on her own two feet the next time he came home.

The room was full of dusk, and the dead limb of the mulberry tree hung like a gigantic question mark against the sky. Why didn't someone put on lights and banish this nightmare-filled half-light?

But before the thought could become a request Fergus was there and taking her in his arms. Then nothing existed but the exquisite comfort of his presence, his hard young arms about her, his face against hers.

'So you're lying in state,' he said. 'And very charmingly you do it.' Then he was kissing her and murmuring, 'Don't mind it, darling. It isn't for long. They really mean to be kind.'

So he understood about the bed, too, and her aversion for it. How could she think that anything else mattered, Uncle Saunders's clumsy remarks, Aunt Annabel's mistaken kindness, Prissie's lightfooted mobility, even the undertone of the cats' frivolities, when Fergus understood so well?

'I don't mind it,' she lied. 'No one's ever been so pampered. The last cripple Nurse Ellen nursed was very poor and hadn't a room like this or a four-poster bed or people to wait on her. She died.'

Fergus started up. 'What are you talking about? What's this nurse been saying to you? I thought she was the sensible kind.'

'Oh, she is. She's perfectly sweet. I adore her already.'

But Fergus was at the door. 'Nurse! Come here a moment.'

Nurse Ellen appeared from the room next door where she slept.

'Oh, it's you back,' she said in her downright way. 'I suppose you've woken my patient.'

'Your patient was awake. What's this you've been telling

her about a case of yours who died?'

'The crippled lady? Oh, yes. I always stay with my patients until the end.'

Brigit caught Fergus's indignant gaze, and suddenly she began to laugh. It was all so ridiculous, Nurse Ellen's unconscious lack of humour, Fergus's indignation, and her own very far-off demise. She might not be able to walk at present, but in every other way she was a young and healthy woman.

Fergus, after a moment sharing her thoughts, began to laugh himself, and it was Nurse Ellen's turn to be indignant, thinking that they were laughing at her professional integrity. The gloom was dispelled. Fergus snapped on a light, and the mulberry's crooked shape disappeared from view. The children were coming, too. She could hear Sarah's chatter as she toiled up the stairs on her short plump legs, and Prissie's voice humming gaily. Prissie was probably the most naturally light-hearted person this old house had seen for generations. Her songs must almost make the walls tremble and send the ghosts to their lairs.

What was it now? Oh, yes, the Clementine song. *Oh, my darling, oh, my darling, oh, my darling Clementine . . .*

Sarah came rushing in first, throwing herself against the bed and beaming at Brigit.

'Mummy's home!' she cried. 'Mummy's home!'

Brigit caressed her tousled hair. 'Yes, darling. Here I am. Come in, Prissie. Where's Nicky?'

Prissie came in lightly, her hair blown, her cheeks as red as hawthorn berries. She looked the epitome of life and vitality.

'Nicky's here. Hurry up, darling, you are slow.'

At last Nicky appeared slowly, almost reluctantly. He stood within the doorway, unsmiling and white-faced. There was a scratch on his cheek, and his knees were muddied.

'Well,' said Fergus critically. 'No wonder you're slow to show yourself, old man. You're still covered in mud.'

'I know, I should have washed him, but Sarah wouldn't wait to see her mother,' Prissie apologized.

Brigit put out her hand. 'Come here, darling. Let me see you. Why, you've even got leaves in your hair.'

Nicky came a slow step forward. He still didn't smile, or relax his air of watchfulness.

'Nicky,' said Brigit.

'Come along,' said Fergus firmly. 'Your mother wants to see you.'

Brigit had one fierce unhappy qualm that perhaps being ill in bed gave Nicky an aversion to her. Then, as the boy came nearer obediently, she saw that his eyes had the fixed frightened look that they had when he awoke from one of his nightmares.

'What's the matter, darling?' she asked gently. 'Who scratched your face?'

Nicky put a grubby hand to the red line on his cheek. Prissie went down on her knees and put her arms round him.

'He fell and scratched himself on a briar. But he didn't cry. Did you, pet?'

Nicky stiffened in her embrace.

'It was Clementine,' he whispered.

'Who was Clementine?' asked Fergus. 'Don't tell me you've been fighting with girls.'

Prissie gave her wide spontaneous smile. 'He hasn't, of course. He only fell down.'

'Clementine pushed me,' Nicky muttered. 'I hate her.'

Prissie went to speak again, but Brigit intervened. 'Come here, Nicky, close to me. Now tell me, who is Clementine?'

'That girl in the park. She pinched me and pushed me over. Does she have to be there when we go to play?'

'There wasn't anyone,' said Prissie over his head. 'He makes these people up. Do you notice how he lives in his imagination, Mrs Gaye? More since you've been ill. I expect it's psychological.'

Fergus looked intently from Prissie to Nicky.

'So there isn't any little girl called Clementine? He's just made her up to make someone the scapegoat for his being hurt?'

'I expect that's why,' said Prissie. 'He said straight away

when he fell that it was Clementine. You have to admit that he really has an astonishing imagination.'

'But why Clementine?' said Fergus, obviously interested in this aspect of Nicky's development. 'It's such an unlikely name.'

'You sing that song, don't you,' said Brigit to Prissie. She could not have explained why she was not as ready as Fergus to dismiss the reality of the fiendish little girl called Clementine. Probably because her's and Nicky's minds worked the same way. She herself could have believed that the mulberry tree outside her window was a petrified witch. Perhaps she had encouraged Nicky too much in his imaginativeness.

'Yes. I do,' said Prissie frankly, 'but I'll tell you what the real reason probably is. The other day I found an old doll in the toy cupboards upstairs and I called it Clementine, just to give it a name. For some reason it seems to have frightened Nicky. I had to put it away again because he wouldn't touch it. He's probably got it on his mind without my noticing.'

Brigit held one of Nicky's muddied hands in hers. She noticed that it was ice-cold.

'Was it that pedlar doll, Prissie? I remember being terrified of it myself when I was a child.'

'I thought it was beautiful,' Prissie said.

'Oh, perfectly made and a work of art, but rather horrible. Witchy.'

'She talks in the night,' Nicky said in a small voice.

Brigit would not allow Fergus his impatience with Nicky's nervousness. She said firmly, 'Fergus, I don't care what you think, but this sort of thing can be very alarming to a sensitive child. Prissie, I think we'll have to get rid of that doll.'

'Yes, I thought that myself after this afternoon,' Prissie said. 'I'm sorry I showed it to him, but I thought it was so cute. The funny thing is he seemed to mind it more shut in the cupboard than when he could see it.'

'We'll burn it,' said Brigit, her arm tightening round Nicky. No use two people in this house having nightmares, she about falling off her horse and Nicky about a harmless wooden doll.

'Seems to me a lot of fuss about nothing,' said Fergus. But he was good-humoured again, and he swung Nicky on to his shoulders, saying, 'What did this oracle used to say to you, anyway?'

'She said she'd know when I told lies. She had a sort of cackling voice.'

'Well, that wouldn't be a bad thing either. You can't go around making up things about being assaulted by people who don't exist. But never mind. Prissie, bring the witch doll and we'll have a bonfire. Everyone can watch her burn.'

The fire was laid in the fireplace in Brigit's room, and it only needed a match set to it to produce flames that soon licked round the macabre figure of the doll laid across the top of the kindling. Sarah danced with delight. But Nicky pressed closer to Brigit and didn't want to look at all.

'Clementine was really there,' he insisted in a very low voice.

'Where, darling?'

'In the park. She had black hair, and—and a red dress.'

But the pedlar doll crackling on the fire had black hair and a red dress, too. Brigit said soothingly. 'She won't be there again. You forget all about her.'

The fire had burned low when, much later, Fergus came in to say good night. For a little while he talked in a light amusing way about what had happened at dinner.

'Aunt Annabel had apparently been stalking a stray cat in the park, and she came in looking far more witchy than that old doll we burnt this afternoon. Uncle Saunders shouted at her through the whole of the meal. He's got some new hiding-place for the housekeeping money, and he's sure this one will defeat her. Guy looked at Prissie all the time—I don't blame him, she looked very attractive——'

'And who did you look at, darling?' Brigit asked, her fingers entangled caressingly in his hair.

'I looked at you. You were sitting opposite me, smiling. I could see you all the time.'

Brigit caught her voice. 'You're as bad as Nicky.'

'Oh, no, I only see the pleasant things.'

Then they were silent, and the fire hissed a little, the flames burning lower. The shadows in the room grew deeper. The bedposts were like straight black trees. Brigit watched Fergus's face, seeing the arrogant lift of his chin, the long straight nose, the lean cheeks, the faint shine of his hair.

'What will the weather be tomorrow?' she asked.

'Fair.'

'You always say that.'

'It always is when I fly. I'll be back on Tuesday.'

'Perhaps I'll be walking by then.'

Fergus laid his head on her breast. His hair was against her chin, soft, thick, familiar.

'Don't be in too much of a hurry. Take this rest while you can. Say perhaps Tuesday week.' His fingers were so tight round hers that she almost had to cry out.

Then the last flame of the fire went out, and the shadows leaped on them. Nurse Ellen, suddenly appearing and switching on the light, said briskly, 'Visiting hours over. The patient has to get some sleep,' and Fergus had his light-hearted face on again.

'Certainly, nurse. Especially since she is to walk so soon.'

When Fergus had gone Brigit, buoyed by his words, again made the futile attempt to move her legs. How *could* they be so numb and responseless? It didn't make sense.

'Nurse, did that one move ever so slightly? Watch.'

Nurse Ellen watched, her eyes kind and attentive. Then she calmly went on with her task of smoothing the bed and tucking Brigit in.

'If it didn't today it will tomorrow. Sleep well, ducky.'

She really thought she would sleep. She was more than two-thirds down the comfortable dark well of unconsciousness when the tiny whispering voice awoke her. *'Don't be so hopeful. It's a waste of time. You'll never walk again!'*

She lifted her head in a panic. The voice seemed to come from the direction of the fireplace. It had had a cackling sound, as of an old old woman. The pedlar doll. Nicky's remark that she had a cackling voice. Oh, no, no, she wasn't sharing Nicky's imagination. She had been dreaming. The voice from the fireplace had been part of her dream. The pedlar doll was in ashes, and it wasn't true that she would never walk again. Of course it wasn't true. Resolutely she settled to sleep again.

It was much later when she was wakened by the moon on her face, and when she thought she heard the high-pitched whispering voice again reiterating her doom, *'You'll never walk again . . .'*

But she was sorry about her panicky ringing of the bell, waking Nurse Ellen who needed her night's sleep. Although it was nice to be reassured by so practical a person and told that all she had heard was Aunt Annabel's cats.

She didn't really want tea, but Nurse Ellen, a cheerful figure in her red flannel dressing-grown, insisted on making it. She said she wanted some herself, and it was lucky Brigit had woken. She was so kind that one could not help relaxing and feeling comforted. Besides, it was nice to lie awake for a little while and think of Fergus sleeping in her old room upstairs, lying in his familiar posture with his face buried deep in the pillow and his fair hair black in the moonlight. She could even pretend drowsily that everything was as it used to be and she was deliberately staying awake, waiting for him to return from a night flight.

The scream from the passage followed by the crash of breaking china dispelled her dream in a moment of icy unreasonable terror.

She tried frantically to sit up in bed. It was only Nurse Ellen tripping over one of those wretched cats, she told herself. Oh, why, why was she so helpless!

A moment later Nurse Ellen, flushed and breathless, appeared in the doorway.

'It's all right, ducky, don't get fussed. I've just seen Mrs Hatchett's ghost and I've dropped the tea tray. Such a mess. It's my first ghost. No wonder I'm in a state.'

'Are you sure it was a ghost?' Brigit asked incredulously.

'He was a little man in a brown suit. I just saw him down

the end of the passage. I screamed and he sort of faded away. Oh dear, now I've roused the whole house. That's Mr Templar calling.'

There was no doubt that it was Uncle Saunders. His voice came echoing down the stairs.

'What's going on down there? Who's prowling about?'

Nurse Ellen gave Brigit a resigned glance.

'That foghorn would wake the very dead.' She began to giggle. 'It's daft, really. Wait till I explain.'

She disappeared, and presently there was a hubbub of voices in the passage, Uncle Saunders's testy questions dominating everybody's. In a moment of silence Aunt Annabel's soft protest, 'It wasn't Renoir because he was with me,' had a chance of being heard.

Uncle Saunders's gigantic scoffing voice dismissed her.

'The time Renoir looks like a little man in a brown coat I'm prepared to live in trees and eat nuts. Fergus, what are you doing with that torch?'

'Just having a look round. There might have been a prowler.'

'First time he's ever been out of the basement.' That was Mrs Hatchett's excited voice. 'I thought it was only my room he inhabited. Probably been a murder or something there once. Sometimes I can't sleep thinking about it, and then I open my eyes and see him standing there, so meek-like, and I don't really think he's a murderer. I think he's just lonely.'

'Well, I wish he'd keep his loneliness in the basement,' Nurse Ellen said. 'Made me spill all the tea.'

'Course he might prowl up here and no one's noticed him before,' Mrs Hatchett reflected.

'What is it, everybody?' That was Prissie's voice. Obviously she was hanging over the stair railing, for her voice came floating down with a far-off sound.

'Nothing to alarm you, my dear,' boomed Uncle Saunders.

'Nurse thinks she saw a ghost,' quavered Aunt Annabel.

'Mine,' said Mrs Hatchett possessively. 'Did he have the hat with the curly brim and a sort of pin-spot cravat?'

'I'd call it a scarf,' Nurse Ellen said flatly. 'And it was too dark to see spots.'

'Yes, that's him. He tries to look sinister, but he isn't a bit, poor lamb.'

'Go back to bed, Prissie,' said Fergus with a note of protectiveness in his voice. 'You'll catch cold. I'm looking for this sinister prowler, real or unreal. He won't do you any harm.'

Prissie gave a far-away excited laugh. 'Oh! One doesn't really believe in ghosts, does one?'

The chatter went on for several minutes, then Fergus, who had obviously been doing a tour of the house, returned saying, 'There's no sign of anyone. Everything looks all right. If anyone got in it could only have been through the downstairs cloakroom window. Isn't that locked at night?'

'It should be,' Uncle Saunders said testily.

'Well, it isn't. But I've locked it now. So you can all go safely to bed. Is my wife disturbed, nurse?'

'She's awake. I was making her tea. Dropped it all over the carpet.' Nurse Ellen's voice was rueful. 'First time I've seen a ghost.'

'They don't do you no harm, dear,' Mrs Hatchett said earnestly.

Fergus's step came to Brigit's door.

'Darling, have you been frightened by all this?'

'Not frightened.' Brigit slowly unclenched her hands. 'Mrs Hatchett has had this ghost for years, but no one else has ever seen him. We always thought she imagined it.'

'I should think she does, too,' said Fergus. 'I'm afraid this might have been a burglar. Someone was careless about locking up tonight. But apparently Nurse Ellen startled him in time. I don't think there's anything missing.'

But there was something missing. In the morning the maid, Lorna, reported that the Dresden shepherd and shepherdess had been shifted. When they couldn't be found it had to be assumed that Nurse Ellen's apparition had really been a burglar. A little later, with loud indignant cries, Uncle Saunders found that the gold angel, that was as fat as a young thrush, was gone also. The burglar, disturbed by Nurse Ellen, had not had time to take more.

It was Prissie who made the surprising discovery that Nicky's coat with the fur collar, left in the downstairs cloakroom to dry after getting wet in a shower yesterday, had also vanished.

SEVEN

The police had to be notified, of course, and during the morning a young constable came and took careful notes. Fortunately both the angel and the Dresden figures were covered by insurance, and the loss of Nicky's coat was negligible.

'Poor man, he must have had a large family,' Mrs Hatchett said. Her sympathies were entirely with the burglar, for she could not be convinced that he had no affinity with her unearthly visitor. It was possible, she was even telling herself, that ghosts liked objects of art, and had to clothe their children.

Uncle Saunders mourned the days when they could afford a butler and then of course no downstairs window was ever left unlocked. Now the house was going to rack and ruin. Aunt Annabel patiently inquired how it could be expected to do anything else, with only a cook-housekeeper, one maid, and a daily.

'Money doesn't come off trees,' Uncle Saunders shouted irately. 'And if it did the Government would take it, royal mint or not. I tell you, existence is practically impossible nowadays.' Suddenly he pounced on Aunt Annabel. 'I suppose you left that window open for one of your deuced cats.'

'Oh, no, I didn't, Saunders. They have their sand-box in the studio.'

'An indoor toilet?' Uncle Saunders's voice was scathing. 'Pampered creatures. Well, let's look at the Stock Exchange reports. If the insurance company pays up, and mind you, I don't expect them to, no one does anything they don't want to nowadays, I might invest in—let me see—Guy, what do you think of these Bolivian oil things?'

Brigit's mind kept running foolishly on the scarf motif. It had been a red-and-white-spotted scarf that had caused her fall from her horse, and now there was this discussion about the scarf the burglar had worn, Mrs Hatchett insisting that it had been the distinctive cravat, green with a pin-spot, and Nurse Ellen saying only that his throat and chin had been muffled by some sort of scarf.

Brigit was sure now that what had originally woken her had been the burglar prowling along the passage, and that the voice she thought she had heard saying, 'You'll never walk again,' had been sheer imagination. She was almost, like Mrs Hatchett, sympathetic towards the burglar for having provided a normal explanation for what had been a nightmare.

Strangely enough, Prissie was the one who was most upset. She was deeply grieved and angry about the loss of the gold angel. 'I adored it,' she said. 'I should think stealing that would bring anyone bad luck.'

'It was probably stolen in the first place from some church,' Brigit said. 'It's only poetic justice about a hundred and fifty years too late.'

'Oh, you!' Prissie exclaimed in sudden impatience. 'You don't appreciate any of these lovely things.'

'Perhaps I don't,' Brigit agreed. 'Perhaps I like best what I can get for myself, even if it's quite simple.'

It seemed to her that Prissie's eyes fleetingly held pity or contempt. At least, for that moment, they were no longer young. They were adult and shrewd.

'If it's your inheritance I don't see why you shouldn't like it.'

When Brigit didn't answer at once she went on almost belligerently, 'Anyway, I adore it all. I can just lap up luxury.'

Brigit noticed that when Prissie was disturbed or upset she always fingered the locket round her neck. It was as if it were her talisman. What had she got in it?

'Prissie, that extraordinary story you told the children about your royal blood isn't true, is it?'

Prissie flung back her head and seemed momentarily to gain height. All at once she had a curious hauteur. Then abruptly she burst into youthful giggles.

'Not exactly. But almost.'

'What do you mean by almost? Either it's true or it's not true.'

Prissie smiled with engaging sweetness.

'That would be telling secrets. And it's silly to do that, isn't it?'

'That would depend whether they are guilty ones or not.'

'Most people's are guilty, aren't they? You ask anyone in this house what their secret is. I'll bet you'll find they've all got one.' Again there was that disconcerting shrewdness in Prissie's eyes. Then excitement seemed to bubble over inside her. 'Life's so *interesting*, isn't it?' she said.

At least wondering about Prissie's own secret, real or imaginary, innocent or guilty, took Brigit's mind off herself. So the funny little creature was performing an indirect service. A psychologist would explain that, after her difficult and lonely childhood, Prissie's stories of past grandeur were simply a defence. She had probably come to actually believe in them because they boosted her morale. On the other hand there was the fact that she possessed natural grace and self-confidence, two attributes that were more likely to come from heredity than from her makeshift upbringing.

No doubt she would one day decide she liked and trusted Brigit enough to tell her the truth. In the meantime, let her enjoy the now somewhat shabby luxury of the Montpelier Square house, and pretend, if she liked, that it all belonged to her. Because that, obviously, was what she was doing. The loss of the little gold angel, particularly, had become to Prissie a personal loss. What a complex little person she was. And would other things, if she were threatened with their loss, grieve her as much? The children, for instance? Was she growing to think of them as hers? And yesterday when she had come in happy and bright-cheeked after meeting Fergus. Was her nature too possessive? Did she unconsciously imagine that everything she cared for or admired should become hers?

But it was foolish to think that way. She must think how lucky she was to have Prissie to care for the children so competently and lovingly. They might have been at the mercy of some thin-lipped dragon. And it wasn't going to be for long. Everyone said so. Soon she would walk again.

Fergus echoed that thought when he came in to say good-bye. He held her closely and reiterated, 'You'll be all right while I'm away? You've got Nurse Ellen. She tells me that burglars will have to get in here across her dead body.'

Brigit laughed. 'I'm not frightened of burglars.'

If only that were all there were of which to be afraid! They could have the entire contents of the house if they wished. They could even take away this bed in which she lay like a princess, if only in return she would regain the use of her legs.

The doctor had said she must relax. Relax and don't worry. That was so essential.

Fergus kissed her again. 'Darling—don't hate being here too much.'

So he knew she hated it. Of course he would know. He hated it, too, hated taking favours from her family. If it came to that it was her family who was to blame for the whole thing. If Uncle Saunders hadn't made that intolerable remark about Prissie and Fergus she would not have left the house in a temper and ridden Polly. She would not have had that fall and lost the baby. But Fergus didn't care about the baby. He had said so. Perhaps he really was glad. Perhaps it had been a shock to him to hear her news that day he had brought Prissie home.

Now his fingers were smoothing the frown from her forehead.

'Biddy—relax. Nothing will happen while I'm away.'

Then he was gone, and it seemed as if a brightness and optimism had gone out of the room.

Nurse Ellen came in and glanced at her.

'Now, none of that down-in-the-mouth business. Sure, I know your husband's a dream, and every pretty girl would try to grab him as soon as look at him. But we haven't time to worry about that now. We've got a busy time while he's away.'

'Me busy!' Brigit said bitterly.

'Indeed you are going to be. I have a Routine, and it's going to keep you fully occupied. First, massage.' She whipped back the blankets expertly. 'I won't say you've got Dietrich's legs, ducky, but they don't miss by much.'

'Are they—starting to waste?'

'Waste, my foot! They're merely the laziest pair of legs I've ever been privileged to see. We've got to get them working so they can chase off all the pretty girls. My, fancy that being a real burglar last night. I'd have passed out if I'd known. Mrs Hatchett won't believe it yet, you know. She's going round like Macbeth muttering "Doomed for a thousand years to walk this earth".'

'That was Hamlet's father,' Brigit corrected.

'Was it, ducky? Well, it's all one now, isn't it?'

Nurse Ellen's face was rather like a sun, a pale London sun shining through mist, as a reminder that there was still warmth and brightness in the world. Brigit tried to respond to her determined cheerfulness.

'Where are the children?' she asked.

'Prissie has taken them over to Harrods to shop. Nicky has to have a new coat, and I think Mrs Templer said something about dresses and shoes for Sarah.'

Brigit started up, her face full of distress.

'Oh, how dare she! I clothe my own children. Sarah's dresses are perfectly all right.'

'Well, I expect you'll get the bill, ducky.'

'No, I won't. That's just the trouble. It will be one more obligation I have to this horrible family of mine.'

'I think your Aunt Annabel is rather a pet,' Nurse Ellen said mildly. 'Just like a nice pussy cat. No claws.'

'Oh, yes, she's all right, but it isn't her money. It's Templar money she's spending. You can't say Uncle Saunders is a pet.'

'He likes to make himself heard, certainly. It's like living on top of the underground the moment he comes in the house. A constant noise and vibration. And he's a bit free with——'

'Yes?' said Brigit, as Nurse Ellen hesitated.

'Well, I guess I can cope with silly old men who like to pinch. My, I wouldn't have qualms about taking his money. Anyway, Nicky has to have a coat, doesn't he, since his own is missing. Do you know, that's the first time I've ever heard of burglars having children. Makes them quite human, doesn't it? One rather hopes he won't be caught, the poor little blighter.'

It did seem a pity to grudge the children their pleasure, even if it were Uncle Saunders's money they were spending. And Prissie's pleasure, too, for the three of them came in later laden with parcels and full of excitement. More accurately, Prissie and small Sarah, who was being a horse, radiated excitement. Nicky, as usual lately, was too silent, and had that pinched look in his face.

'We've had such fun!' said Prissie, with her way of speaking in italics when she was excited. 'Come, children, show your mother your new things. Sarah, I might say, would have given her eyes for a ballet dress, the sweetest thing in pale-pink tulle. She ought to have dancing lessons, you know, she's crazy about dancing.'

'I don't know where she gets it from,' Brigit said matter-of-factly. 'You didn't buy her the dress, I imagine?'

'Oh no, of course not. I was quite sensible. Although I had hard work not to be. The lovely things in that shop.'

Sarah galloped round the bed, shaking her fair head until she almost lost her balance, then rubbing it affectionately against Brigit's hand.

'Nice horsey, nice horsey,' she said winningly.

'Oh, she saw the horse-guards go past,' Prissie explained. 'Really, we've had the most exciting time. Haven't we, Nicky? Come and show mummy your new coat, darling.'

Nicky, being spoken to, came forward slowly. He was wearing the new coat, a well-cut tweed that gave his little figure a poignantly mature look.

'Oh, that's very nice,' Brigit said with genuine pleasure. 'Just what I would have chosen for him. Don't you like it, Nicky?'

Nicky nodded. Then suddenly, as if he were driven to, he burst out, 'Clementine had a new dress, too.'

'Clementine! You mean——'

Prissie frowned a little and shook her head. 'I'm sorry, he will persist with this make-believe of his. And after us burning that cute little doll, too.'

'You mean he's still turning her into a little girl that goes around with you?'

'All the time.' Prissie shrugged good-naturedly. 'I suppose children do that sort of thing. Look at Sarah, she's a different animal every day. Yesterday she was carrying sticks in her mouth because she saw a spaniel doing it, today it's a horse. I'll have her galloping about until bedtime.'

Brigit took Nicky's hand and drew him near. 'Nicky, darling. This Clementine. Where does she live?'

Nicky hesitated. He gave Prissie a quick glance. 'In the cupboard in the nursery,' he said. 'At least I think so.'

'But, darling, no little girl could live in a cupboard. She would have to eat and have a bed to sleep in. There was that doll who lived in the cupboard, but we burnt her yesterday, don't you remember?'

Nicky's eyes were too big, their pupils enlarged in a strained and worrying way.

'She's still there, mummy. She cackles in the night.'

All at once for no reason at all, a swift feeling of premonition, of apprehension, of fear—what was it, this cold airy feeling that came from nowhere—stabbed Brigit. The cackling voice—she had heard it, too. From the fireplace, where the pedlar doll had been burnt, in the dark and quiet of the night. '*You'll never walk again!*' What was it? Were she and Nicky under some spell?

'Oh, darling, you only dream that,' she said swiftly. 'I have funny dreams, too, but they're only dreams.'

'She pinches me,' said Nicky, rubbing his arm reminiscently.

Prissie said softly, 'You see? Something's got into him. I don't know whether he's being deliberately contrary, or whether he really believes there is this peculiar person. It was my fault in the beginning for my habit of going round singing. "Darling Clementine" has always been a favourite song of mine.' She sang it lightly and gaily, looking at Nicky for approval. 'But I shouldn't have called that nasty doll Clementine on the spur of the moment. The name seems to have become associated in his mind with bad dreams and horrid things.'

'He's always had too much imagination,' Brigit said. 'Has he been having nightmares?'

Prissie put her hand protectingly on Nicky's shoulder.

'Only little ones. Haven't you, sweet?'

Brigit was worried. This thing of Nicky's seemed to be becoming an obsession.

'Tell me, darling, if Clementine was getting new clothes, too, this morning, what did she get?'

Nicky frowned with thought.

'A blue dress with a velvet collar. Red shoes.'

Prissie whipped open one of the packages, and spread a miniature blue dress with a velvet collar and buttons on the bed.

'You see, he does have imagination, but not enough to make Clementine's dress even a different colour. This is Sarah's new dress. And her red shoes, too. She longed for them to be red. I hope you don't mind, Mrs Gaye.'

'Not a bit. Red shoes are pretty. Sarah will adore them. But, Prissie, before you shop for the children again please tell me.'

Prissie's eyes flew wide open.

'Of course, Mrs Gaye. But I thought you knew. Mrs Templar said——'

'Oh, I know Aunt Annabel thought they were shabby, and I know Nicky's coat disappeared. No doubt Aunt Annabel meant it as a wonderful surprise.' Brigit closed her eyes a moment. Her head had begun to ache and she felt exhausted. 'But they're still my children, Prissie. I like to be told what is happening. I even have pride about buying and paying for their clothes myself.'

'Of course, Mrs Gaye.' Prissie's voice was warm and understanding. 'I should have thought. I just get carried away with enthusiasm.'

She really was only a child herself, full of her vivacity and thoughtlessness. Brigit said wearily, 'And, Prissie. You still call me Mrs Gaye. You don't call my husband Mr Gaye or Squadron Leader.'

The colour mounted charmingly in Prissie's imp-like face. 'I suppose it's because I've known him longer, working with him and so on. But somehow it hasn't seemed right to call you anything but Mrs Gaye.'

'We're friends, aren't we?'

'Oh, of course!' Again came her warm rejoinder. 'It's just terribly sweet of you. I can't tell you how grateful to you I am for being here, in this lovely house——'

'My accident was lucky for you.'

'Oh, no, Mrs Gaye! I didn't mean that at all. I just mean your making me a friend and letting me have the children, just as if I were their mother. People in the street look at me and say, "Isn't she young to have two such beautiful children!"' Prissie laughed in pleased reminiscence. 'It's not fair being happy while you lie there helpless, but I can't help it. I just can't.'

Brigit could not help being carried away by her youthful enthusiasm. 'Go on being happy. It's nice.'

It was only later that she thought of Prissie's innocent remarks about her pleasure in being mistaken for the children's mother, about the friendly way in which she called Fergus by his name, while she kept Brigit at arm's length, and about the way she danced confidently about the house as if she belonged there. Was possessiveness Prissie's one failing? Or was her own sick mind placing undue emphasis on these things?

The one thing that did emerge from that visit to her room was her uneasiness about Nicky. Why did he have this strange obsession about a child called Clementine?

It was Prissie's afternoon off that day, and she seemed particularly eager to get away to visit her aunt in Putney.

She came flying in to say good-bye to Brigit.

'Mrs Templer is taking the children in the park,' she said. 'They might track down that starved cat, she says. So if Nicky has his face scratched again you'll know what's done it this time. I'll be back in time to put them to bed. Aunt Maud does enjoy my visits, and what she'll say when she hears about the burglar last night, I can't think. I was so terrified I was shaking. Fergus had to tell me not to be silly. Good-bye, Mrs Gaye.'

Fergus ... Mrs Gaye ... Was the distinction deliberate? But Prissie was such an alive pretty little figure in her cherry hat and coat that one couldn't really accuse her of these subtleties.

After Aunt Annabel, wrapped in her grey furs, had taken the children off, chattering all the way about 'that sweet little pussy striped just like your Uncle Saunders's new tie', Brigit looked at Nurse Ellen, and Nurse Ellen nodded and said:

'Yes, ducky, that cupboard. I'll go up and take a look at it right away.'

She came back soon enough.

'It's a whole wardrobe,' she said. 'You can step right inside it.'

'I know. There are shelves for toys, and the chilren's clothes hang in the middle.'

'That's right. There isn't anything there to worry about. All the toys are harmless things, nothing to frighten Nicky now that doll has gone. Certainly the cupboard is big enough for someone to hide in, but who is going to be silly enough to do that?'

'Who indeed?' said Brigit. 'Well, that's that. Nicky is just being too imaginative. His father has always said so. We'll have to cure him of it.'

'That's right,' said Nurse Ellen cheerfully. 'Time for your nap, ducky.' She was humming as she smoothed the sheets. Then she exclaimed, 'Oh, my God! Now I'm doing it.' She had broken off half way through 'Darling Clementine'. 'Is that wretched tune going to be the theme song in this house?'

EIGHT

SARAH came back from the park being a dog. Aunt Annabel had found not the starved tabby she sought but a black kitten, plump and playful, and simply miles from home, she said, but of course she would advertise it, and if no owner turned up perhaps Brigit would like it. It would bring her luck. Although Renoir would be simply furious, he hated kittens of all colours.

Even Nicky had pink in his cheeks. In response to Brigit's question he admitted that they had had fun catching the kitten and that Clementine hadn't been there that afternoon.

'It's nicer without her,' he said.

'Of course it is, darling. You forget all about her.'

Then Prissie came home and she, too, was bright-eyed and bright-cheeked.

'I've got simply heavenly material for a dress,' she said. 'May I show it to you?'

She unwrapped the parcel and spread the brilliant peacock-coloured silk over the bed. Brigit looked at it, then slowly at Prissie.

'That's the colour my mother is wearing in her portrait.'

'I know. That's why I chose it. I thought it was so heavenly.'

The black kitten on Brigit's bed pounced at the brightly-coloured silk. Catching it, Brigit said rather stiffly:

'What is the dress for, Prissie?'

'Guy wants to take me to dinner. And I hadn't a thing to wear.'

'Oh,' said Brigit slowly. Was the sudden pang she felt envy because she couldn't put on a pretty dress and go dining and dancing? That Guy should be attracted by Prissie was a very natural thing. She was gay and full of light chatter, and he, lately, had grown even more quiet and secretive. Hadn't she wished he could find a nice girl to make him happy and light-hearted? Surely Prissie was exactly the answer. Except that her acquisitive notions and her love of luxury would blend only too well with the Templar traits, and would this be altogether wise?

'Guy needs cheering up,' Prissie was continuing. 'He works too hard and he looks awfully thin. A night out will do him good.' She glanced at Brigit. 'You don't mind, do you, Mrs Gaye?'

'What you do in your spare time is your own business, Prissie.' Then, regretting the slight coldness of her tone, she said, 'You really have taken us on as a family, haven't you? Me helpless, the children dependent on you, Guy needing cheering up, though goodness knows why.'

Prissie's face sparkled with her wide spontaneous smile. 'But I love it, Mrs Gaye. Truly.'

'I believe you actually do,' said Brigit. Then suddenly she was gay herself, because Prissie seemed so excited at the prospect of going out with Guy, and therefore could not be cherishing too much secret affection for Fergus. 'Tell that brother of mine to come and see me. He's scarcely been near me since I've been ill.'

Guy, no doubt at Prissie's behest, came in after dinner that evening. It was true that he had got even thinner than usual. His face seemed drawn, and his eyes didn't quite meet Brigit's. Has he done something wrong? flashed through Brigit's mind. All her life she had been afraid for Guy because he had inherited so many of the Templar weaknesses, without the saving grace of the dashing impudence and confidence that Uncle Saunders had. If Guy were found out in a wrong deed, Brigit realized, he would have no courage.

Now he worked in a stockbroker's, a position Uncle Saunders had obtained for him. Had he been gambling? Brigit wondered. Was he in debt and afraid to tell Uncle Saunders, who could be terrifying in his wrath?

'Hullo, Guy,' Brigit said lightly. 'I hear you and Prissie are having a night out.'

'Any objections?' Guy flashed at her.

'Of course I haven't. Prissie's charming, and I should think would be great fun to take out. Don't be so prickly.'

Guy smiled, a little shamefacedly.

'Sorry, Biddy. I'm touchy these days.'

'You certainly are. What have you been up to? You're terribly thin.'

'Working too hard,' he said quickly.

'Guy—now don't jump down my throat—you're not in debt, are you? You're not worried about money?'

At first it seemed that he was going to lash out at her again. But he controlled himself, and gave his slow rather charming smile.

'I'm always worried about that. I've got to practically exist on my salary, you know. It seems so damn silly while Uncle Saunders sits on the fleshpots. After all, half of them should be ours.'

'I imagine they'll all be ours one day,' Brigit said wearily. 'For my part you're welcome to the lot. You know I've always hated the Templar money.'

'You must take after father. I don't. I'm all Templar. I long to have lashings of cash.'

'Then you have a willing confederate in Prissie,' Brigit said dryly. 'She has similar ambitions. I don't know whether she will be good for you after all.' She added, 'Is that really all that's wrong, Guy? Shortage of money?'

He gave her his quick uneasy glance.

'What do you mean, wrong? There's nothing wrong at all.' He smiled crookedly again. 'Well, that money won't cure.'

Money! It was a topic of absorbing interest in this household. This was the day of the week that Uncle Saunders was expected to hand over the housekeeping money, but since he had developed this latest elephantine joke of hiding it, the evening developed into a wild scramble, with Aunt Annabel, Mrs Hatchett, and the maid, Lorna, darting from room to room searching, while Uncle Saunders followed them ponderously, bellowing gleefully, 'Cold! Colder!' then reluctantly, 'Warm now. A little warmer. No, cold again. Ten minutes to go. Come along, Annabel, you're expert enough at catching your deuced cats. Surely you can ferret out a little bit of money.'

Aunt Annabel protested, 'Oh, Saunders, you are exasperating. This is all so childish!'

'Is it in the bedrooms this time, sir?' inquired Mrs Hatchett.

'No, no. I play fair. Bedrooms out of bounds. It's on this floor.' Uncle Saunders began to whistle gaily, and Brigit could visualize him, his face flushed, his pale blue eyes protruding with the fun and excitement he was having, his thick lips hanging open in a pleasurable smile. His heavy footsteps went tramp, tramp, tramp from one room to the other after the scurrying women. He would be dropping cigar ash down his waistcoat and over the carpet, while he held his large gold watch in one hand, consulting it repeatedly.

'Five more minutes!' he announced. 'If I win this week I've got a very nice parcel of gold mining shares sorted out. Very cheap. Should show a hundred per cent profit. Wouldn't that be worth starving one week for?'

'You, too, will starve, my dear,' Aunt Annabel pointed out.

'I'll eat at my club, ha, ha! It's your deuced cats you're worrying about, not yourself. No, no, my dear, I told you the sideboard was cold, ten minutes ago. Ah ha, Lorna's getting warm. Very warm indeed. Oh, no! No, not that flower pot, my dear. That—oh, she's smelt it out, the little rat. Yes, there it is. Dig it out of the earth. Shake it clean.'

'Oh, Saunders!' Aunt Annabel cried. 'My hyacinths! You'll have ruined the bulbs!'

'Money doesn't ruin anything, my dear. Yes, there it is. Count it. Divide it up. Turn it into butter and eggs and floor-polish and cats' meat. Watch it disappear. If it had been invested in my gold shares it would have come back a hundred times. But there you are! All this passion for food and household goods. You women! You'll never learn to appreciate money.'

His mournful voice, decreasing in volume, faded away. The house settled down to silence again. Nurse Ellen, in Brigit's room, drawing the curtains and putting out the lights, said, 'Well! How he likes to liven things up,' and smiled at Brigit and said, 'No burglars, no ghosts tonight. Sleep well, ducky.'

Upstairs on the top floor Prissie was interrupted in her writing by Nicky, who was wakeful, asking for a drink of water. She went to the bathroom to get it, and when she came back Nicky had got out of bed and was standing by the table concentratedly trying to read what she had written.

'Love-ly seeing you today,' he read laboriously. 'But it's so odd a-bout the an-gel——'

'Nicky!' Prissie exclaimed peremptorily. 'Don't you know it's very bad manners to read other people's letters?'

Nicky shrank back. She had spoken sharply, and lately he couldn't bear sharp voices. They made him feel as if pins were sticking into him.

'I was only seeing if I could read,' he muttered.

Prissie set down the glass of water. She picked up the half-finished letter and put it on the mantelpiece. Then she spoke in her usual soft kind voice. 'So you were, darling. But you mustn't practise on people's private things. That's very bad.'

'Yes,' Nicky whispered obediently. He sipped some of the water, and his mind went back with curiosity to what he had just read. 'Did you see an angel today?' he asked interestedly.

'An angel! You mean—Oh, no, my aunt had a nice dream about one. She's very old and she dreams things like that. Silly, isn't it?'

'Like my dreams about Clementine?'

'A bit. Now off to bed with you, and no more calling out. I'm going to put your light out and you have to go to sleep.'

'Yes,' said Nicky again obediently. He did feel sleepy now, and was sure that he would cuddle down at once into that warm friendly world of sleep.

He did, too. He must have slept for hours and hours. But it was still dark when he awoke, and the cackling voice was in the cupboard again. It was saying, 'Nicky, listen to me! Nicky, if you tell lies about Clementine again, even once again, I will know. I will know, ha ha!'

The voice, ending in that croaking laugh, was indescribably frightening. Nicky cowered rigidly beneath the blankets. He wanted to draw them over his ears but he couldn't bring himself to move his hands. The tip of his nose was frozen, the hair felt stiff on his head.

'It's all lies, Nicky!' came the voice again. 'You know it is.'

Before this he had heard the voice crackling in laughter in the night. But this was the first time it had said actual words. He was so petrified with terror, expecting to see the cupboard open and the small black witch-like shape of the doll advancing upon him, that he could scarcely breathe.

'Remember!' the voice was saying. 'Remember!'

Downstairs the moon shone on Brigit's face again, but it was barred with clouds tonight, and anyway it had not woken her. She had been awake. She had scarcely slept at all. No voices or other sounds, beyond an occasional soft scurry from the cats overhead, disturbed her. The house was silent. If Mrs Hatchett's ghost were prowling about it was doing so noiselessly. There was nothing to keep her wakeful. Yet she remained intensely wakeful, and deep inside her that cold fear was stirring. And it was not now fear about her physical condition, but another fear, unnamed and unexplainable, like a ghostly finger on her shoulder...

'Nothing will happen while I'm away,' Fergus had said.

Even as she remembered his reassuring words Brigit imagined she heard a faint stirring in the direction of the fireplace, then, a second later there was no doubt about the sound of hoarse breathing. Brigit raised her head and looked intently into the indistinct shape of the fireplace. There was nothing to see, only the mouth of the chimney a square of deeper blackness than the surrounding tiles. The sound had stopped now. It hadn't been Nurse Ellen because tonight she was sleeping in her bed in the dressing-room next door. Brigit had insisted that she do so. She could ring, she said, if she wanted anything.

But she wouldn't ring just because she imagined she

heard breathing in the fireplace. It was the wind, sending breathy gusts down the chimney. Was there a wind? There was no rustle of leaves outside the window.

Her heart still beating violently as much from her premonition of danger as from what she thought she had heard, Brigit lay back. It *couldn't* have been anything. She was as bad as Nicky who imagined someone dwelt in the big dark cupboard in his room. But Nicky was only a child. She at least was old enough to know better.

'Silly!' came the small throaty voice from the chimney. 'You think you are yourself. But you're not. You're me.' There was a dreadful ghostly little cackle of laughter. Then the voice, with its macabre mirth, 'I am you and you are me...'

Now there was a gust of wind stirring outside. It rustled leaves, crackling them like brittle paper, then swept down the chimney, sweeping the voice away.

Had there been a voice? Even now, in the silence, Brigit could not have sworn to it. She lay drenched in chilly perspiration, helpless, unable to move or cry out.

Yet in the morning, with the fragile late autumn sunlight coming in the window, and the house full of normal sounds, the children scampering downstairs, Uncle Saunders shouting, and Nurse Ellen tripping in and out of the room, it seemed that it must have been a nightmare. How could a voice speak from the chimney? It was all so absurd. She must have thought she was awake and yet been dreaming. Anyway, the words the voice had spoken didn't even make sense. *You are me* ... Who was *me*? No, when Fergus came home this evening she could not tell him this latest flight of fancy. He would be as impatient with her as he was with Nicky.

Nurse Ellen's routine was well under way now. First there was the early morning cup of tea, then the refreshing wash, the clean nightdress, the hair brushing, and the application of a decorous amount of make-up ('just to keep up your morale, ducky') then the brief rest before breakfast.

Her breakfast tray was obviously prepared by Nurse Ellen with great care, and always bore a rose or a carnation, as well as the morning papers and any mail that might have arrived for her. By the time it came in Brigit was ready for the comfort of food and hot coffee for she was invariably suffering from intense dejection at the discovery that still her legs were numb and useless. Each morning the frail but tenuous hope would come to her—perhaps today one of her feet, or even one toe, would consent to move. When nothing happened her spirits would begin to sink lower and lower. In hospital at this time the sister had frequently found her in tears. But now that she was at home, with the children likely to come in at any moment, and everyone being so kind, she felt that the least she could do was to keep bright and cheerful. On the nights that Fergus slept in the house it was even more imperative to present a smiling face to him. But the mask, she was afraid, was going to wear thin. Oh, how much longer could this go on?

'Now, ducky, you're needing this, I can see,' Nurse Ellen said briskly, as she crossed the room with the tray. '*And* a surprise for you this morning. Just look and see!'

'What?' said Brigit feebly, biting on her trembling lip. Nurse Ellen had nearly witnessed the shame of her cowardly tears this morning.

'A cable from Rome. Really that husband of yours spoils you disgustingly.'

'Oh, from Fergus!' Brigit cried in delight.

'That, and a letter, too! Now don't let your coffee get cold. The news will keep.'

The cable might have been Fergus speaking.

DIDN'T I TELL YOU NOTHING WOULD HAPPEN WHILE I WAS AWAY SO STOP WORRYING. ALL MY LOVE FERGUS

Brigit smiled, and blinked back tears, and holding the cable lovingly in her hands forgot to pour her coffee while it was hot. She temporarily forgot the other letter, too. Anyway, it didn't look very important. Her name and address were printed in rather crude letters. It was probably from one of the patients with whom she had made friends in the hospital.

She opened it languidly after she had savoured the delight of Fergus's brisk business-like cable that covered so much thoughtfulness and understanding.

Then she dropped the sheet of paper the envelope contained as if she had been stung. She gazed at it lying on the clean white sheets in complete horror, as if it were some horrible insect. The scrawled printing did, in fact, look like the wandering trail of a slug. But the words were quite legible.

DID YOU KNOW THAT YOUR BROTHER IS THE HIT AND RUN DRIVER WHO KNOCKED DOWN A MAN AND KILLED HIM OUTSIDE DORKING ON THE NIGHT OF THE FIRST OF OCTOBER. I HAVE PROOF OF THIS BUT I WILL KEEP MY MOUTH SHUT IF YOU PAY ME A HUNDRED POUNDS BY MIDDAY TOMORROW. THE MONEY MUST BE IN SINGLE POUND NOTES. YOU CAN GET THESE EASILY ENOUGH. I HAVE WATCHED THE HOUSE AND KNOW WHO LIVES IN IT. SEND THE NURSEMAID WHO LOOKS AFTER YOUR CHILDREN TO THE BANK FOR THE MONEY, THEN PUT IT IN AN ENVELOPE AND ADDRESS IT TO MR GEORGE SMITH, 15 PELHAM ROAD, HAMMERSMITH. I KNOW YOU CAN GO TO THE POLICE BUT THE SENTENCE I GET WON'T BE HALF WHAT YOUR BROTHER WILL GET. IS THAT CLEAR?

Nurse Ellen came bustling busily into the room. Automatically Brigit crumpled the loathsome piece of paper into her hand.

'Why, ducky, you haven't eaten a thing! What's the matter? You don't look so good.'

'I—I'm not hungry this morning,' Brigit managed to say. 'Later, perhaps. I want to see my brother.'

'Sure, you can see your brother, but there's plenty of time. Lie still and relax for a bit.'

'No, now,' Brigit insisted. 'Before he leaves for the office. It's—it's quite important. And, nurse, if you'd mind just leaving us alone for a few minutes.'

Nurse Ellen's blond head went in the air huffily.

'Certainly, Mrs Gaye. I'm not interested in other people's conversations, even though there might be other people in this house who are.'

'What do you mean?' Brigit asked swiftly.

'Nothing. Nothing at all.' Nurse Ellen swept up the untouched breakfast tray. 'And what the doctor will say when he knows you're deliberately starving yourself, I can't think.'

But for all her brief display of temperament she sent Guy. He came into the room, thin and slightly hollow-cheeked in his dark city suit. He looked as if he hadn't slept, and his beautiful lips drooped peevishly.

'Hullo, Biddy,' he said languidly. 'Anything wrong?'

'I—I hope not, Guy,' Brigit said carefully. She was still in the peculiar unreal state following shock. 'But someone has just written me a very nasty letter. It concerns you.'

Guy looked at her fully for one moment, his eyes startled and aware. Then they slid away, and now he was speaking as carefully as she.

'Concerns me! What on earth about?'

Brigit pushed the crumpled sheet of paper towards him. 'Read it yourself. I can't bear to look at it again.'

It couldn't be true, of course! Guy was weak and perhaps even cowardly, but he couldn't have done this. Surely he couldn't have.

Guy echoed her thoughts. After glancing at the paper he flung it on the bed, saying hoarsely, 'It's damned lie! Some swine—oh, my God, fancy inventing a filthy lie like that!'

But Brigit had glimpsed his eyes again, darkened and full of fear. Her heart sank.

'The first of October was the day before my accident,' she said, speaking almost casually.

'Was it? I can't remember.'

'It was, because that was on the second, and you had driven Uncle Saunders down to get Aunt Annabel. Don't you remember? He was complaining very loudly about your careless driving, because you had bent the bumper bar of the car the night before. You said you hadn't had time to get it straightened. Guy!'

'Yes!' he said violently.

'Had you been afraid to take it into a garage to get it straightened—in case they should recognize the car?'

'No! My God, no!'

'Didn't you use to know a girl in Dorking not very long

ago? I remember Aunt Annabel saying you had been going down there rather a lot.'

Guy flung round, his face white and drawn.

'Biddy, what is this? A cross-examination?'

She sighed deeply, and put out her hands.

'Tell me, Guy. It's true, isn't it? I knew it was true from the moment you couldn't look at me. Anyway these'—she gestured towards the letter—'these insects are usually pretty sure of their facts. Or so I've been told.'

Abruptly Guy sat down and buried his head in the bed-clothes. He began to sob.

'Yes, it's true. My God, it's been a nightmare. But the chap was over seventy. And he hadn't any family. I know that. I found out. And he had heart disease, too, so he couldn't have lived long. It isn't that bad, Biddy.'

'What is bad,' said Brigit in her quiet inexorable voice, 'is your behaviour. Why didn't you stop? Why didn't you go back?'

'I know,' said Guy, rolling his head back and forth. 'But I panicked. And then it was too late. And anyway he was dead. I couldn't bring him back to life.' Suddenly he raised his head. 'Biddy, what are you going to do?'

Brigit looked at his tormented face. She saw the weak chin, the beautiful drooping mouth, the desperate eyes—all the hated Templar characteristics, she thought despairingly. And now cowardice added to them.

'Guy, I want you to go to the police.'

'The police! At this stage! Are you mad?'

'No. Only—only honest, perhaps.'

'But, Biddy, it's all right now. It's over. They've never even for one minute suspected me. And the chap's dead and he has no dependants. There's absolutely no good can come of my going to prison now. And supposing I did go to prison. You know the Templars. I'd be kicked out, just as mother was. I'd be disinherited. Isn't that a nice Victorian word? Disinherited.'

'So you're thinking of nothing but money, too.' Brigit's voice was too weary even for scorn.

'I'm not, Biddy. Truly. I'm thinking of much more than

that. I think I'm in love with Prissie. It's the first time I've ever been in love. It's so wonderful to feel a little happy. Oh, Biddy, you know what it's like to be happy with someone you love. Don't spoil it for me.'

His face was suddenly young again, the lines of strain and fear temporarily smoothed out. He was the little boy Brigit had defended through so many childish troubles, since she had had to be his mother as well as his older sister. She had always longed for his happiness. She had thought that being happy would work a miracle in him and turn him into a normal confident person. But now—how was happiness to come on top of guilt? And blackmail?

If Guy went to the police and confessed there was no doubt that he would have to serve a prison sentence. Equally, there was no doubt as to Uncle Saunders's reactions. Prissie—would she love him enough to be loyal to him, supposing she loved him at all? Fleetingly Brigit remembered Prissie's covetous fingers on the silk sheets, and she was sadly certain that Prissie's love of luxury would prove too much for her loyalty.

Besides, Guy had said that the old man had had no dependants, so that beyond justice being done nothing more could be remedied.

But was one so weakly to play the horrible game of this blackmailer with his writing like the slimy trail of a garden slug?

'Biddy!' said Guy, his dark shadowed eyes looking deeply into hers. 'If you tell the police about this I'll kill myself. I mean it.'

NINE

SHE was doing this not only to save Guy's life (for she knew by the haunted look in his eyes that his threat to take his life was no idle jest), but for Prissie, too. Prissie, she thought ironically, who was so well able to take care of herself.

Fergus would say she was just the person for Guy, someone gay and light-hearted, and yet as strong as steel. For there was no doubt that Prissie's soft laughing exterior had a very definite and, to Brigit, almost frightening strength.

So indirectly she was playing this unknown blackmailer's despicable game to enable Prissie to obtain possession of the things she coveted, the pictures and china, the Persian rugs, the walnut and rosewood furniture, the silk sheets . . .

Brigit had reached the conclusion that Prissie had found out all she could about the Templar family before she had come to work for them. Her illness on the plane may have been a fortunate coincidence that had brought Fergus's attention to her, but if it had not happened that way she would have contrived something else. She was a fortune-hunter. She loved luxury, and was determined to possess it. No doubt she had known all about Brigit's unmarried brother long before she came to the cottage in the country.

The lucky coincidence that was not of her contriving was the enforced move to the house in Montpelier Square. She must secretly have been jubilant about that. Indeed, her jubilation showed all the time in her sparkling eyes, her plain little face transformed into a fascinating liveliness, her quick dancing movements. It was amazing how she had brought life into the quiet gloomy house. One should be grateful to her.

But if Guy were falling in love with her, was she genuinely returning Guy's affection, or was her warmth and friendliness to be translated into eagerness for possessions? If so, Guy should be warned.

But wasn't he old enough to look after himself? Brigit thought with sudden weariness. Wasn't it enough that she, ill in bed, should suddenly be burdened with this horrible blackmailing thing? If she could succeed in getting Guy out of this scrape she could not be responsible for his love life, too. And after all, it was very probable that Prissie, given the things she wanted, would be a charming and devoted wife. She adored children as was proved by the affection that she gave to Nicky and Sarah. Or could it be that she coveted them, too . . .?

Brigit dismissed that thought impatiently, telling herself that she was developing a sick mind as well as a sick body. Oh, if only she could get well, and take the children home. Would she ever get well in this house?

'Nurse,' she called.

Nurse Ellen came bustling into the room. She looked clean and fresh and so full of energy that Brigit's tiredness seemed to sink more deeply into her body.

'Nurse, get me my writing things, will you, please. And I want to sit up.'

'You're not going to start writing letters now! You should be having your morning nap.'

'Oh, nurse, I'm not a baby!' The irritability in her voice drew a second glance from Nurse Ellen. She said:

'Who's been upsetting you, ducky?'

'Nobody. I just want to do some writing, and if you don't mind, it's none of your business.'

Nurse Ellen went to the bureau at the window to get the leather folder which contained all Brigit's papers. She said over her shoulder:

'Everything about a patient I nurse is my business. If you ask me, I think your family worries you. If you would prefer it, we'll have rules about the times they can see you. All this running in and out of your room—I don't think the doctor would approve. And he's coming this afternoon, so you must be looking your best.'

'Yes, nurse,' Brigit said more meekly. 'And now will you ask Prissie if she will come in for a minute. I have an errand for her.'

Whether she was protecting Guy for his own sake, or for Prissie's, it was ironical justice that Prissie should be the one to do this errand for her. In any case, who else could she send?

But it was hateful having to lie about it.

She wrote the cheque for one hundred pounds (how fortunate Uncle Saunders had given her just that amount for her birthday, and more fortunate that she had not yet spent it) and handed it to Prissie. Fergus could never be told about this, it would only make him despise her family even more than he did already, and who knew when he might at last accuse her of having the bad Templar blood. Her face was quite stiff and expressionless as she said:

'Would you mind going to the bank for me, Prissie? I need this money suddenly—oh, and it must be in single notes. If they ask questions at the bank, tell them I want it for paying bills.'

'But why not pay them by cheque?' Prissie asked, wide-eyed.

'I prefer it this way,' Brigit said stiffly.

'Why, yes, of course, but——' Prissie folded the cheque in her tiny tapering fingers. She had the fingers of a lady, Brigit thought. Though what was a lady? Nurse Ellen was one, and her fingers were short, strong, and capable.

'But what?' she asked.

'There's nothing the matter, is there?' Prissie said impulsively. 'I mean, this is quite a lot of money to get in single notes——'

'You think so?' said Brigit politely. It was the first time she had used the grand lady act with Prissie, and she despised herself for doing it now. Especially when Prissie flushed and said defensively.

'Well, to me it is. And I thought you were looking worried about something. You would tell me if you were worrying about anything, wouldn't you?'

Prissie looked so earnest and anxious, her brow running into furrows, that Brigit relented.

'I don't see why I should bother you with my worries. And anyway this isn't one. Now run along. Nurse Ellen will mind the children while you're away. I may want you to post some mail for me later, too.'

Prissie was back within an hour, flushed and with moisture shining on her smooth dark hair. It was raining, she said, as she tumbled the bank-notes carelessly on to Brigit's bed. She wouldn't be able to take the children in the park, so perhaps Brigit would like them all to have tea round the fire in her room.

'It would be company for you,' she said, with her quick enchanting smile. 'And besides it would give me a chance to get on with my dress. If I'm to allow your brother to take me out I have to be suitably clad. Shall I help you count that? I did it carefully in the bank, but just to make absolutely sure . . .'

'No, no, it will be right,' Brigit said quickly. 'Yes, bring the children down. And your sewing. It will do me good.'

Nurse Ellen was upstairs with the children. There was just time, while Prissie was away, to pack the notes into the chocolate box she had emptied, and to quickly wrap the box into a parcel and address it. Mr George Smith, 15 Pelham Road, Hammersmith, she wrote, and wondered despairingly who this man was, and why he had had to do this horrible low-down thing. Though to have gone to the police would have been worse for Guy, anyway. Why, she wondered, hadn't Mr Smith acted more quickly? It was now three weeks since the night of the accident. Probably he had been snooping about, finding out all he could about the house and its inhabitants, planning to whom to address his poisonous letter. Involuntarily Brigit glanced out into the misty afternoon, half expecting to see a figure lurking outside the gate, watching. She must have been watched ever since she had come home from the hospital. And there had been that burglar, about which the police had not yet a clue. Had he been the mysterious Mr Smith, actually invading the house itself? No, that must have been an unconnected crime. The whole thing made her feel as if she were enclosed in a mesh of nastiness. It wasn't fair of Guy, first to have behaved so despicably, and then to have placed her in the vulnerable position of being the only person who would care enough about him to try to keep him out of trouble.

It was nice to have Prissie back with the children, Sarah tumbling about happily, and Nicky playing in a concentrated way with his building blocks, while Prissie, with yards of green silk spread over her knees, sewed and talked and sang, and told the children stories.

Brigit almost relaxed. The black worry in her mind eased. It was comfortable in the big room, with the rain bringing an early twilight, and the fire glowing. She drowsed a little, and woke to hear Prissie saying, 'It was only years and years later that they found the true baby, the tiny little skeleton buried in the wall, while all the time the wrong baby had grown up and become king . . .'

Brigit roused herself.

'Prissie, what *are* you telling the children?'

'Only that old story about the skeleton of the baby found in Edinburgh Castle. I think it is fascinating. The poor little baby that died, and never got its rights——'

'But Prissie—the children——'

Sarah, busily knocking down Nicky's bricks, had obviously paid no attention at all to the story. But Nicky's ears were almost standing out. What a pity he was such a sensitive child, and how could Prissie not notice the way these things affected him? She had had one experience with the pedlar doll.

'I think everyone should know these things,' she said serenely, re-threading her needle with the shining green silk. 'I hate injustice.' Then she began to sing softly, and in the midst of her song Fergus walked in. There was rain in his hair, too, and his lips, as he kissed Brigit, were cold, as if he had brought the rain into the room.

'Fergus!' she whispered happily. 'You're early.'

'What are you all doing?' he asked. 'What's Prissie up to, sitting there like a little queen?'

It was true, Brigit realized. Prissie did have a quaintly regal look, sitting on the stool with the shining silk spread about her and the children at her feet. She looked amazingly attractive. It was little wonder that she had drawn Fergus's eyes.

'I'm making a dress,' she said and stood up and draped the material about her. Her small head rose proudly from the flurry of silk.

Fergus stared. Then he said, 'You know what you look like, don't you?'

'I mean to,' said Prissie composedly.

'What are you talking about?' Brigit asked. 'Oh!' She drew in her breath. 'I know. It's the portrait of my mother.'

With her quick change of mood Prissie flung down the silk and was herself again, eager and young. 'You don't mind, do you, Mrs Gaye? I think that portrait's terribly attractive, and I long to look like it. I won't, of course, but I'm copying the dress as well as I can.'

'Guy is taking Prissie to dinner,' Brigit told Fergus, and was instantly aware of Fergus's eyes fixed on Prissie speculatively. He doesn't like it, Brigit thought in a flash. He's thinking of Prissie looking like a little queen in all that shining silk.

'Will he appreciate you looking like his mother?' he asked ironically.

'Fergus, don't be silly,' Brigit reproved. 'Anyway, Guy doesn't remember mother very much.' She was going to add, 'Fortunately,' and only stopped herself in time. It was such a dreadful thing to have those bitter memories of one's mother.

'What's this?' Fergus asked, picking up the parcel on Brigit's bedside table.

Brigit felt the colour draining out of her face. She had momentarily forgotten about that parcel. She hadn't wanted to disturb Prissie, and hadn't anticipated anyone, least of all Fergus, coming in and seeing it.

'Oh—that's something Prissie is going to post for me. Prissie, if you don't mind. It isn't too wet, is it?'

Prissie sprang up. 'No, of course not. There's a post office at the corner, anyway.'

'Who is the mysterious George Smith?' Fergus asked. 'Wasn't that the name of the brides in the bath murderer?'

'Fergus, don't be so idiotic!'

'Well, wasn't it?'

'I believe it was. This, if you must know, is a child I knew in the hospital. I promised to send him something. It's only a box of chocolates. But I do want it to go this afternoon.'

'Come along then, Prissie,' said Fergus. 'I'll come with you and see that you don't step in a puddle.'

Prissie gave her quick delighted smile. 'Oh, good! Shall we take the children? We can put on their macs. It will be some fresh air for them.'

Before Brigit could reflect that it would be practically the complete Gaye family going out walking, as they had done so often in the past, Nurse Ellen came in with her air of authority.

'Out, all of you! Out! Doctor's due in half an hour and I must see to my patient.'

Brigit welcomed her bustling intrusion. She let her think that her paleness and quietness was from exhaustion, and meekly submitted to a scolding.

'The moment I leave you you try to do too much. Writing business letters, having the children underfoot, wrapping parcels. Nothing's that important.'

'What do you think the doctor will say, nurse?'

'Why, that I'm not doing my job properly, I should think. Now let me wash your face and you can put on a bit of lipstick, and then close your eyes and rest.'

The lipstick and the face powder were no use, because when Nurse Ellen left her to rest she promptly began to weep. The tears slid childishly down her face and every time she mopped them up they came again. She was getting as wet as Prissie and Fergus in the rain would be. Why did she mind Fergus going out with Prissie? It didn't mean a thing. It was only that she envied so much their ability to stride freely, while she lay here like a dead thing. And those horrid things that had happened had got on her mind. Burglary and blackmail. What would be the next thing beginning with 'b'? She reflected idly, and the word that came into her mind was bitch. Oh, no, she thought, that isn't a respectable word anyway. The Templars, for all their avariciousness and licentiousness, would not approve of a daughter of their family using a word like that. Even knowing a word like that. And of course it didn't apply to anyone in this house.

Doctor Brown was not particularly pleased with his patient. Although he was cheerful and non-committal Brigit could sense his disappointment.

'There's no improvement, doctor?'

'Oh yes, indeed there is. You're better in yourself——'

Brigit cut him short. 'Doctor, when will I walk again?'

'Well, that's not altogether possible to predict. The paralysis may cease tomorrow or it may hang on for another say three or four weeks——'

'You mean I might never walk again?'

'I mean nothing of the kind. I'm going to prescribe a tonic. Nurse, you might see that this is made up in the morning. Ah, Mr Gaye, come in. We're doing very nicely indeed.'

'That's fine,' said Fergus. 'Have a drink, doctor. My wife can have a drink, can't she?'

'Yes, indeed. Do her good.' The little doctor's eyes took in the luxurious room, the bed with its carved headboard, the glowing fire, the flowers. 'You're very comfortable here. I wouldn't mind having a long rest in a room like this myself.'

'That's exactly what I say,' said Aunt Annabel, coming suddenly into the room, the big grey Persian tucked under her arm. 'Brigit's a lucky girl. And with the children nicely cared for, and all. Oh, Fergus, are you bringing drinks? Then Saunders must come. And perhaps Prissie would like a little sip of sherry, too. She's so sweet with the children. My niece hasn't a thing to worry about, doctor. Everything is organized. But tell me, doctor, what would one do for a cat that cries all the time? It literally cries. Obviously it has been badly treated from the time it was a kitten——'

Aunt Annabel, her grey hair shaken loose round her vague kind face, her large eyes full of earnestness, discussed the new cat that no doubt was going to keep them all awake with its mewing. Uncle Saunders came stamping in shouting, 'Whisky for me, Fergus, my boy. Such a day I've had in the city. The market's all gone to the pack. We'll be selling up shortly. Annabel, put that deuced cat down. It's got four legs, hasn't it? Two more than you have, so let him use them. Well, Brigit, I don't suppose you'd sneeze at legs like that yourself. Do you think she's bluffing, doctor? She looks well enough. All this paraphernalia, nurses and so on, for a bit of neurotic fancy. Ah ha, Prissie my dear, who's been putting colour in your cheeks? Pretty as a rose, eh?'

Did Prissie move nearer to Fergus? Brigit couldn't tell for at that moment Fergus came over to her bedside and gave her hand a brief squeeze. Then he caught the doctor's eye and said, 'I think we might finish the party in the other room. Be back soon, darling.'

But Brigit was hardly aware of their noisy exit. She was so wrapped up in her own misery. The doctor had deliberately evaded her question. He had given her no clue as to when she could expect to walk again. Which meant that it might be never.

That treacherous voice that whispered in the night was right. It had said ... Wait! There it was now, right this instant. Hoarse and sibilant and triumphant, directly from the cavern of the chimney. 'Didn't I say so! Didn't I tell you you'd never walk again!'

'Nurse!' called Brigit. 'Nurse, nurse!' But before Nurse Ellen could reach her from her room next door the voice had gone, died away like a breath of wind.

'What is it, ducky? Are you feeling bad?'

'Nurse, did you hear a voice just then? From the chimney?'

'I never heard a sound except your Uncle Saunders. From the chimney! Now, don't be daft! Who lives up there except that witch doll of Nicky's.'

'That's what I mean,' Brigit whispered.

Nurse Ellen eyed her with concern.

'It has been too much for you. All those people in here at once. You're beginning to imagine things.'

'No, no——' But was she? The room seemed to be going dark and then bright in a curious way, the mulberry tree shook a skinny fist at the window, the bed tipped up, then slowly righted itself, from a long way off a pale and drained-looking moon moved in front of her ... But it was only Nurse Ellen's face. The voice in her ears was not saying, 'Save your brother ...' It was Nurse Ellen, indignantly, 'Too much fuss and bother. You'll be all right presently, ducky ...'

When Fergus came in to say good night he asked gently, 'What frightened you, darling? Nurse says something frightened you.'

Brigit was aware of the concern in his face. He looked

grave and the youthfulness had gone out of his face. Suddenly it came to her that he looked like that too often now. She was doing this to him, prematurely taking away his youth and vitality.

'Nothing frightened me,' she said.

'But you've been crying.'

That was another thing. He was always having to look at her drained and unhappy face. No wonder he had eagerly sought Prissie's gay lively company. If she were to go on like this—— Another fear, not of the unexplainable, but of something all too possible, chilled her. She seemed to be seeing Prissie's sparkling radiant face above the green silk. The picture filled her mind with bright menace. All at once the knowledge came to her that she had to surmount all these things, her crippled state, the threat of the blackmailer, the unwanted hospitality of Uncle Saunders, and, most of all, Prissie's pretty thieving fingers, clinging to the children, to Fergus's arm, to the lovely valuable knick-knacks scattered about the house.

At last belatedly but strongly a core of stubbornness and a refusal to be defeated came to life in her. From now on there was to be no crying. She was not going to lie there weakly and let other people fight for her. She was going to do her own fighting.

Gravely she moved her fingers over the lines in Fergus's face.

'You don't have to worry about me, my darling. I'm going to be all right.' She smiled steadily, and now, with the spirit strong inside her, it was even easy to smile. 'You might not believe it, but I'm not even going to cry any more!'

TEN

Nicky had been dreaming about the little baby hidden in the dark hole beneath the wall in Edinburgh Castle. In his dream it had not been a dead baby, still and curiously light and empty, as had been birds and once the tiny corpse of a field mouse he had found, but a little live baby that fought and struggled to get out of its dark hole. It even had a tiny gold crown on its head to show that it was really the true king. In his dream he became the buried baby, fighting and struggling and screaming, and he still struggled even after he found that it was not a box but Prissie's arms that held him.

'Now, now,' came Prissie's soothing voice. 'It's only a bad dream. Keep still, honey. Go to sleep again.'

Nicky opened his eyes and looked into her face. It was a pretty face, soft and smiling and happy.

'See,' she murmured. 'It was only a dream.'

But Nicky was suddenly stiffening in her arms, trying to draw away. For inexplicably her face was the face of the dead baby in his dream. The only difference was that she wore no crown. But the crown would be in the locket round her neck that she never opened. That would be where she hid it. A little secret crown. If one could only get the locket and look in it . . .

'What's the matter?' Prissie asked, laughing. 'You funny little scrap. Surely you're not frightened of me!'

It was truly silly to be frightened of her. She was so kind when she smiled. But she had that dead baby's face . . .

'I'll just go back to sleep,' Nicky announced, in his new aloof mature voice.

'You didn't hear that doll in the cupboard again, did you?' Prissie asked.

Nicky tried not to shiver. Even mentioning that doll wasn't safe. It might bring back the cackly voice. He shook his head vigorously.

'I—I haven't talked about Clementine today.'

'Well, that explains it, doesn't it. Just let me tuck you in. That's a good boy. Kiss me good night.'

Obediently Nicky kissed her. Her cheek was quite warm and it smelt nice. Something told him that the cheek of a dead baby would not be nice to kiss. So that old dream was silly, after all. It had almost gone now. But he wished his own mother could have tucked him in and wished him good night . . .

When Prissie went back into the next room she sat down at the table and picked up her pen to continue the letter she was writing.

> You should see my dress. It's going to look wonderful. But you will see it, of course. Don't you think I am clever? Please say I am clever. I am still desperately upset about the little gold angel. It was such a heavenly thing. I hope whoever took it will be caught. And for your information I am not falling in love with Fergus. How absurd!

But she stopped writing, and began to remember the quick walk with Fergus, his light chatter about the parcel addressed to Mr George Brides-in-the-Bath Smith, and the rain in their faces.

A tap at the door made her hastily slip the sheet of paper under her writing desk. Who was this? That silly old Mrs Hatchett with her tales of ghosts. Ghosts, indeed! Or—her heart missed a beat—was it Fergus, come up for a little cheerfulness after his wife's depressing company.

'Come in,' she called in her light welcoming voice.

The door opened and Guy came in.

Prissie exclaimed, 'Oh, how nice of you to come and see me! I was feeling a little lonely.'

'You! You wouldn't ever need to be lonely,' Guy said.

'Everyone is lonely some time.' Prissie picked up her sewing, and threaded a needle. 'Sit down and talk to me. Tell me what you do all day juggling money.'

'I don't juggle much money,' said Guy. 'I wish I did. I'm afraid that's left to Uncle Saunders.'

'Does he have that much?' Prissie asked. Her smooth

head was bent over her sewing, her voice politely interested.

'Enough, I should think.'

'Never mind,' said Prissie soothingly. 'It will be all yours and your sister's one day. Or do you hate it the way your sister does?'

Guy smiled wryly. 'I only hate the lack of it.'

'Oh, come!' Prissie patted his arm. 'You're a Templar. You must know ways of making money. They all did, didn't they? I'll bet your Uncle Saunders has done some things he wouldn't talk about.'

'I shouldn't be surprised at that.'

Prissie looked up eagerly, her face alight with interest.

'Do you know anything? Oh, do tell me. I adore scandal.' Then she drew back. 'I shouldn't ask you those things. He's your uncle. We shouldn't talk about him. But I'm disgustingly inquisitive. I just can't resist knowing about people. They're so fascinating.'

'I shouldn't mind talking about Uncle Saunders if I knew anything,' Guy said. His thin face was momentarily bitter. 'He doesn't rate any loyalty. On the surface he doesn't appear to be a miser, but you find out about him, really. You'll be at the mercy of his grudging allowance as I have been all my life—what's the point when he has so much?'

'Yes, what is the point,' Prissie said sympathetically. 'But I really don't see why you couldn't be clever, too. There must be ways.' Her eyes rested on Guy speculatively. Then she laughed. 'That must sound awful and calculating. But I'm on your side, you know.'

'Darling!' said Guy, pulling his chair closer to her.

'You want to be clever, too,' Prissie murmured. 'Match your brains with his.' Again she gave him her considering gaze. Then she exclaimed, 'Guy, you're looking awfully tired and worried. Is there something wrong?'

'No, nothing.' His answer was too swift. Prissie said intuitively:

'Guy, you're in trouble!'

'I'm not in trouble. For God's sake——' He stopped and gave a tense apologetic smile. 'Sorry, I'm a bit edgy these days. Tell me, did Brigit ask you to do anything for her today?'

Prissie re-threaded her needle. Her voice was cool. 'Why don't you ask her yourself?'

'I meant to, but the nurse wouldn't let me in. Said she was sleeping.' He pouted, his mouth suddenly childish.

'Your sister was tired and upset,' Prissie said. 'The doctor came and I don't think he gave her very much hope of walking, poor thing. Just imagine that. Never being able to walk again.'

'This is—worse,' Guy muttered.

'What did you say, Guy? You are in trouble! Is it money?' Suddenly she exclaimed, 'Oh, that's why she wanted the hundred pounds.' Then she clapped her hand over her mouth. 'I shouldn't have told you that. It was private.'

'Then she did get it,' Guy said eagerly.

'Yes, but don't tell her I told you. I didn't tell you, anyway. You wangled it out of me.' Prissie was hurt and offended, her cheeks flushed, her eyes reproachful. 'Guy, it wasn't fair of you.'

But Guy was suddenly happy, the tension gone from his face and his eyes admiring.

'Prissie—you're the most attractive girl I've ever met. You like me a little, don't you?'

'Of course I like you, but——'

'Then why don't you kiss me? Come.'

Prissie's body stiffened. She tried to draw away from his embrace. For all their bony fragility his hands were steel. She felt her arms bruised as she resisted. *Silly!* she told herself. *Silly!*

'You little puritan!' Guy muttered. And then the full sensuous lips of the Templars, painted on half a dozen portraits over the stairs, were on hers.

She forced herself to relax and respond.

But afterwards, when she was alone, she finished her letter in agitated emphatic words, 'I can't endure Guy kissing me. Must I? Must I?'

ELEVEN

In spite of her resolution it was still difficult to wake up in a cheerful frame of mind. Brigit's first feeling as she opened her eyes in the early dawn was dread as to what might be in the mail. It was said that blackmailers never stopped at their first demand, but that the horrible vampirish letters kept on coming, making more and more demands. She hadn't thought too seriously about that yesterday. It had been enough to take the fear and guilt from Guy's face.

But now she was afraid she had been foolish and impulsive, and too ready to obey the blackmailer's instructions. She should have told Fergus about it. He would have communicated with the police and the house in Hammersmith could have been watched.

And Guy would have been arrested ... Guy who was perhaps at last going to find the miraculous happiness with Prissie that she had found with Fergus. No, she could have done nothing else. She had had to give Guy this one chance, at least. She could only pray that the blackmailer had some sort of honour, and would now keep his promise to trouble her no more.

It was going to be a nice day. The sky beyond the skeleton arm of the mulberry tree was luminous. A nice day for Fergus flying, Brigit thought, and listened to the house stealthily coming to life. One of the cats was mewing plaintively. From far off there was a steady rattle of dishes in the kitchen. A sudden series of bumps overhead indicated that one of the children had decided to get out of bed. Sarah, probably. She never waited to be told it was time to get up. She came bouncing out in her definite imperturbable way. Nurse Ellen appeared abruptly, said, 'Good morning, ducky. Sleep well? No ghosts last night, thank goodness. I'll be back in a minute with your tea,' and disappeared. As she went the black kitten that Aunt Annabel had brought home yesterday suddenly pounced on the bed. It made Brigit jump. She said, 'Naughty,' and fondled it. The kitten purred and settled beside her contentedly. It seemed to be asleep when all at once it stiffened and made a spring at her toes.

Why had it done that so suddenly? It couldn't be—surely it couldn't be——

With wildly beating heart she watched the mound of bedclothes as she wriggled her toes. They moved. They did move! They really did!

An exclamation of excited joy caught in Brigit's throat. She repeated the exercise, and again there was a faint but definite movement of the bedclothes. The kitten pounced eagerly.

Hitherto when she had had the sensation of her toes moving nothing whatever had happened. It had been an illusion. But today, on this wonderful wonderful day, life was coming back to her.

On the verge of calling excitedly for Nurse Ellen, Brigit suddenly checked herself.

No, she wouldn't tell Nurse Ellen yet. Nurse Ellen would promptly tell the whole household, and some caution urged her to keep it a secret from Fergus until she was quite sure that she would walk again. It would be so awful to send him away full of hope this morning, and to come back tomorrow to find that it had been all an illusion. No, she must be certain, absolutely certain. So, in the meantime, if she could manage it, the joyful news would remain her secret.

How can I be so calm as to plan this? Brigit wondered incredulously. Indeed, she could not keep the colour and excitement out of her face. Nurse Ellen spied it at once, and said, 'My, we are perky this morning!'

'Oh, I was playing with the kitten. He's so funny. Has the mail come yet?'

'Yes. I'm afraid there's nothing for you.'

Brigit sighed with relief. Even the blackmailer was silent. Life was beginning to take on colour and warmth again. Where was Fergus? She wanted Fergus.

But it was Aunt Annabel who was her first visitor. She came in with Renoir in her arms and two timid long-legged alley cats at her heels. Nurse Ellen tripped over one and gave an exclamation of impatience. The cats scuttered away.

Aunt Annabel said amiably, 'No one likes my cats.'

'I like this one,' said Brigit, stroking the black kitten. 'He's a sweetie.'

'Do you, dear? Then you must take him home with you when you go.'

Yesterday the obvious uncertainty in Aunt Annabel's voice would have struck her to the heart. But this morning she could say confidently, 'Thank you, I'd love to,' and resist the temptation to wriggle her toes.

'It's our monthly meeting today,' Aunt Annabel went on. 'I do hope Saunders stays in the city, otherwise he's liable to—well, to join in with us. And he will insist on making absurd and facetious suggestions.'

'You'd like the children out of the way, too,' Brigit said.

'Oh no, dear, they're no trouble.'

'But it's a lovely day. They can spend the whole day in the park. I'll tell Prissie.'

A little later Prissie came in with the children to say good morning. She wore a red sweater and a black skirt that swirled about her.

'I sat up until after midnight finishing my dress,' she said. 'I feel half dead this morning.'

If that were being half dead, Brigit reflected, how did she look when she was really alive? Oh, if only Guy were going to be happy. Otherwise keeping Prissie might just possibly be a mistake.

Brigit could not have explained why she had that intuition. Certainly it was not because Fergus, coming in at that moment and overhearing Prissie's remark, put his arm round her and said, 'Don't look too bewitching tonight. Save that for me.'

Prissie giggled and took the children out. Fergus came over to the bed and looked down at Brigit.

'Hi, darling! You look very up and coming this morning.'

'I told you I wasn't going to cry any more.'

Fergus bent to kiss her. His lips lingered on hers.

'Good girl,' he whispered. Then he caught up the black kitten.

'Who does this thing remind you of?'

'Why, nobody.'

'Yes, it does. It's just like Prissie. Smooth and soft. And no one knows what it is thinking.'

'Do you wonder that, too, about Prissie,' Brigit asked involuntarily.

'I wonder it about all pretty girls,' Fergus's voice was light. 'Darling—no tears before I come back?'

'No tears,' Brigit promised.

If a man couldn't guess what a girl was thinking he usually grew more and more determined to find out, and in the process of satisfying his curiosity he grew more and more interested in the girl. Nonsense, Brigit told herself firmly. Fergus was no more interested in Prissie than he would be in any attractive girl—even if it were possible that she was making that dress to lure him, and not Guy at all. But that, too, was a sick fancy that belonged to her illness now past. She began happily to concentrate once more on the miraculous movement of her toes.

Even Guy paid her a visit that morning. He said, 'Anything more?' in a low voice, and when she shook her head his thin dark face cleared and brightened. 'Thanks a lot, Biddy,' he said.

It was the first time she could remember him giving generous unsolicited thanks. She said, 'Guy, it's all wrong. But now it's done, for heaven's sake try to be happy. You owe that much to me, and to that poor old man. It's the least thing you can do.'

'I'll be happy. Everything will be all right.' His tone had never been so jaunty and confidant. He even looked young and carefree. 'I'll have some luck and pay you back,' he promised. 'I'm beginning to feel lucky.'

But if Guy's happiness were to depend on Prissie—*why* had she this insistent lack of faith in Prissie? The girl had done nothing to merit it. Rather the opposite. She had proved that she could be relied on in a crisis. Beneath her tender and gentle exterior she was practical and competent and intelligent. Whatever her childhood background had been she would make a wonderful wife for Guy, especially after he had come into his share of the Templar fortune. No doubt already in her mind she was adorning this house as its mistress.

So how could one imagine that her glances kept turning sideways to a fortuneless airman who was already married?

Brigit did not ponder on these things too long. The morning, clear and sparkling, was too lovely for problems or gloom. Besides, her biggest problem was being solved. She thought that if she were alone for long enough she would be able to move her legs. She couldn't bear anyone to watch in case the lovely miracle vanished. Even Nurse Ellen, with her vociferous enthusiasm, might ruin it. She must find some way to get Nurse Ellen out of the house for an hour or two.

'What are you lying there smiling about?' Nurse Ellen had appeared in her abrupt way and was standing over Brigit.

'I was just imagining I was walking through the park, scuffling through the leaves. It's such a lovely day, the trees must look like fires burning. Wouldn't you like a walk in the park, Nurse?'

'This afternoon I might while you have your nap. I want to do a little shopping, too. I'll slip over to Harrods.'

'You might match some wool for me,' said Brigit. 'I'm not going to have enough to finish Sarah's cardigan.'

'Right. If I can't get it there I'll go to some other places. My, the children will be enjoying their outing this morning. They were going to the Round Pond. That ought to put some colour into Nicky's cheeks. Should you have that cat on your bed, ducky?'

'Oh, he's only a kitten. Leave him.'

'Well, they never taught me it was hygienic to tuck one's patient up with a cat. But I suppose he's the right colour. He might bring you luck.'

'Oh, indeed he might.'

It was midday when the children came back. Sarah came into the room first. She immediately crouched on all fours and began making curious leaps, accompanied by a guttural sound in her throat. Nicky, following her, seized her hair and pulled it hard. Sarah screamed with pain and indignation. Prissie came in swiftly and separated them.

'Nicky! I'm sorry, Mrs Gaye—I'm afraid Nicky's being difficult this morning.'

'Oh, on such a lovely day?' Brigit looked reproachfully at her small son who now stood sullen-faced and silent. 'What's the matter, Nicky? Why did you do that to Sarah?'

'Because she was being a toad and she knows I hate them.'

'A toad? What a curious thing. I didn't know she had ever seen a toad.'

'She saw one this morning over at the Round Pond,' Prissie explained. 'You know all the horrid things children there collect. Jars of worms and tiddlers. Ugh! I don't know how they do it.'

Nicky came suddenly to Brigit. His face was dead white, and now Brigit saw the way the pupils of his eyes were enlarged, as if with fear. But what could it be that he was frightened of?

'Nicky!' she said gently, stroking his small cold grubby hand.

Tears formed in Nicky's eyes. His lips quivered uncontrollably.

'It was Clementine had the toad,' he sobbed. 'She put it on me. It was cold and slimy like a slug. Mummy, I *hate* toads!'

Brigit said slowly, 'Clementine again?'

In the background Nurse Ellen's practical voice came, 'That name has a familiar sound.'

Prissie shrugged her shoulders helplessly.

'I'm sorry, Mrs Gaye. I don't know why he does it. Every child he doesn't like he calls Clementine.'

'Was there a child he didn't like this morning?'

Nicky, between sobs, said, 'Her face was dirty and she laughed at me all the time. She wanted to hurt me. She said toads bite.'

'Thev don't, you know,' Brigit said soothingly. 'They're

really nothing at all to be frightened of.'

'She laughed like the—like the——' But there Nicky stopped, for he could not now put into words his intense fear of the witch doll in the cupboard.

Sarah, on hands and knees again, was giving her sideways leaps and croaking happily. So there had been a toad, at least, Brigit realized, or Sarah could not have done her clever imitation.

'Prissie—couldn't you have stopped this?'

'I did as soon as I saw what was happening. I didn't know Nicky was frightened until I heard him crying, and then all the children ran away.'

'The children?'

'Oh yes, there was a bunch of them. You know the way they all make friends instantly.'

'And there was a toad?'

'Well, yes, there must have been. But as I said, the children ran away.'

'And you didn't see the one Nicky calls Clementine?'

Prissie shook her head. 'I told you, it's the particular one he doesn't like at the time that he calls Clementine. It's just a thing he has about that name.'

'If you ask me,' said Nurse Ellen suddenly, 'it's all very well having grown-up theories about the reason for a child's fears, but are they the right ones? Personally I believe there is a little horror called Clementine who has decided to persecute Nicky, and I'm going to find out if she does exist. At least we'll know then whether what's frightening Nicky is real or imaginary, and we'll be able to deal with it. With your permission, Mrs Gaye, I'll take the children to the park this afternoon.'

Brigit was aware, first of all, of the resentment in Prissie's face. It flashed over it like a shadow, turning it suddenly hard and cold. Then it passed, and Prissie turned a hurt but acquiescent look towards Brigit.

'If you don't believe what I tell you——'

'I do believe you, Prissie. But it won't do any harm for Nurse Ellen to take the children out. I promised her an afternoon out today, anyway. I'm fully prepared to believe that Clementine has no more reality than Mrs Hatchett's ghost. But like the ghost, she might be taking another form. If there is a horrid little girl who persecutes Nicky it must be stopped.'

Prissie was still sulking a little.

'Then if I'm not required this afternoon may I go and see my aunt? She wasn't very well yesterday and I'd really like to see her.'

'Of course you may. This is a very good opportunity. Aunt Annabel is having a committee meeting so there'll be no one in the house except myself. And I can't disturb her.'

Brigit smiled at everyone. She didn't want trouble between Prissie and Nurse Ellen, but she was extremely grateful to Nurse Ellen for her offer to investigate the thing that was troubling Nicky. If there were something that Prissie was lying deliberately about—but there couldn't be. There was no reason for it.

'Take the children for their lunch, Prissie. And have a nice afternoon with your aunt.'

Prissie pouted slightly. She was being as childish as Nicky. She didn't speak directly to Nurse Ellen, but said to no one in particular, 'The children will need their top coats. There's a cold wind out.'

At last she was alone. Nurse Ellen had tucked her up and left her to sleep, but as soon as she was sure that Nurse Ellen and the children were safely out of the house she propped herself up, and began the magical movements with her toes again. She knew now that she could move her legs. She threw the blankets off and slowly drew her knees up, first one then the other. They ached a little and felt strangely as if they did not belong to her, but they had life again. It was so wonderful that she cried a little. Then she briskly dried her tears, and began a system of gentle exercise. She wanted to be able to get out of bed unassisted, to stand, and later to walk. Now she could tell Nurse Ellen what had happened because it was really true. Later today, or perhaps in the morning, she would persuade Nurse Ellen to help her to walk, so that when Fergus came home in the evening she would be able to walk to meet him.

But in the meantime she must take things easily lest she got too tired and her new-found mobility left her. She would do as Nurse Ellen expected her to, and sleep.

Aunt Annabel's committee women had arrived and filed into the drawing-room. From that direction there came the distant hum of voices. Otherwise the house was silent. Brigit, her mind free from care, fell asleep almost at once. She slept soundly except for once waking momentarily and thinking she heard a strange forlorn cry. But she was asleep again instantly.

Prissie was the first to arrive home. She was flushed and a little out of breath. She said she had run from the bus stop because she was afraid she was late. Her aunt had been in bed and she had stopped to do things for her.

'It's all right,' Brigit said. 'The children aren't home yet.'

'Not yet? Are you sure?' Prissie seemed surprised and Brigit noticed for the first time that it was growing dusk. The dead leaves on the trees hung like withered jewellery against a lemon-coloured sky.

'Nurse Ellen was going to match some wool for me. She's probably doing that. But it is getting late. They must be here soon.'

'And you haven't had any tea,' said Prissie. 'I'll tell Mrs Hatchett.'

Brigit called to tell her not to bother, but Prissie had already gone. Indeed, she seemed in a hurry to get out of the room. After she had been to the kitchen Brigit heard her running upstairs. It was not long before she was down again. She came back into Brigit's room and said breathlessly, 'I think the mythical Clementine must have kidnapped the children. Do you mind if I go out and look for them?'

Brigit laughed. 'Don't be silly, Prissie. Nurse Ellen knows the way home.'

'Yes, but it's getting terribly cold out, and she didn't take the children's coats as I told her to. I've just looked, and they're still in the wardrobe.'

'That's odd. She must have thought they didn't need them.'

'They might not have earlier, but they do now. I'll take them over to the park. Nicky catches cold so easily.'

Was that a maternal note in Prissie's voice? Or was it just covering what was suddenly an extreme anxiety that showed itself in her edging towards the door, eager to be gone? Was there something in the story of this strange menacing child Clementine after all, and Prissie knew it? Brigit was baffled and beginning to grow anxious herself. But before she could say anything more Mrs Hatchett appeared with her tea-tray and Prissie took the opportunity to slip out.

'Well, I declare,' said Mrs Hatchett. 'You should have had your tea long ago. I thought the nurse was looking after you.'

'No, she took the children out this afternoon.'

'And when was that?' Mrs Hatchett asked, putting the tray down.

'Why, about two o'clock, I should think.'

'Well, they were still playing in the garden at half past three. I know because I had to go out and tell them to make less noise. The mistress's ladies were in the meeting, and what with shouting children and miauling cats—though I don't expect the cats would worry the ladies, that being their business so to speak.'

'At half past three?' Brigit repeated. 'But you must be wrong.'

Mrs Hatchett made a disapproving sound. 'I suppose I can trust the evidence of my eyes, can't I? You might laugh at me about my ghost, poor innocent that he is, but at least I know whether or not two children are trampling over the master's chrysanthemum beds.'

'Then when did they go?' Brigit asked.

'Soon after I spoke to them. I didn't see who took them. I suppose it was Miss Hawkes, but it could have been the nurse. And after that I forgot all about them. I was so occupied listening to the supernatural.'

'To the what?'

'The supernatural, dear,' Mrs Hatchett's face became rapt. She stood with her plump arms folded across her plumper bosom, and her head slightly on one side in a listening attitude. 'Do you know, that's the first time I've ever heard him in the daytime, in broad daylight, mind you.'

Brigit was losing patience. 'Mrs Hatchett, just what are you talking about?'

Mrs Hatchett's voice became pained and formal.

'My ghost, madam. In the past he has only made his appearances at night, and silently. But this afternoon he has been calling, oh, so sadly. It would break your heart!'

In spite of her practical sense, Brigit had to repress a shiver. Hadn't she awakened to a far-off forlorn cry?

'And tomorrow we'll find the silver is missing,' she said sceptically.

Mrs Hatchett shrugged her shoulders.

'You may joke, madam. But you'll live to find out.'

With this cryptic remark she departed, and Brigit was left in the rapidly growing dusk to sip her tea and realize that this queer worry and apprehension had taken away all her pleasure in her suddenly regained mobility. Where was Nurse Ellen? Why had she delayed so long in taking the children out, and why didn't she bring them home? What had gone wrong?

She jumped violently as Renoir slid like a substantial grey ghost into the room. He was followed, a moment later, by Aunt Annabel who was dressed in a once elegant black satin afternoon dress, but who still contrived to look as if the wind had been blowing her in all directions.

'Darling, what do you think?' she exclaimed. 'The ladies have made me treasurer of the society. Isn't that an honour? I bank the money and draw the cheques. Oh dear, oh dear. I shall have to be so methodical. I'm afraid Saunders will laugh at me. Dear, are you listening?'

'Aunt Annabel, forgive me, but when did you last see the children?'

'Why, after lunch, I think it was. They were waiting to go

out. The sweet little innocents. They were waiting for their coats, I think. No, let me see, it was much later that I heard them playing in the garden. Really, dear, I couldn't say when they went to the park. Don't tell me they're not home yet.'

Brigit shook her head.

'But gracious, it's almost dark. Nicky will be quite frightened. Oh, listen! Isn't that them now?'

Surely enough, it was. Brigit breathed a sigh of deep relief as she heard Nicky shrilly making some explanation, and then the rapid patter of feet approaching her door.

Prissie came in first. Now, instead of being agitated she was brightly flushed, and her eyes were shining with what looked like intense excitement. Or was it apprehension?

'Mrs Gaye, I found the children in the park. Nicky said he didn't know it was so late. He said he had managed to get Sarah across the road quite safely. The cars had stopped for him.' Prissie gave a breathless almost hysterical giggle. 'They were alone, Mrs Gaye,' she said.

'But Nurse Ellen? Where is she?'

'That's what we don't know. Nicky said they waited an awfully long time for her and when she didn't come he decided to take Sarah himself.'

'I did, Mummy,' Nicky said eagerly. 'She was quite safe with me.'

'You mean the children crossed that road alone!' Aunt Annabel demanded in a horrified voice. 'But that nurse! Brigit, we must speak to her. How could she have let them do it?'

'She wouldn't have let them do it,' Brigit said urgently. Her apprehension had not been without reason. Now it had flowered into this very real problem. 'Something has happened to her. We've got to find out what it is.'

TWELVE

But no one could find out anything. No one had seen Nurse Ellen leave the house. Her hat and coat and bag were gone, but no one had seen them on Nurse Ellen's short plump brisk figure. They might have walked out of the house alone. It seemed that from the time she had left the children waiting while she assumedly went to fetch their coats Nurse Ellen had not been seen.

She had had to match wool, Brigit kept saying. Perhaps she had slipped over to Harrods before taking the children, and then, unable to match the wool there, had gone elsewhere. But she was not an irresponsible person. Had she done that she would have telephoned. It seemed that there could be only one explanation, and that was that she had had an accident.

By this time it was quite dark. Uncle Saunders had come home, and on being greeted with the news had exclaimed with lewd enjoyment, 'There's a man, of course. No woman ever disappears unless there's a man in it. And that young woman didn't look the spinster type.'

Brigit protested heatedly, 'She wouldn't just go off like that leaving all her clothes.'

'What would she want with clothes?'

Aunt Annabel sighed in exasperation. 'Saunders, do be serious! Apart from Nurse Ellen's very odd disappearance here's Brigit with no one to look after her. Something will have to be done.'

'Don't worry about Mrs Gaye,' came Prissie's soft eager voice. 'I can look after her until another nurse can come.'

The thought of having to submit to Prissie's ministrations was, to Brigit, the final exasperation. She felt she could not endure those white hands, childishly small and delicate, which had caressingly touched her possessions, now touching her body.

'Why do you say "another nurse"?' she asked sharply. 'Why are you so sure Nurse Ellen won't come back?'

The colour flew into Prissie's cheeks. Her eyes looked strained and enormous. Brigit realized then that she was misjudging the girl. Her excitement about the turn of events was superficial. Beneath it she was alarmed and frightened. Her eyes, with their enlarged pupils, had almost the same look of repressed fear that Nicky's had had.

'The police must be informed,' Aunt Annabel ventured nervously.

Uncle Saunders swung round on her. 'I won't have those damn useless police in my house again. They came to investigate a burglary and what have they done—nothing at all! No fingerprints, no clues. Just a waste of time. My goods have vanished and the insurance company will have to pay up. Police!'

He made an exclamation of disgust.

Brigit found herself longing desperately for Fergus. How could she, helpless in bed, manage a situation of this kind? Her eyes, moving restlessly round the room, caught sight of Nurse Ellen's sewing, the needle stuck in a half-made stitch, as she had put it down on the chair by the window. It seemed, for one eerie moment, as if that vital cheery presence were in the room begging for help. Nurse Ellen wouldn't just deliberately disappear. She must be in trouble somewhere.

'I suggest,' Brigit said, struggling for calm, 'that someone ring the police and inquire if there has been an accident in this area. I think she must have been hurrying over to Harrods and been knocked down by a car. Probably she's still unconscious. I can't think of anything else.'

'I'll do that now,' said Prissie with a return of her practical good sense. 'We should have thought of it long ago.' She turned at the door to look back. 'If there hasn't been an accident shall I report her disappearance?'

'I think not until tomorrow,' Brigit said slowly. 'If she hasn't had an accident she must be all right and——'

'And she wouldn't thank us for prying,' Uncle Saunders finished jovially.

Brigit's eyes returned to the sewing on the chair. Nurse Ellen sewed beautifully and took great pride in her work. If she had been deliberately going away she wouldn't have left things about. Anyway, Uncle Saunders had the horrid diseased mind of all the Templars. One could not expect practical help from him.

Guy came presently, but he too was of little help. At first he looked alarmed, but when he heard that the immediate crisis had nothing to do with him or his complex affairs, he dismissed it lightly.

'Nothing happens to a woman in broad daylight,' he said. 'She'll turn up.'

Prissie came back to report that there had been no accidents in the Knightsbridge area that afternoon and Guy said, 'Didn't I tell you? Nurse Ellen can take care of herself.'

He took Prissie's hand in a possessive way, and Brigit sadly realized that already he had forgotten the mystery of Nurse Ellen. He was still completely selfish.

There was always the hope, of course, that at any moment Nurse Ellen would walk in, with vociferous apologies for her absence. When, at ten o'clock, she had not done so Brigit was seriously alarmed. It was difficult to wait until morning before notifying the police, but perhaps Uncle Saunders was right and it was foolish to panic so quickly about a normal uncomplicated person like Nurse Ellen temporarily disappearing.

Prissie was the only one who was aware of her alarm. She was unexpectedly perceptive about it, and indeed seemed on the verge of tears. The colour had left her cheeks and her great dark eyes seemed to have grown. When her hand trembled as she handed Brigit her cup of hot chocolate, she laughed shakily and apologized.

'I'm sorry. I've got the jitters. It's just so queer Nurse Ellen vanishing like this. Do you think she was cross with me for not wanting her to take the children?'

'I can't think that would have worried her,' Brigit said honestly.

'Well, I don't like anyone interfering with my job, and that's true. But I didn't expect this to happen.'

'Prissie, it's nothing to do with you. At least let's be

thankful the children are all right.'

'Yes, there is that.'

Prissie bustled about tidying the room. 'They seem to have had an enormously successful time just by themselves. Yes, Mrs Templar? Did you want me?'

Aunt Annabel was at the door saying that Prissie was wanted on the telephone. Brigit said at once, 'Take it here, Prissie.'

For one moment Prissie stood as if poised for flight. Then, with the least perceptible reluctance, she came forward and picked up the white telephone by Brigit's bedside.

With her back to the bed she said a guarded, 'Yes, who is it?' Then very quickly she went on, 'I can't discuss that now. We have some trouble here. I'm very busy. No, it isn't serious, at least I hope not.' Then suddenly and piteously she said, 'I can't——' and stopped as if a hand had been clapped over her mouth. She listened a moment as the voice at the other end seemed to be saying something earnestly, then her head went up slightly, and she said in her normal voice, 'Yes, I know you're right. I'm so glad you're feeling better. 'Bye, darling.'

She put down the telephone and turned to Brigit. She was smiling, with a return of her light-hearted gaiety, but Brigit had the queer feeling that it was gaiety superimposed on fear, that if one stripped it off there would show a terror as stark and inarticulate as Nicky's for the mysterious Clementine.

'That was Aunt Maud,' she said. 'She suddenly wanted to discuss an argument she is having with the people in the upstairs flat. Apparently it came to a climax this evening. I told her I just can't be mixed up in them. I'm afraid Aunt Maud loves arguments. It's so bad for her when she isn't well. But apparently this one has done her good. She says she is feeling much better.'

Prissie was talking too much and too quickly. Brigit said:

'You needn't have been quite so abrupt with her, the poor soul.'

'Oh, but I've told her she mustn't ring me here. Honestly,

you don't know her. She's incorrigible on the telephone. You literally have to hang up in her ear.'

Prissie's voice, although it had its undertone of excitement, was quite self-assured again. That momentary desperation had left it. Could one garrulous old lady who liked to fight with her neighbours reduce her niece to desperation? Perhaps, in time, she could. But that was Prissie's problem, and unrelated to the one that confronted them in this house tonight.

It was impossible to reconcile oneself to Nurse Ellen's absence. Something very strange indeed must have happened.

But no one except Brigit and perhaps Prissie with her air of tension was going to worry a great deal about it. Uncle Saunders went stumping up to bed at his usual time, followed presently by Aunt Annabel. Guy, who had been playing records in the drawing-room, obviously hoping Prissie would go in, followed later. The house, apart from the sudden springs and pounces of the cats in the studio overhead settled to quiet.

It was Nicky who woke first. The witch doll in the cupboard was talking again. He knew that before the sound reached his ears, because he had woken in that familiar state of rigid fear. Something had woken him. It must have been the cackling voice of the doll.

He tried not to listen, but he knew that he would have to. Some awful fascination compelled him. Surely enough, presently the voice began again. It seemed very far away and it had a new tone tonight. Almost as if it were crying. 'Let me out!' it said. 'Let me out!'

But that was a trick to make you get up and open the cupboard. And then out would come the horrid little black person with the beady eyes and clutching hands.

Oh, yes, she was being clever, saying, 'Let me out!' as if she were in desperate trouble. But it was a trick.

With a great effort of will Nicky moved his hands enough to pull the blankets over his head. That way, although it was hot and suffocating, he couldn't hear the sad crying voice any more.

There was no voice in Brigit's chimney tonight, not even a whisper of wind. But the silence, if anything, kept her awake. She kept worrying about Nurse Ellen's completely unexplainable disappearance. Why, in between leaving this room and going to fetch the children, had she vanished? Certainly her hat and coat and bag had gone also, but everything else was here, even her sewing on the window-sill. She had told the children to wait until she got their coats. She had gone up to the second floor presumably to get the coats. No one, apparently, had seen her since. Had she come down the stairs again? Or was she concealed somewhere in the house?

Slowly, in her mind, Brigit began to reconstruct Nurse Ellen's probable movements. She would go into the bed-room where the children slept. Their coats would be in the big wardrobe in which Nicky declared the doll called Clementine was still hidden. She would reach in for them. Could she have stumbled and the door closed on her, locking her in? But then someone would have heard her calling for help.

And anyway Prissie had been up to ascertain whether or not the children had their coats. She would have opened the door to check on that. Nevertheless the feeling was growing in Brigit that the interval between telling the children to wait in the hall and going upstairs was the vital one.

Suddenly she thought, 'If I were to trace her steps,' and on an overwhelming impulse she sat up in bed, switched on the light, and threw back the blankets. Slowly, very slowly, she swung her legs over the side of the bed. Could she stand? With trembling hands she grasped the bedpost (surely no Spanish infanta had ever got so feebly and ignominiously out of this bed!) and gently let her weight go on to her feet. Her knees buckled ridiculously, but she did not fall. She could feel the chill of the polished floor on the soles of her feet. She could stand and feel!

Even as she was savouring this miracle, feet came shuffling rapidly along the passage and stopped at her door. Brigit, sinking on to the bed, saw Mrs Hatchett, a rotund figure in a pink flannel dressing-gown, standing uncertainly in the shadows.

'Oh, madam, you're awake,' she said thankfully. 'I'm that worried, I can't sleep. It's the noises.'

'What noises?' Brigit demanded sharply.

'My ghost. No one else.' Mrs Hatchett's voice was a mixture of proprietary pride and anxiety. 'He seems to have got shut in somewhere. He keeps calling "Let me out!" It's never happened before. It's downright heart-rending. I can't stand it.'

'What sort of a voice?'

'Oh, high and wailing.'

'A man's?'

'Well, it doesn't sound like a man's, I must say. But do ghosts have a sex? That's one thing I've yet to find out. Why, madam, you're all uncovered.'

'I was too hot,' Brigit said, impatient with the diversion. Her voice became urgent. 'Mrs Hatchett, will you do something at once?'

'Certainly, madam. Did you want a cup of tea?'

'No, I want you to go upstairs and look in the big wardrobe in the children's room. It's a very large wardrobe built into the wall. All their clothes and toys are kept in there. Go right into it, will you?'

'At this time of night, madam? I'll wake the children.'

'Never mind if you do. But go at once.'

Mrs Hatchett's round plain face was growing apprehensive.

'You're not expecting a—b-body, madam?'

'Not if you can still hear that noise. But go quickly. Please!'

Brigit lay back, listening tensely to Mrs Hatchett's dubious footsteps going towards the stairs. Oh, this was probably a mad fancy she had, but events could add up—the interval of a few minutes to get the children's coats, the almost sinister wardrobe, and now the persistent voice crying . . .

It was fantastic, it was horrible, but—Her thoughts broke off as a scream echoed and re-echoed through the house.

It was Mrs Hatchett and she was possessed of impressive vocal chords. She screamed, 'Save me! I'm falling! Save me!' until everyone was awake and running upstairs.

Brigit lay stricken with terror. She could not have moved now even had she tried. She muttered over and over to herself, 'Nicky, don't be too frightened. Please don't be too frightened,' but she knew that Nicky's small body would be paralysed as completely as her own.

It seemed hours before anyone came. Then it was Aunt Annabel, an unreal figure with flying grey hair, saying for Brigit not to worry, there had been a dreadful accident. But it was all right. It was all *right*!

'What?' Brigit managed to whisper.

'It's that big wardrobe, dear. The floor has rotted and it's over a well. Now we never knew that. All these years and we never knew there was that enormous hole. Being right next to the chimney, of course, it's probably been a builder's fault that they covered up.'

'But what has *happened*?' Brigit demanded.

'Mrs Hatchett nearly fell down it, dear. She just managed to save herself. She said she was ghost hunting. Of all things!' Aunt Annabel played feverishly with the tie of her dressing-gown. 'But there is someone down it at the bottom,' she blurted out, her face going grey.

'Nurse Ellen,' Brigit whispered.

'I'm afraid so, dear. But she's alive. She spoke. Saunders and Guy are thinking of the best way to get her up. Mrs Hatchett said she thought the noise of crying was her ghost. Bother that woman with her ghosts!' Aunt Annabel finished, glad to release her pent-up emotions in anger.

'At least Nurse Ellen has been found,' said Brigit. She began to tremble violently, and wanted to laugh hysterically. The terror of the unknown leaving her, now she suffered from this absurd reaction.

'Aunt Annabel, go up and help them. Bring the children down to me and then try to help them.'

Aunt Annabel's face puckered in helpless worry.

'All this is so bad for you.'

'Never mind me. See that Nurse Ellen is all right.'

It was Prissie who brought the children down. She carried Sarah, who was sleepy and bewildered, and held Nicky by the hand. Nicky looked as if he were sleep-walking. (Oh, Nicky, Nicky, when I get you home safely in the country I'll make all this up to you, Brigit cried silently.)

Without a word Prissie put Sarah in bed on one side of Brigit and Nicky on the other. Then she began to sob.

'I never knew there was that hole in the floor. I looked to see if the children's coats were gone, but they hang in the front and I saw them without putting the light on. She must have gone right into the wardrobe for them and the floor collapsed. Oh, it's awful!'

She didn't cover her face with her hands. She stood there with her mouth twisted and the tears running unchecked down her cheeks.

'I never heard a *thing*,' she said. 'To think she's been calling since this afternoon. O-oo, I can't stand to think of it!'

'Don't take it to heart, dear. It's not your fault.' Brigit's sympathy was instinctive. 'After all, it might have been you if you had been a heavier person.'

'I've walked in and out of there getting the children's toys——' Prissie shuddered violently. 'Guy's going to get a rope. She says she can get up on a rope. It's only her leg that's hurt.'

'Thank goodness for that.' Brigit's mind sought and then slipped away from a worse horror. 'Oh, thank goodness she's alive.'

'Clementine said bad things would happen,' Nicky said suddenly in his considering, too unnaturally calm voice.

'Clementine!'

'That's what she said,' he declared, wrapping his cold arms tightly round Brigit.

THIRTEEN

In the morning the events of the night were mercifully blurred in Brigit's mind. Doctor Brown who had been called to Nurse Ellen had given Brigit a sedative that had made her sleep without stirring and left her in a drowsy unreal state long after daylight. It was even difficult to remember what had happened after Nurse Ellen's rescue. Nurse Ellen had insisted on being taken into Brigit's room before leaving for the hospital to be treated for shock and a broken ankle. She had lain back in the easy chair by Brigit's bed and turning her white dust-marked face to Brigit said hoarsely:

'I'm sorry I'm letting you down, ducky. I'll be back as soon as I can hobble.'

Brigit had been going to say quickly, 'There'll be no need,' for by the time Nurse Ellen's ankle was mended she hoped to be walking normally. But there were too many people in the room, Uncle Saunders, enormous in a checked dressing-gown, looking irritable at having had his night's rest ruined, Aunt Annabel fluttering about nervously, Prissie still tear-stained and distraught, Guy with his gloomy fatalistic look—why did she think it might be wise to keep her mobility a secret, that it might be a trump card later on?

'Don't worry,' she said soothingly to Nurse Ellen. 'Just go away and forget about all this.'

Nurse Ellen's blue eyes, paler now, and rimmed with dark circles, went round the watching faces. She frowned a little, as if there were something she couldn't understand. Then she said, in a ghost of her old jovial voice, 'Can't understand why it took so long to make myself heard. There I lay in that musty dark hole, with the damn cats walking over my grave. Irreverent creatures, cats.' She smiled determinedly, then grimaced with pain, and grew, if possible even whiter. But as if she would not allow the watching faces to intimidate her, she clung to consciousness and said clearly to Brigit, 'Don't let that Clementine fool you!'

Then, probably to her intense disgust, she fainted, and before she regained consciousness the doctor was there.

What had she meant by telling Brigit not to let Clementine fool her? In the cold dreary morning light Brigit could not concentrate. She remembered vaguely Doctor Brown saying that he would send another nurse, and Prissie saying in her clear self-possessed voice that she could take over very well from Nurse Ellen, at least in the meantime.

So it was Prissie who brought her breakfast tray with the letters on it. When she saw the one with her name and address printed in block letters she automatically slipped it beneath the others. The blackmailer again! Oh no, this was too much.

'Is there something the matter, Mrs Gaye?' Prissie was looking at her concernedly.

'No, I'm all right. It's just that drug the doctor gave me last night. I can't wake up properly. I feel as if I'm in a nightmare.' She did, too. Everything was nightmarish, the grey sky hanging close to the window, the trees with their phantom-like leaves, the persistent wailing of one of Aunt Annabel's cats, even Prissie's charming concerned face that seemed strangely as if it might be distorted into something entirely different any moment.

'Have your coffee quickly and you'll feel better. After all, there's nothing to worry about now. Nurse Ellen is safe, and everything is all right.'

Everything—with that letter on her breakfast tray!

As soon as Prissie had left the room Brigit's trembling fingers opened the envelope and took out the slip of paper. The sprawling printing in a flamboyant violet ink read:

> YOU HAVE MADE A MISTAKE MY DEAR. IT WAS A HUNDRED AND FIFTY POUNDS I ASKED FOR. YOU SENT ONLY A HUNDRED. THE OTHER FIFTY HAD BETTER ARRIVE BY TOMORROW OR ELSE!

What was she to do? What was she to do?

Brigit was still lying back nervelessly when Aunt Annabel bustled in.

'I've come for your tray, dear—oh, my dear, you haven't touched it!'

Brigit said, 'No,' and then could say no more.

She was aware of Aunt Annabel coming close and peering at her with her kind short-sighted eyes. Her shaggy head looked like a sheep's.

'Brigit, there's something else wrong.'

Brigit whispered, 'No,' again, but Aunt Annabel, bending over her, said in a suddenly brisk voice:

'You never could tell lies, my dear, even as a little girl. There is something wrong. Don't mind telling me. I might be able to help you.'

'You can't this time,' Brigit said flatly. 'After all, Uncle Saunders never gives you any extra money, does he. You've got to be a pauper as well as everybody else in this house.'

'Is it money then, dear?'

Brigit nodded. 'It is, and yet it's so much worse. Oh, Aunt Annabel, how much do you love Guy?'

Aunt Annabel patted Brigit's head, and then stroked it with a sure touch, as if she were one of the cats, even the most treasured Renoir.

'I love you both. I have no children of my own, you know. I could have shown my affection so much more if—if it had been easier.' Suddenly her eyes glinted and she said fiercely, 'I've always been a coward. Saunders is so overpowering. But if Guy is in trouble of course I will help. And not a word to Saunders. Tell me, dear. What is it?'

So, with the gentle kindly old face above her, the whole story tumbled from Brigit's trembling lips.

'I haven't *got* another fifty pounds,' she sobbed. 'And even if I had, presently another one of these horrible letters will come.'

Aunt Annabel, who had taken the story of Guy's cowardice very calmly, continued to pat her head soothingly.

'Now don't worry, love. It's so bad for you. As it happens I can easily put my hands on fifty pounds.'

'Oh, Aunt Annabel! Can you?'

'Quite easily, dear. I'll bring them to you later.'

Brigit was filled with hope, then despair.

'But is it any use? If this sort of thing is going on indefinitely——'

For a moment Aunt Annabel looked frightened, her eyes going blank. Whatever shock the story had given her she was determinedly hiding, for Brigit's sake.

'Don't let's look on the black side. This person, whoever he is, might get run over, or fall down some stairs, or even die of pneumonia or something quite respectable like that. I've got into the habit of living from day to day. With Saunders one must ... Well, well, I mustn't complain. Now drink your coffee, dear, and you'll feel a lot better. And supposing we don't tell Guy about this new letter until tomorrow. He doesn't deserve to be protected like this, but poor boy, he hasn't been happy until now. He and Prissie are having their party tonight. It would be a pity to spoil their fun. Oh, we'll manage this little old blackmailer, don't you worry. After all, there have been much worse things in the Templar family than hit and run drivers and blackmail. We always cope.'

Aunt Annabel's words may have been merely bravado, but there was an unsuspected strength in her that Brigit found immensely reassuring and comforting. Suddenly, with the awful anxiety taken over by someone else, she was too tired even to think. With the last thought in her mind that Fergus would be home that evening she fell asleep with a frail ray of morning sunlight struggling through the gloom and falling across her face.

It was Nicky, that morning, who refused to be reassured. Although Prissie kept saying, 'But there's nothing to be frightened of, you silly boy,' he knew very well that there was. Although the sound had stopped long ago, he kept hearing as a faint echo in his ears that thin voice shrieking 'Let me out!' and he shuddered every time he thought of Nurse Ellen at the bottom of that deep black hole. It was no use to say that the floor of the wardrobe was rotten and had given way with Nurse Ellen's heavy body. One knew that that wasn't true. One knew that Clementine was responsible. Either Clementine, the witch doll, had pushed her into the dark hole, or that other Clementine ... Though how the Clementine of the cold slimy toad and the malicious pinching fingers and jeering voice could have got into the house and into the wardrobe he couldn't explain. He only knew that she was magic.

And more bad things would happen. He knew that, too, even though no one would believe him. Prissie, indeed, had lost patience with him, and had told him shortly to stop in the nursery and mind Sarah, and to keep out of her way because she had no time that day for whining little boys. She had his mother to look after, too, now that Nurse Ellen had gone.

Actually Nicky was very glad to keep out of Prissie's way because as well as being full of this strange fear he was also guilty. He had taken something of Prissie's. He hadn't been able to resist it. In all the excitement and bother last night Prissie had left her treasured locket lying on the dressing-table unguarded. And Nicky, who had been consumed with curiosity as to what it contained ever since Prissie had told her romantic stories about princesses and royal babies, had picked it up and opened it.

He didn't know what he had expected to see inside it. A tiny withered baby, he thought. Or perhaps a miniature crown of diamonds and rubies. Or even a curling golden lock of hair. All there was was a piece of paper neatly folded which, on opening, proved to be a letter. Nicky couldn't even read it, the writing was so spidery and faint. He was disappointed and disillusioned, but some instinct made him slip the folded letter into the pocket of his pyjamas and close the locket and put it back on the dressing-table. He would ask his mother or somebody to read the letter for him. It might have something about a royal baby in it. But whatever it contained, it could not compensate for the vague exciting thing he had expected to find in the locket.

In the morning he was not allowed to go into his mother because she was very tired after the disturbance last night. Also, Prissie said in her laughing voice that always seemed to Nicky to carry a threat beneath the laughter, Nicky was being such a difficult little boy that he only worried his mother, he must learn to be placid and happy like Sarah. So there he was confined to the nursery with the letter in his pocket still unread, and the fear on him that at any moment Prissie might discover that her locket was empty.

He wished desperately that his father were home. When suddenly Guy came into the nursery looking for Prissie it seemed to the frightened little boy that Guy was the next best thing to his father. He approached him timidly with the folded piece of paper.

'Please, Uncle Guy, will you tell me what this says?'

Guy looked at the paper Nicky held out. It seemed that he drew back for a moment, alarmed, as if the scrappy grubby piece of paper frightened him.

'Where did you get that?' he asked sharply.

'It's out of Prissie's locket. Oh, please don't tell her! It's about her being a princess, I think, but I can't read it.'

Guy's face lightened and he snatched the letter from Nicky.

'Ah ha! This will be interesting. The little minx, she's been holding out on me. She with her delusions of grandeur.' His tone was affectionate and tolerant. He obviously liked Prissie a lot.

'But you won't tell her!' Nicky begged.

'No, I won't tell her. At least, we'll see what this says——' His voice died away. His face seemed to stiffen, and then to grow very pale. 'My God!' His voice had become a thick whisper. Nicky couldn't hear what he was saying. Was it '... can't be true ...'? Nicky wasn't sure, and he couldn't ask Guy to repeat it, for Guy suddenly thrust the scrap of paper back at him and turned and went out of the room.

So there was Nicky with the unintelligible writing on the paper and no information at all as to what it said. He muttered, 'I don't want to know, anyway. I don't care what any old letter says,' and he sat on the floor and began to tear it to pieces. He made the pieces smaller and smaller until they looked like confetti at a wedding. Sarah was enchanted and pounced on the fluttering scraps of paper and flung them about. When Prissie came in with the empty locket dangling innocently round her neck she exclaimed,

'Oh, you naughty children! Look at that mess all over the floor. Now you can just tidy it up. Run down to Mrs Hatchett and get a broom and shovel. Quickly!'

Curiously, the act of destruction had made Nicky feel better. It was funny that Prissie could be looking at her precious letter scattered all over the floor and not knowing what it was, just thinking it was a page out of some old story book. Of course, some day she would find out that the letter was missing from her locket. But she would think Clementine had taken it. That was it. Clementine!

Nicky ran whooping down the stairs.

It was not Nicky's sudden noisiness but the search for the housekeeping money that woke Brigit. She was still heavy and tired, and the momentary relief that Aunt Annabel's shouldering of the burden of the blackmailing letters had given her seemed to have gone. Indeed, all her apprehension was back. Too many strange unpleasant things had happened, she thought. They could not all be coincidence. There was her accident, then the burglary, then the horrible letters from the blackmailer, and nastiest of all, Nurse Ellen's fall last night. What would be next?

She could not even smile at the sound of the pantomime going on in the adjoining rooms. The search had apparently grown desperate for Prissie was wandering farther afield, while Aunt Annabel called, 'Not upstairs, dear. That's out of bounds. Isn't it, Saunders?'

'Yes, out of bounds!' roared Uncle Saunders. 'I promised not to go out of this territory and I keep my word.'

Prissie's voice came back pertly, 'But supposing I don't trust you!' and Uncle Saunders gave his great peal of laughter.

'Quite right, too, my dear. Never trust a Templar.'

Alone in the big bedroom Brigit slowly and carefully moved her legs. Thank goodness they still responded. Later, when the coast was clear, she would get out of bed again and try to walk across the room. She had meant to walk into Fergus's arms tonight, but now she was not so sure that she would divulge her secret even to him. It was strange how imperative it seemed to her to keep that secret. There was a dim audacious plan forming in her head. If it came to fruition it would be very necessary to keep her mobility a secret.

Was it really true that the floor of the wardrobe had collapsed from dry rot last night? Was it?

'Oh, Saunders, we give up today,' came Aunt Annabel's exasperated voice. 'Really, we haven't time——'

'Then you lose,' declared Uncle Saunders merrily. 'That's the rule. Damme, it's time I won. I haven't won for six weeks. And what have you to worry about, my dear? Haven't you access to the funds of the lame cat society? So what are you worrying about?'

'*Saunders!*'

'Come now, don't be so shocked. You know as well as I do that honesty has never paid what one would call a thumping dividend. Hi, there, Prissie, you look like the cat that stole the cream. What have you found?'

'She can't have found anything, Saunders. That's out of bounds.'

'I just thought Mr Templar might have cheated,' came Prissie's audacious voice.

'Well, that's a nerve, I must say,' Uncle Saunders, in high good humour, declared. 'I've a good mind to spank your b—h'mm—well, come downstairs, you little minx, and make up your mind to bread and water this week because we're bankrupt.'

'It's too bad for you,' Prissie said primly, 'but at least I'm going out to dinner tonight.'

She came lightly down the passage to Brigit's room. Her cheeks were glowing, her large eyes more brilliant than ever. Was it the thought of going out with Guy that produced that excitement?

'Have we disturbed you, Mrs Gaye? Honestly, your Uncle Saunders is a character. Do you feel better after that nap? I'll go and make you a cup of tea.'

'Thank you,' said Brigit. Why should Prissie be so full of life today? Didn't Nurse Ellen's accident weigh on her at all? Perhaps she was glad it had happened, because then there could be no more awkward questions about Clementine. Clementine! Brigit's tired mind slid away from that mystery. She concentrated on Prissie's injunction that she must be bright and cheerful for Fergus. After all she had promised him. No more tears, she had said, even though Nurse Ellen had nearly died, and the blackmailer was at work again. Fergus had to believe that all was serene and happy in the Templar household. He must not despise her family any more than he already did because when would that feeling, like a contagious disease, spread to her?

It began to rain later so that the children could not go out. Brigit lay watching the colourless drops sliding down the window and listening to the intermittent sound of the children and the scampering of Aunt Annabel's cats. Prissie was in and out all the time, determined not to allow her to brood, so there was no opportunity for her to make her attempt to walk. The carpenter came to mend the floor of the wardrobe, the hospital where Nurse Ellen had been taken reported that the patient was as well as could be expected, Aunt Annabel bobbed in to nod her head mysteriously and say that that little matter they had discussed that morning had been attended to, the day wore on uneventfully towards evening when Fergus would be home.

But all the time the apprehension and gloom deepened in Brigit. She felt as if the cold raindrops were falling in her heart. When, in the half dusk, she dozed and awoke to the sound of the hoarse whispering voice in the chimney she felt no surprise. It was as if she had been waiting for it. Almost, she had known what it would say.

'You're not Brigit Gaye. You're not even Brigit Templar. You're me!' And then, with a gusty macabre chuckle, it said, *'You're a thief, a thief!'*

There was no Nurse Ellen to answer her frantic ringing. She sobbed aloud, and pressed her finger on the bell again and again.

But when at last Aunt Annabel, breathless and distressed, arrived she had regained control of herself. A voice in the chimney. She had imagined it. It had been a nightmare in the daytime. They were always worse.

'I'm so sorry,' she apologized to Aunt Annabel. 'I woke with a nightmare. I'm as bad as Nicky. Where are the children?'

'Prissie's bathing them. They'll be down to say good night. How cold and gloomy it is in here. No wonder you had a nightmare. I'll put on the lights and shut out the rain.'

'Isn't it early for the children to go to bed?'

'A little, but Prissie's going out, you remember? She has to have time to dress. She's so excited. If Guy is really going to become serious about her we must find out something of her background. There's this old aunt in Putney. I shall make it my business to call on her. But there! As long as Guy is happy, I won't let Saunders interfere!'

The bravado in Aunt Annabel's voice sounded a little tremulous in the gloom. She could face a blackmailer's threats with aplomb, and yet quail before her loud-voiced husband. Brigit wanted to reassure her, but Renoir, the colour of dusk, swept in with his dignity and insolence, and Aunt Annabel was already happy again, gathering him into her arms and crooning to him.

Then she suddenly muttered into Renoir's fur, 'Oh, my darling, have I betrayed you?' and hurried from the room.

Brigit could find no explanation for that cryptic utterance. She shrugged her shoulders, and all at once found herself inclined to giggle. When Fergus arrived and said, 'Everything all right?' she would answer, 'Well, Nurse Ellen did fall down that awful hole in the wardrobe, and Nicky was chased with a toad by someone called Clementine who doesn't exist, and a blackmailer has taken our last penny, and Nicky's witch doll talks to me from the chimney, and Aunt Annabel has betrayed her cats, but otherwise, yes, everything is all right.'

When Fergus did arrive she didn't burst into tears. At least, thank goodness, she didn't do that, but she found herself unable to say a single word to him. For his plane had been delayed and he was three hours late. Guy, who was not flying planes but simply coming home from the city, had not arrived at all.

FOURTEEN

'BUT it was only fog, I tell you,' Fergus kept saying. He gently undid her clinging fingers. 'There's often been fog in the past and you haven't let it worry you.'

'It isn't fog with Guy,' Brigit said bleakly.

'What, isn't Guy home yet? But, darling, surely there's nothing exceptional about him having a night out?'

'On any other night, no. But this was the night he was to have gone out with Prissie, if you remember. She's waiting for him. She's wearing her new dress. And Guy had been counting the hours until tonight. I know.'

Fergus looked round.

'Where's Nurse Ellen?'

'She had an accident. She broke her ankle.' Briefly Brigit related the details.

Listening, Fergus's face seemed to close. It was the first time, Brigit realized, that he had withdrawn from her into thoughts she could not interpret. Was he surprised at Nurse Ellen's accident? Did he think it had been an accident?

'Sweetheart!' he said, feeling for her hand.

But now, in an uncontrollable nervous reaction, she snatched her hand away.

'Oh, do something, Fergus. Why doesn't somebody do something?'

Fergus roused himself from whatever thought he had been pursuing.

'Guy will turn up,' he said. 'It's only ten o'clock. If he isn't here by morning we can start some inquiries.'

'Last night we said that about Nurse Ellen,' Brigit told him sombrely.

'Well, Guy wouldn't fall down a hole that he knew about. As a matter of fact I think I'll take a look at that hole.'

'You can't. It's been covered up. The carpenters were here today. It couldn't have been left like that with the children. Not that Nicky would go near that wardrobe. He's terrified of it. He still believes that Clementine lives in it.'

'Clementine?'

'Yes, darling Clementine. Now don't ask me who she is. I only wish I knew. But I'm beginning to be like Nicky and believe in her existence, whatever she is, a real person or just a malicious evil spirit.'

Fergus looked at her a moment, pondering, then he said suddenly. 'Poor little Prissie. I must go and see if she's worrying about Guy,' and left the room.

Was he impatient with her for what he could consider was her increasing neuroticism? Brigit gave a despairing sigh. This was the night that she was to have told Fergus that she was getting better, that she could walk again. They were to have been so happy and jubilant.

But how could she have thought that anyone could be happy in this house?

Prissie, sitting alone in the nursery, was finishing a letter. She had been crying, and there were still the marks of tears on her cheeks. She wore the dress she had made. She looked very slim and small. Her dark straight hair and thin arms were childish. But there was nothing childish in her face, or in her narrow shoulders rising from the glowing green silk. They had a maturity and sophistication that rivalled that in the portrait of Brigit's mother on the staircase. The tight-waisted full-skirted dress, made with clever success, was full of seduction.

But Prissie was alone, and had only her forlorn letter for company.

'What *can* have happened to Guy?' she wrote. 'I have done nothing, said nothing ... I even kissed him although I hated it. His disappearance worries me terribly. I'm frightened.' She paused a moment, her dark eyes full of anxiety, then determinedly she continued, 'But I'm sure he's all right. I refuse to brood about him. Isn't it a joke about what I found this morning!'

There was a tap at the door. Was it Guy at last? Prissie hastily closed her writing pad and called, 'Come in.'

It was Fergus who stood in the doorway. He was still in his flying uniform, and he stood straight and tall, his fair hair shining, his eyes resting on Prissie suddenly full of admiration.

Prissie stood up slowly, wiping away the last traces of her tears childishly with the back of her hand.

She did not want to cry any more, even for Guy, although she was still frightened for him. For in that dazzling instant she knew why she had really come to the Templar family. Deny it as she would she had been in love with Fergus from the first moment of meeting him. Looking at him standing there, tall and lean, his brown face creased with laughter lines, his blue eyes shining, she knew that at last she had found a person worthy of her love. Everything now had a goal.

'You're very grand,' Fergus said admiringly.

Prissie held out her wide skirt.

'Do you like it? Do you think I'm clever?' Now her face was glowing with animation, all her fears about Guy resolutely pushed out of her mind.

'Very clever. But hungry, too, I expect.'

'Yes, I am,' Prissie admitted. 'Guy hasn't turned up yet. Isn't he a stinker? After me going to all this trouble, too.'

'What do you think has happened to him?' Fergus asked casually.

'I haven't the least idea. I don't know much about his habits except that he's inclined to drink rather too much at times. I expect he's got lured somewhere with some friends.'

'I expect so, too,' Fergus agreed. 'Anyway, he's not at the bottom of the wardrobe.'

Prissie shivered. 'Don't talk of that. It was horrible.'

Fergus looked at Prissie's face. She couldn't decide whether he was studying it or thinking about something entirely different. Then suddenly he touched her lightly under the chin and said:

'I'm hungry, too. And all this glamour of yours is too much to waste. Shall we go out and eat?'

They came in to see Brigit before they went. Prissie had flung a silk stole casually over her narrow shoulders. Now her face was solemn and deferential, but she glowed, in the dimly-lit room, like a green jewel. Her hand was lightly on Fergus's arm.

'Mrs Gaye, do you mind terribly?' she asked in her soft eager voice. 'Poor Fergus hasn't eaten since breakfast, and as you know rations are short here. We didn't find the housekeeping money this week. Anyway, I think Mrs Hatchett has gone to bed.'

'What an excellent idea!' Brigit exclaimed. Did her voice sound quite spontaneous and sincere? They were so heartbreakingly attractive, the two of them standing there. 'If Guy comes in I'll tell him it's no more than he deserves.'

Fergus came swiftly over to the bed to kiss her. 'Sleep well, poppet,' he whispered.

Then they were gone, and all the life had vanished from the room. It was a dead empty place, and she switched off the bedside light so that, in the complete darkness, its emptiness did not matter. Even herself was not there, but just a part of the darkness.

If Fergus no longer loved her it would be pleasant to become one with the peaceful quiet darkness.

But even the darkness was not to remain for her. As her eyes grew used to it shapes became clear, the pitch-black fireplace, the paler shape of the window, the dim form of the mulberry tree. Oh, couldn't she peacefully disappear, and not linger on half alive, half dead like that tortured tree?

In the morning Guy had still not come home. Now it appeared that he had not been at the office where he worked at any stage the previous day, but they reported a telephone call from him saying that he would be away for a few days. Uncle Saunders was furious. He stood in Brigit's room, seeming to fill it with his bulk.

'The young scoundrel never had any thought for anyone else. Born selfish, that's what he was. His mother all over. He shall hear about this from me when he turns up again. Putting us to all this worry. Standing up a pretty girl like Prissie, though from what I hear she did all right for herself last night. They didn't get in until after midnight, the pair of them. Don't you mind, Brigit? Don't you think your husband is a bit too handsome to be trusted?'

It was no use being angry with him. Once before she had been angry, and her anger had brought her to this state, a cripple in a trouble-ridden house.

In any case Brigit's painful difficult courage was foremost in her again. She knew now that, crazy as it may seem, she had to carry out her plan. First in secret she had to practise walking until she was reasonably strong. Then she had to investigate what, to her, seemed the heart of the matter. The mystery of Clementine.

If Fergus was falling in love with Prissie, that could not be due to Clementine, neither could Guy's disappearance, nor Nurse Ellen's accident, nor the work of the blackmailer. Reason told her that the nervous state to which her illness had reduced her, and Nicky's constant state of concealed terror, were giving her this obsession. But her obsession was stronger than reason. It told her that first and foremost the riddle of Clementine had to be solved.

When she was alone after Fergus had left that morning (he went reluctantly, saying that he would telephone from Rome that night—he even held her in a hard desperate embrace as if he really loved her, and hated the way his admiration for Prissie was growing) she cautiously got out of bed and practised her slow tottering steps.

Gradually, as she gained confidence, her spirits rose. It seemed incredible to her that she had been able to refrain from telling Fergus of this miracle—had she been half-afraid he would not welcome it, that it was now going to be much more convenient for him to have a bed-ridden wife?

No, she would not think those bitter thoughts. She would secretly grow strong and well. She would sit before the mirror and assure herself that she had regained her beauty. Then she would fight Prissie proudly on an equal basis.

When Doctor Brown called unexpectedly she found herself observing the same secrecy with him. She answered his questions in monosyllables, yes, she was feeling well in herself, yes, she was sleeping, and no, she did not wish another nurse to be sent at present. She was being cared for very well. Another nurse would upset her plans, wouldn't she?

And anyway, she had a feeling that it would be disloyal to Nurse Ellen who had cared for her with genuine friendliness as well as skill. Nurse Ellen, Doctor Brown said, was progressing nicely, and had recovered from the shock of her fall.

'She was luckier than me,' Brigit could not help observing.

'Your cases are very dissimilar,' Doctor Brown answered.

Of course they were dissimilar in everything but that they had been accidents. Odd, unexpected accidents. Not the kind that killed but the kind that crippled.

But those thoughts, too, were strictly not allowed. She had to concentrate on one thing only, and that was to walk.

She got Prissie to unpack her clothes that afternoon. They had been left in the suitcase ever since they had been brought up from the country. They had been meant for her to go home in, but as yet they hadn't been needed. Her grey alpaca coat, her brogues, a fine wool jumper and skirt, nylon stockings, a yellow tam o'shanter that Fergus liked.

Prissie did as she was asked, but this time she did not attempt to disguise the pity in her eyes.

'That coat needs pressing,' she said. 'Oh, well, I suppose it doesn't matter.'

'It does matter,' Brigit said in a light pleasant voice. 'Ask Mrs Hatchett or Lorna to do it.'

'Why, I'll do it myself, Mrs Gaye.' Prissie was obviously humouring an invalid suffering from a chronic ailment.

'That's kind of you, Prissie, but it seems to me you're doing too much already.'

'Not really. I'd rather be busy today, anyway. It takes my mind off Guy. Where could he have got to? You're his sister, Mrs Gaye. You ought to know his haunts. Where do you think he is?'

The fear was in Prissie's eyes again. It had come and gone last night, but today it was there almost all the time. Brigit had not seen her frightened before. She had, at times, had some intense secret excitement, but never fear. For some reason Brigit found this fact increased her own uneasiness.

Had something happened between Prissie and Guy that would drive him away? If he had known about the second blackmail letter that might have led him to seek some hiding place. But he hadn't known. Aunt Annabel swore he hadn't.

'I haven't any idea, Prissie,' she answered. 'Guy didn't tell me his secrets. Did he tell you them?'

'None at all.' Prissie met Brigit's inquiry with a direct gaze from her frightened dark eyes. 'I didn't know he had any. I thought——' Suddenly her voice trembled with incipient tears. She turned abruptly away.

'You thought he cared for you,' Brigit said gently. As usual her treacherously soft heart had taken command and she had forgotten Prissie's glowing pleasure at Fergus's company last night. Could she seriously care about Fergus if she could weep for Guy?

'I hadn't done anything to hurt him,' Prissie sobbed. 'Truly I hadn't.'

'No one's suggesting you had,' Brigit said. 'Don't worry, dear. Guy's a strange moody person. He'll walk in any time. There's nothing wrong at his office, Uncle Saunders says, so there's no reason for him to disappear.'

'N-no,' muttered Prissie. She seemed to brighten as she hung up Brigit's clothes. 'There,' she said, straightening the coat on the hanger. 'You'll be wearing these again in no time.' Her voice indicated that she was once again speaking to a hopeless invalid.

'In no time at all,' said Brigit cheerfully. And then, she thought to herself, I'll find out not only about Clementine and other things, but why Prissie has this guilty fear about Guy's disappearance. Although of course by then Guy would be back again and would have explained everything...

While she waited for Fergus's telephone call that evening another one came for Prissie. Brigit heard her voice low but sharp and clear from the hall.

'Didn't I tell you not to ring me here! Please remember that this time!' The receiver was slammed down and Prissie's high heels went tapping angrily away. The caller may have been the sick aunt in Putney, but the greater possibility was that an attractive diverse little person like Prissie had other men friends. Indeed, thought Brigit suddenly, that would be exactly what it was. Guy had discovered that she had another friend and was playing a double game, so in disgust and despair he had left her. It would be the tortuous way his mind would work. 'I'll teach her a lesson,' he would say to himself. 'She'll think she isn't going to get the Templar money after all.'

But the thought of losing what she coveted might bring chagrin and disappointment to her eyes, not fear...

Fergus's call came through at last, and Brigit felt the familiar sensation of pleasure at the sound of his voice. Oh, would she never recover from this foolishness of love. Even the clipped brisk voice Fergus used on the telephone reduced her to this sweet trembling weakness.

'Guy back?'

'No, he isn't.'

'No news of him?'

'None at all, but Uncle Saunders said if anything had happened to him we would have heard by now, and if he's all right he wouldn't thank us to interfere.'

'That's exactly what I think,' came Fergus's brisk unemotional voice. 'Is everything else all right?'

'Yes, thank you.'

'You?' Did his voice grow warmer, or was it deterred by the knowledge of so many miles of telegraph wire between them?

'Oh, I'm fine.'

'Prissie?'

'She's upset about Guy.'

'I know. She was last night. I tried to get it out of her.'

'Get what out of her?'

'How much she cared for him, of course.' (Had that been impersonal or very personal curiosity on Fergus's part. A picture of them sitting side by side in the restaurant, the waiters deferential as to a pair of lovers, flashed into Brigit's mind. She could see Prissie laughing up at Fergus. She could almost hear her saying in her light laughing voice,

'Oh, Guy. He's sweet, of course...') 'She hadn't much to say,' Fergus went on. 'We'll talk about it tomorrow, darling.'

He was on the verge of hanging up. Brigit longed desperately to keep his voice in her ears.

'Did you have a good trip?'

'Reasonable. Darling, this call is a little expensive——'

'Fergus, hurry home.'

'I always do.' His voice deepened to a warmer note. 'You know I always do.'

After the sound had ceased Brigit still cradled the receiver against her cheek, trying to retain its magic. Prissie, in her red jumper, flashed into the room and said eagerly, 'Oh, was that Fergus?' before she could stop herself.

Brigit put the receiver down. 'Yes He was asking after you.'

It was useless for Prissie to conceal the light in her face. It came as naturally as a flower opening. Then her lashes drooped.

'That was nice of him,' she said primly.

'He seems to think you care a good deal about Guy,' Brigit said deliberately.

'He's quite right, too. I do. More than he thinks. Oh, why doesn't that darn fool boy come home!'

The moment of Prissie's flowering had gone. Had it been for Fergus or Guy? Fergus, undoubtedly. Brigit sighed and moved her toes surreptitiously. She still refused to be defeated.

In her room Prissie wrote, 'I had to unpack her clothes and hang them up this afternoon. Just a whim, of course. Perhaps she thinks looking at outdoor clothes will bring her nearer to wearing them. What a hope, poor thing. But I wish Guy would come home. I have this awful feeling that something has happened. You know that I'm not in love with him—how could I be? And as for Fergus, you know that, too. Didn't I tell you?'

FIFTEEN

AUNT ANNABEL stood just within Brigit's door. She was trying to conceal something in her hand. She was also trying to smile, but was quite unsuccessful in preventing the trembling of her lips. Her eyes held a look of shocked disbelief.

'Aunt Annabel, what is it?' Brigit demanded. 'Not Guy?'

'No, not Guy, dear. There's still no news from him.'

'Then what—Oh! You've got a letter.'

'It says I stole the money,' she burst out in a quavering voice. 'From my cats!'

'Show me,' whispered Brigit.

Aunt Annabel came forward slowly with the shameful scrap of paper. This time the message was impertinent and vulgar. It said:

> YOU SILLY OLD GEEZER, DID YOU THINK I WOULDN'T KNOW WHERE YOU GOT THAT FIFTY POUNDS. YOU ROBBED THE CATS' HOME AND WHAT WILL THE COMMITTEE SAY WHEN THEY FIND OUT. YOU'D BETTER SEND ME ANOTHER FIFTY POUNDS TO STOP THEIR FINDING OUT. THE SAME WAY AND PRONTO.

'But how does he know?' Aunt Annabel asked. 'Is he a magician, do you think?'

'How do you know it's a him?' Brigit asked cryptically.

'Why, you don't imagine a woman—but his name is George. I never heard of a woman called George.'

'It could be short for Georgina. It could even be short for Clementine.'

'But, darling, Clementine and George—oh, I see. An assumed name. Of course. He would. I mean she would. Oh, darling, do you really think a woman could do a horrid thing like this? Why, women usually adore cats.'

'I'm not saying it's a woman,' Brigit said patiently. 'I'm only mentioning that we have no way yet of knowing its sex. All I can say is that it is someone who has ways of knowing what goes on in this house.'

'Yes, like a spy. I quite see that.' Aunt Annabel ran her hands through her hair, increasing its storm-tossed appearance. 'Darling, this is so awful. I've only been treasurer one day and now they'll say already that I'm a thief. I only *borrowed* the money, you know.'

Brigit reached for her hand.

'I know you did. Dear Aunt Annabel. You were helping Guy and me. That's what you must explain when you tell Uncle Saunders.'

'Tell Saunders!' Aunt Annabel backed away. 'Oh no, I couldn't do that. Besides, he's had news this morning that has upset him.'

'What news?' Brigit demanded sharply.

'I don't know, dear. Something that came in the mail. He clapped his hand to his head like this'—Aunt Annabel pressed her own plump one against her forehead—'and cried "My God, I'm ruined! Ruined!" Then he got up from the breakfast table and disappeared. I think he's in his study but I don't dare disturb him. You know how he is when he's worried.'

'Yes, I do,' said Brigit, remembering Uncle Saunders's terrifying black rages directed against the whole world.

'Oh dear! And now I'm worrying you, and it's so bad for you. Well, there's only one thing.' Aunt Annabel's voice became more brisk. 'I shall have to borrow some more money.'

'No, Aunt Annabel. You can't do that.'

'But, dear, we're not in the red yet.' Aunt Annabel looked proud of her knowledge of modern banking jargon. 'We have over two hundred pounds.'

'Don't you see that that's only going from bad to worse?' Brigit said worriedly.

'Yes, I do. I quite see that. These letters will keep on coming until we are paupers. But what can we *do*?'

'I don't know,' said Brigit slowly. 'But I have a plan. I hadn't meant to try it quite so soon, but I think it will have to be today. Don't do anything about that letter until this evening. By that time——'

'Yes, dear?'

'I'll perhaps know a little more.'

'Darling, this plan?' Aunt Annabel's face was full of worry. 'Is it dangerous?'

'Now, sweetie, what could be dangerous to a cripple lying in bed? Run along and feed your cats, and don't worry.'

'I'll try not to. But my poor darlings, I'm afraid, are on bread and milk today. Saunders won the housekeeping money this week and we're all on short rations and no one's at all happy.'

Brigit took care to give Prissie instructions to take the children out that afternoon. It seemed to her that Prissie looked relieved, as if she had been afraid she might have had to stay in.

'But what about you, Mrs Gaye?' she asked. 'Mrs Templar is going out to a meeting, I think.'

'Oh, I'll be all right. If I want anything Mrs Hatchett will get it for me.'

But privately she was thinking that it would do her good to get out of the house, too, and her heart began to beat rapidly from excitement and nervousness. Would she be able to manage it? Was she strong enough? In another day it would have been much better, but events did not wait for the gathering of her strength.

This morning, during the hour when she was supposed to rest, with drawn curtains, she had walked to the window and back six times. Then she had sat at the dressing-table and studied the slightly ghostly person in the mirror. She had lost weight and was very pale. Beside Prissie, with her glowing vitality, she must indeed have seemed a poor washed-out creature.

But that was over now. She could be glowing and vital too. She would show them. Tonight she would show them.

Everything went as planned. Prissie, still with that lurking look of fear in her eyes, left the house first, and later Aunt Annabel, who seemed to have recovered her good spirits, said she would go part of the way with them. Who knew, they might find a kitten in distress on the way. Sarah instantly began to mew plaintively and Brigit could hear

Nicky saying earnestly that he liked kittens much better than toads.

Uncle Saunders, looking like thunder, had departed noisily for the city some time ago. Lorna, the maid, was having her afternoon off. So only Mrs Hatchett was left in the house, and she was probably in the warm kitchen dozing, and expecting Brigit to be dozing, too.

Brigit had two clear hours before anyone was likely to come to her room. That should be time enough.

As soon as Aunt Annabel's and the children's voices had died away she got stealthily out of bed and began to dress in the clothes that Prissie had unpacked for her yesterday. She felt weak and a little dizzy, but it was surprising and reassuring how being dressed in daytime clothes made her feel once more a normal self-respecting person. When she was completely dressed, with hat and shoes on, she had to sit down for a few minutes to rest. Although she was so eager to be on her way she must take things quietly and not become so exhausted that she collapsed on Mr George Smith's doorstep.

Or was it Miss Clementine Smith's doorstep? Soon she would know.

On her slow, careful way through the hall she collected one of Uncle Saunders's walking-sticks. This aided her progress, and she was able to go out at the front door and negotiate the steps without accident. Excitement at this achievement temporarily banished her feeling of weakness. She hailed a conveniently passing taxi, and safely ensconced inside it gave the driver her destination. The house in Hammersith. The abode of the blackmailer.

What did she expect to find there? Brigit could not have said, except that she had this overwhelming intuition that that was the place where the answer to all the mystery lay, and it would be plain there for her to see.

It was a thin slice of a house standing with one wall bare to the ruined shell of a bombed house. It was also as Brigit had hoped it would be, an apartment house with the names of the occupants inserted in slots beside the front door. With no clear plan as to what she would do if the name 'Mr

George Smith' were really written there, bringing to life a person who should be only a figment of someone's imagination, Brigit asked the taxi driver to wait, and climbed out. Now she could scarcely stand.

The driver made a move to come and help her, but she waved him back. She would be all right when she got to the top of the steps. It was only her violently beating heart that made her dizzy. At this stage she must not collapse.

The front door was open slightly. Brigit clung to it as she read the names in the slots. Miss Emmeline Collard, Mr James Hunter, Mr and Mrs Jacques Clare.

No George Smith. No Clementine. But she hadn't really expected there to be. They wouldn't flaunt their names openly. They would hide behind a name like Emmeline, or Jacques.

She would ring Miss Emmeline Collard's bell first. She would say 'Clementine told me to come,' and watch the woman's face. She would go on then, 'You don't know Clementine? Then you know her husband, George Smith?' It was all quite absurd, the reasoning, Fergus would say, that one could expect of a woman. But if the Collard woman expressed nothing but astonishment she could go on to Mr James Hunter, and then to the Clares, although she did not think a married couple fitted into the picture.

Her finger was on the bell. Her heart was beating suffocatingly again, making her head whirl. She leaned a little harder on the door for support, and it swung in slightly so that she could hear voices from within.

At first they sounded far away as if she were hearing them inside her head. They were singing in a high happy chant. The tune was familiar. What was it?

Oh, *yes! Oh, my darling, oh, my darling, oh, my darling Clementine!*

Prissie's song! Brigit pushed the door wide open and stumbled inside. There was no one in sight. She stared up a flight of stairs to a landing overhead, and a closed door. That was where the noise was coming from. There were sundry thumps and shrieks as if a lot of people were playing a game.

Brigit began to hurry across the linoleum-covered hall, leaning on her stick. The outline of the stairs wavered slightly. She couldn't faint now, not at this moment on the verge of discovery. She had to get to the top of those stairs, and open the brown door. It wasn't very far. If the floor were not so slippery . . .

A door opened and shut suddenly behind her. A man's voice said suddenly, 'Can I help you? Where are you going?'

She couldn't see his face clearly. It seemed to recede from her into the mistiness that also hung over the stairs that she had somehow to climb. It was white and black, that was all she could notice about him. She vaguely indicated the stairs, and his voice came again:

'Oh, to Clementine's party.'

A woman's voice suddenly came from upstairs on a high-pitched note, 'Jacques, it's not——' and then, in an unexplicable way the house seemed to be full of noise, of feet running, of shouting and screaming. She was on the floor because she could feel the linoleum cold and hard beneath her. But all the faces and bodies and legs round her she could not explain. Her last impression seemed to be of beady black eyes in a white face, and long stringy black hair. Then there was nothing.

When she opened her eyes again Aunt Annabel was bending over her. At least it looked like Aunt Annabel, but what would she be doing in this house? From far off Brigit heard a voice, and that, too, was Aunt Annabel's.

'Thank goodness, dear, you're coming round. You fainted, you know. Dear me, what a fright we've had.'

Brigit blinked resolutely. Yes, surely enough it was Aunt Annabel's round pale face with its halo of wildly flying hair. But what was she doing here?

'Aunt Annabel—you shouldn't have brought the children here.'

'They're not here, dear. They're still in the park with Prissie. I left them having such a frolic.'

'But how did you get here?' Brigit repeated slowly and intensely. 'I told you to do nothing about that letter until this evening. You didn't have to come to this hou——' Her voice faltered as she realized for the first time that she was in bed. She turned her head slowly, unable to believe that it was the familiar furniture in her own room she was seeing, and that here she lay, as usual, in the royal Spanish bed.

'I haven't done anything about the letter, as you said. I did wait. My dear child, what is it? I believe you're wandering a little. Look, this is me, Aunt Annabel. And you're safely back in bed.'

'Back in bed!' Brigit repeated.

'Yes, darling. Mrs Hatchett came in and found you on the floor. Such a fright she got. She got you back somehow, and now she's sent for the doctor. I came in just as this was happening. It's my fault, really. We should never have all gone out and left you. What Fergus will say, I can't imagine.'

'But Aunt Annabel, I was out of bed. I was——'

'I know, dear. However did it happen? Do you remember falling?'

'But I didn't fall. I walked. I've been out in a taxi. I went to the house in Hammersith, you know the one where Mr Smith is supposed to live——'

At the name Aunt Annabel looked round uneasily.

'Brigit dear, you're romancing. I know that is the horrible Mr Smith's address, but you haven't been there. You've only imagined it, poor soul. It's been on your mind and you've had a nightmare.'

Brigit started up, but she was so weak and exhausted she had to lie back, breathing quickly. The very aching exhaustion of her body proved that she had had that dreadful trip.

'My clothes,' she said. 'I had them on. That proves——' But her voice died away as she saw that she was clad, as usual, in her nightdress, and that the wardrobe door was shut on the outdoor clothes which someone had taken off her.

Aunt Annabel smiled gently and patted Brigit's hand.

'Just rest, dear. The doctor will be here in a moment.'

There was nothing to do but obey. Brigit closed her eyes,

thinking that when she opened them she would see not Aunt Annabel but the white-and-black man called Jacques, and that other face, the one with the bright beady eyes and long dangling black hair. Instead, she remained in her own bedroom and when she opened her eyes it was to look at Doctor Brown's slightly reproachful face.

'And how did you come to fall?' he asked in his dry professional voice. 'Can you tell us? Did you actually attempt to get out of bed?'

'I *did* get out of bed,' Brigit announced. Her voice was meant to be strong and triumphant, but her exhaustion was so great that it was scarcely more than a whisper. 'I walked.'

'So.' Doctor Brown's voice was completely sceptical.

'But I did, Doctor. It's quite true. I've been walking for two or three days. I was keeping it a secret to surprise my husband. But today I had some urgent business in town, so I got up and took a taxi.'

'You dressed?'

'Of course I did.' Brigit's voice became impatient. 'You don't imagine I would go out like this. I expect Mrs Hatchett put my clothes back in the wardrobe when she undressed me.'

'You remember collapsing?'

'Yes, indeed. I was in this house full of strange people——' Brigit's voice died away as she saw the doctor's sceptical eyes.

'And how did you get back here?'

'Why—I don't know. I just opened my eyes and found myself here, in bed.'

'H-mm!'

'But I was out, doctor. I was! You can ask—well, the taxi driver, anyway.'

Doctor Brown threw back the blankets. 'Well, let's have a look at your legs, anyway.'

He began his usual methodical examination.

'Can you feel this? This?'

To Brigit's complete dismay she could feel nothing at all. She was back to the old dreadful days of numbness. The doctor's fingers might not have existed for all she could feel them on her flesh. She tried desperately to move her toes. Nothing whatever happened. Nothing.

'But I could before!' she insisted. 'Really I could! I suppose I've done too much. I'll be all right when I've rested. Doctor, you must believe me!'

Doctor Brown gave his small tight smile and, as Aunt Annabel had done, patted her hand.

'There, my dear, in your anxiety to walk these dreams become very real. You appear to have had a singularly vivid one. I think a small sedative. Yes?'

He was now exerting all his bedside manner to take the look of white dismay from her face. But it was no use. He was not going to believe her, and until he, or someone, believed her, she knew she could not get well.

Because they would all finally convince her that she had not walked, and so, as in a fairy story, the magic gift would leave her . . .

'And if you had been out somewhere, dear,' Aunt Annabel, coming back, said, 'who do you think brought you back? Because you couldn't have walked if you were unconscious.'

'I don't know. Someone from that house. Perhaps the blackmailer.'

'And how would he get into this house *and* into your bedroom? Oh no, Brigit dear, that's asking too much even for me to believe. And there's nobody else. I've been looking for cats, Mrs Hatchett has been baking, Saunders has gone to the city, Prissie has had the children in the park—they've just come in now. Sarah is still being a cat, bless her.'

'Prissie!' murmured Brigit.

'Now you're not suggesting that Prissie left the children in the park and rushed off somewhere to rescue you!'

'No-o. But did she have the children in the park? Aunt Annabel, ask Nicky to come and see me.'

'You're supposed to be resting,' Aunt Annabel reproved. 'Oh, very well, just for five minutes.'

Nicky came in slowly. For a moment he looked as if he were afraid even of her. His eyes were darkened and wary.

He stopped a little distance from her bed and said in a cautious voice, 'Are you worse again, Mummy?'

'No, darling. I'm very well. Did you have a nice time in the park this afternoon?'

'Yes, thank you.'

'What did you do?'

'We made a pile of leaves and pretended it was a bonfire.'

'Did Prissie help you?'

'No, she just watched.'

'And you spent the whole afternoon doing that?'

'Yes.' Nicky nodded his fair head uncertainly.

'You didn't see the little girl you call Clementine?'

Nicky's head turned quickly. What was he looking for, Prissie or the ghostly child? He saw that there was no one else in the room and he said loudly, 'No.'

'Nicky, who is Clementine?'

'She isn't anybody.'

'But you've always said she was somebody. Come, there's no one listening. Tell me.'

'She isn't anybody!' Nicky said again, firmly. Then he added, 'I made her up.'

'And you were really in the park all the afternoon?'

Nicky's voice was sulky. 'I told you I was.' Suddenly he said more animatedly, 'I can do a trick. Would you like to see it?'

'Of course, darling.'

'It's with these handkerchiefs. You see, one is red and one blue. You roll them up into your hands like this——'

As he laboriously handled the coloured squares Prissie appeared.

'Oh, there you are, Nicky. Is he worrying you, Mrs Gaye?'

'No, I wanted to see him.'

Prissie put her arm round Nicky's shoulders.

'You'll have to practise that trick a little more before you can show it off, dear. It's one I used to do when I was a child, Mrs Gaye. It's quite simple, really. Nicky, have you been telling your mother about the bonfire you made?'

Nicky put the coloured handkerchiefs back into his

pocket. He nodded, his head bent.

'That's a good boy. Now run up to Sarah because your mother isn't very well today.'

Nicky went as if he were glad to escape. Brigit tried to dismiss her uneasiness about him.

'Prissie, you shouldn't have said that. Nicky's so sensitive. And anyway I'm very well. I've even been out.'

Prissie smiled tolerantly. 'Yes, I heard about that. I'm so glad you didn't hurt yourself.'

'Hurt myself?'

'When you fell out of bed, Mrs Gaye.'

For a moment Brigit looked at her desperately, weighing in her mind whether she should try at least to make Prissie believe in her exploits. But it would be no use. Prissie wouldn't even want to believe it. Somehow she knew that. There was only one person who would believe her, and that was Fergus. He *must* believe her.

'It must have been a very vivid dream you had,' Prissie went on. She opened the wardrobe door as if at random, showing Brigit's clothes hanging innocently where she had put them the previous day. For a moment Brigit had a frantic feeling that it must all have been a dream, that everyone else was right and she alone wrong. Perhaps it was even a dream that she had got out of bed and walked.

'I heard people singing,' she said. 'The strange thing was that they were singing that song of yours. "Darling Clementine".'

'Then that proves it,' said Prissie gaily. 'Who else would be singing that old-fashioned song, except in a dream?'

The awful thing was that Fergus completely agreed with Prissie and with everyone else. There was Brigit lying in bed helpless, quite unable to move her legs, even her toes. And yet she persisted in this completely impossible story that she had got up, dressed, got a taxi, and taken a journey to a strange house in Hammersmith.

It seemed incredible that a thing so vivid in her own mind should be so impossible for anyone else to believe. The trouble was that she hadn't a shred of proof unless she could find the taxi driver who had taken her. He would remember her, she knew. But how could she set about finding him when she was indeed lying helpless in bed, with even her newly-found ability to move her legs deserting her.

'But I could walk, I tell you,' she insisted to Fergus whose face had that same tolerant look of disbelief that Prissie's had had. 'I had kept it a secret to surprise you. I was going to show you tonight. I hadn't even told the doctor. But now—now——' Her lips trembled. She tried uselessly to move her legs.

'Darling, don't mind it so much,' Fergus said gently.

She grew angry then. 'I do mind it. Because it was true. It was true! I dressed and put on my shoes, and walked to the front door and down the steps.'

Fergus sat on the side of the bed and took her hand.

'But even if this were true and not a daydream or wishful thinking or whatever the doctor attributed it to, why get up and go to a completely strange house in Hammersmith? It doesn't make sense.'

'Because——' Brigit began and stopped. She could say no more. She couldn't make explanations because that would involve Aunt Annabel and Guy, and Fergus, while smiling gently and tolerantly, would grow inwardly sick with shame and dislike for her family and their dishonesty and cowardice.

'Well, why?' he persisted.

'You wouldn't understand,' she said lamely. 'It was something to do with this—this Clementine of Nicky's. A hunch I had. And there was the house, and they were singing "Darling Clementine".' Her voice grew excited as she remembered.

'Who were singing "Darling Clementine"?'

Her excitement faded. 'I don't know. Some children, I think. But then there was this man——'

'What man?'

'I couldn't see him properly. His face was in the shadow. That was when I fainted.'

'And you saw no one else at all?'

'Just the——' Again she hesitated. 'Oh, just someone with long stringy black hair and black eyes—the person Nicky talks about——'

'You mean the witch doll?' Fergus demanded incredulously.

'I don't know who it was!' Brigit, full of her own perplexity, grew petulant.

'And then Mrs Hatchett found you,' Fergus said. 'you were lying on the floor beside the bed in your nightgown. At least that's what she said, and she has no reason to lie about it. So if you had been dressed and out, how did you undress again?'

Brigit rubbed her hand over her eyes. Why did Fergus worry her with these unexplainable things? Why couldn't he just believe her? Oh, why was everything so utterly awful?

'I'm tired,' she whispered. 'I want to sleep.'

'Yes, darling, of course. Best thing for you.'

And you'll wake up in a saner frame of mind, his eyes said. Oh, Fergus, what is this evil thing that is going on, that is separating you from me much more than my physical state is? And can't you see it happening? Or do you want it to happen? Is Prissie making you want it to happen?

'Brigit——'

'No, Fergus.' She shut her eyes tightly, not wanting to see his awareness of her sudden panic. 'Go and see the children. Get Nicky to show you his conjuring trick. You'll find him more amusing than me.'

'His conjuring trick?'

'Yes. I feel it should explain something. But I don't know what.'

Whether her adventure that day had been reality or waking dream, the voice that night was certainly part of a dream. It said with croaking maliciousness, 'How can you hold a man like Fergus when you are a hopeless invalid? Let him go free...' And then, 'He wants to be free ... free...'

The word was echoing in her head as she started awake.

There was no one in the room, of course, and now there was utter silence. Outside, in the dark night, the moon, a slender horned shape, hung lightly in the arms of the mulberry tree. Like a shining cap a jester had tossed off. A malicious merciless inhuman jester.

Had she walked or had she imagined it, just as she imagined the persecution of this evil voice which must come from inside her own head? Had she worn the clothes that hung innocently now in the wardrobe? Was there a taxi driver in London who could tell a story of a woman walking into a tall narrow shabby house in Hammersmith and a little later being carried out? Or was all this as much imagination as Nicky's terror of an imaginary child called Clementine?

There was no one to answer her questions, and no one to be on her side. She knew now, desolately, that she was alone.

SIXTEEN

PRISSIE had almost persuaded herself to stop thinking about Guy. After all, she didn't know him very well. He was probably accustomed to doing these irresponsible things, and his disappearance had nothing whatever to do with her or—— She switched her thoughts abruptly, and reflected on the fact that the drama surrounding Brigit had temporarily put Guy out of everyone's mind.

That was a good thing, because he would come back soon. Of course he would. It was ridiculous to think that anything serious had happened to him, or to be so frightened...

She should be glad he wasn't here, shouldn't she? She didn't need him any more, and now she didn't even have to endure his kisses. But she couldn't quite get rid of the cold fear in her mind. Supposing...

None of this must show in her letter. She wrote gaily:

Such a do today with Brigit's accident. Fergus didn't believe her wildly improbable story about a visit she had made somewhere by taxi. Poor soul. Perhaps her mind will become affected. I'm sure mine would. The children have been very good, especially Nicky. I think he is on my side at last. I am beginning to feel, after the last few weeks, that these children are really my own——'

Prissie stopped and allowed the forbidden thought to come into her mind. Supposing Nicky and Sarah were hers, and Fergus her husband. Supposing Brigit never got well——

Oh, *poor* Brigit, but one couldn't expect to tie a virile handsome young man to an invalid.

Supposing...

'Supposing we have a drink,' came Fergus's voice from the doorway. 'I'm sure you need one after all this fuss and bother.'

Prissie sprang up, glowing with pleasure.

'Oh, I could do with one. The children are asleep and——'

'Brigit's asleep, too,' said Fergus. 'The doctor gave her something. Poor darling, she's been so upset about this dream of hers. Extraordinarily vivid it must have been. And yet Mrs Hatchett swears she was lying on the floor in her nightdress.'

'Yes, I'm afraid she was,' Prissie said soberly.

'Tell me, where was it that she so badly wanted to go? She had some place on her mind.'

Prissie flung out her hands.

'I really couldn't say. Your wife doesn't confide in me. Sometimes I think she doesn't like me.'

Fergus smiled, his eyes full of their familiar heady admiration.

'Oh, nonsense! I never heard anything so improbable. Come here and tell me more about yourself.'

As Prissie approached him there was a taut look of excitement that she had never seen before in his face. Her own pulses began to race. Oh, this was what she had wanted all the time, and she hadn't completely realized . . .

'What about myself?' she said in a low provocative voice.

'Why, who you are, what secret you guard so closely in this locket?'

Prissie quickly laid her hand over the locket, guarding it from his curious fingers. But she was smiling. Later was time enough for that. Later . . .

'Don't be so inquisitive,' she reproved.

His face was close, his blue eyes narrowed to brilliant slits.

'You're quite right, my secretive little monkey. At the moment—this is more important——'

Only afterwards when the intoxication of the kiss was over but not faded from her mind did Prissie realize that her half-finished letter lay there open for his gaze. She had a momentary pang of dismay, but after all it was all right. She hadn't written anything that mattered. And anyway, Fergus would have had his eyes closed. No one kissed like that with open eyes.

Brigit didn't know why she should have awoken with that heavy premonition of disaster hanging over her. Perhaps it was the grey morning, with the daylight no more than an apology for the departing night. Perhaps it was her feeling of utter exhaustion, as if she could find no strength even to lift a finger. Or more probably the depressing fact that her legs still remained numb and motionless, so that even she was beginning to wonder if she had ever climbed out of this aristocratic bed and walked.

Her despair was unreasonable. There had been no more events to cause it. Aunt Annabel had slipped in early, with three cats playfully following the trailing cord of her dressing-gown, to whisper that there were no more of *those* letters in the mail, and a little later Prissie had come to switch on the lights, light the fire, and make the room cheerful.

Her sudden aversion to Prissie's expert and gentle ministrations was unreasonable, too. But all at once she felt she could not endure having her face washed and her hair brushed by those little white hands that were always lingering covetously on the beautiful objects in the house. It was humiliating, as if she had become one of Prissie's possessions, a tiresome one that required just the right amount of politeness and care.

Prissie, she felt, must know where Guy was, who Clementine was, if indeed she were a person at all, even the identity of the blackmailer. If one could strip off the bland smiling mask of her face and expose all those secrets . . .

'Mrs Gaye, you're not looking at all well this morning. Didn't you sleep?'

'Yes, I slept, thank you.'

'You look so tired. Of course, it's the shock of your fall yesterday.'

'I didn't have a fall,' Brigit said distinctly. 'I can brush my hair myself, thank you. If you'll just give me a mirror. And tell my husband I'd like to see him, please.'

'Yes, Mrs Gaye. Of course.'

There—it wasn't fair to be so cold and ungrateful to Prissie. The girl was looking hurt. But suddenly she couldn't endure her in the room. It was absurd, it was neurotic, but there it was. Prissie had become, absurdly, part of her premonition of disaster. It wasn't fair that Prissie should be standing there with the glow of health in her cheeks and eyes and lips, as a contrast to her own state of fragility and weakness when Fergus came in.

Did she flick him a swift secret glance before she went out? Brigit was sure she did. Fergus had his head turned and she could not see whether he reciprocated the glance, but his gaze lingered on Prissie until she was out of the room. Then he turned belatedly to his wife.

'Energetic little creature, isn't she?' he said cheerfully.

'Fergus,' Brigit said abruptly, 'why don't I trust Prissie?'

Fergus looked at her in astonishment.

'Don't you?'

'No, I think she's up to something.'

Did Fergus's gaze flicker slightly? Oh, but in the past he had never failed to meet her eyes.

'And what would that be, darling?' he asked with good-humoured tolerance.

'I don't know, but she should be more upset about Guy's disappearance. Guy was in love with her and she encouraged him. Now she doesn't seem to care at all.'

'I thought she was quite worried about him going off like this.'

'Oh, worried, yes, but for some private reason. I think she's even a little frightened. But she isn't affected emotionally. I think she's quite heartless.'

Fergus sat on the side of the bed and patted her hand.

'You're lying there making up things, my little silly. You're disappointed because your match-making efforts didn't come off.'

'Oh, no!' Brigit exclaimed. 'It's true I wanted Guy to be happy, but Prissie—no, she was only interested in him for his possessions. I'm sure of that. Fergus, I want you to get me another nurse, and I want Prissie to go.'

'But what about the children? They're so fond of her.'

'Are they?' Brigit asked. 'I wonder. Nicky seems to have changed so much. Yesterday he scarcely answered my questions. He spoke like an automaton.'

'Darling, little boys do those things when they're in the mood.'

'Nicky never used to have those moods. And why should he suddenly start doing conjuring tricks?'

Fergus laughed. 'You can hardly accuse Prissie of teaching him those. Anyone less like a conjurer——'

'Oh, you're besotted with her, too!' Brigit cried suddenly and angrily. 'You think I don't notice anything lying here all day.'

'Biddy——' Fergus began.

But Brigit was now in a state rare for her of becoming thoroughly upset and unreasonable.

'It's Prissie, Prissie, Prissie all the time. You don't believe anything I tell you—I can dress and go out and nearly kill myself, but you don't believe a word of it—Prissie can tell you I was here all the time and her word is the absolute unshakeable truth!'

'But, darling, Mrs Hatchett said——'

'Couldn't I have been brought back and undressed and

left on the floor!' Brigit demanded. 'Wouldn't that have been a possibility you could have considered had you had any faith in me at all?'

'And who,' Fergus asked gently and reasonably, 'do you imagine brought you back? Prissie, I suppose, although she is smaller and lighter than you, and couldn't under any circumstances lift you, let alone carry you. And anyway she was with the children, as you very well know. Ah, come now, darling, don't upset yourself' (for Brigit was muttering sadly, 'You don't believe me any more') 'I would believe anything that was humanly possible to believe. For instance, why did you want to go to this particular house?'

But that was the one question Brigit could not answer. She could not bring herself to tell him of this new shameful thing regarding her family. Anything but that.

'It was to find out about this mythical Clementine,' she said unconvincingly. 'I'm sure there is something to be found out. Nicky——'

'But where did you get that address?' Fergus interrupted. Then suddenly he jumped up. 'I have it! The Brides-in-the-Bath man—the parcel the other day! Darling, what is this curious business——'

His sentence remained unfinished, for at that moment Aunt Annabel came flying in, her face full of distress.

'Fergus! Brigit! There's a message—Guy is very ill—it's from an hotel in Brighton. Someone will have to go——'

Uncle Saunders's heavy step followed. 'What is it, Annabel? Why don't you tell me these things? Is the boy dead?'

Brigit gave a little cry and was aware of Fergus holding her hand in a sudden protectiveness that gave her a frail feeling of warmth even though it seemed he no longer loved her.

'Well, speak up!' Uncle Saunders demanded. 'Is he dead? And if he is, why did he have to go to Brighton to die. Extraordinary!'

His voice was far from inaudible. Wherever she had been Prissie must have heard it, for suddenly she was at the door. Her face was white, her eyes enormous.

'Dead!' she whispered, and gripping the doorpost she slid quietly downwards.

Afterwards Brigit remembered more clearly Fergus picking Prissie up in his arms and carrying her like a child to the couch at the foot of the bed, then Aunt Annabel explaining breathlessly that Guy was not dead but dangerously ill. Apparently he had taken an overdose of sleeping tablets. And Uncle Saunders reiterating, 'But why do it in Brighton? Damme, that's where one goes to have a good time.' It seemed that the graver aspect of Aunt Annabel's news had not yet occurred to him.

Fergus was bending over Prissie with concern. When almost at once she opened her eyes he smiled reassuringly, and said, as if it were a conversational opening, 'I wonder why Guy would take sleeping tablets.'

Then he straightened and said briskly, 'What about getting Prissie a little brandy, Aunt Annabel? I must go and see about trains.'

'Trains, dear?' Aunt Annabel said vaguely. 'But your plane?'

'My dear aunt, if I were dead someone else would fly the plane.'

It was not a fortunate remark, for it made Prissie give a little cry and relapse into partial unconsciousness again. Uncle Saunders stamped across the room muttering melodramatically in a rumbling undertone. 'What the devil has the boy done? Are we all ruined?' Then he stood over Prissie exclaiming impatiently, 'Oh, for heaven's sake, girl, if he was your lover why couldn't you have been kinder to him? You can't mess about with people like Guy.'

'I didn't kill him!' Prissie said, in a high clear voice, as if the words were forced out of her. Then she sat up, clapping her hands to her mouth, her eyes wide with fear.

There was a moment's complete silence, as everyone looked at her. Then Aunt Annabel flung out her hands in a helpless gesture.

'What are we talking about? Guy isn't even dead.'

Prissie wrote on the bottom of her unfinished letter, 'No!

No! No!' and then left it lying brazenly on the table when Aunt Annabel called that she was wanted on the telephone. Nicky read the indignant words written in heavy black lettering, and wondered what it was that Prissie didn't want to do. He hadn't thought that she, too, would be faced with unwelcome or frightening things. Not like the things he had been faced with. But he hadn't done anything or said anything he shouldn't have this time, had he? There had been no threatening voice from the wardrobe, no gaping dark hole that would swallow up bad people.

Sometimes he wondered what Nurse Ellen had done that was so bad. He had thought she was nice and kind, but for some reason she had been made to fall down the dark hole. And the witch doll had pretended not to hear her calling. Probably wherever she had been hiding she had been laughing in her cruel cackling voice, waiting for Nurse Ellen to die.

Instead, it was Uncle Guy who was to die ... Why?

Nicky fumbled with the coloured silk handkerchiefs in his pocket. The slinky feel of them and their bright colours delighted him. He shook out the crimson one and pulled it slowly through his fingers, and was filled with sensuous pleasure. He had begun taking the handkerchiefs to bed with him, because in the night, a sudden creak might indicate the beginning of the croaking cackling voice from the wardrobe, if he felt the smooth silk beneath his pillow he was calmed and soothed at once. He almost didn't mind now about Clementine.

Prissie came back into the room after answering the telephone. She was breathing quickly and there was a spot of red colour on either cheek. Her eyes were sparkling as if she were angry—or frightened. Nicky didn't know which it was. He spoke timidly, 'Is Uncle Guy dead?'

Prissie whirled on him and he saw that regrettably the emotion that filled her was anger.

'No, of course he isn't, and don't you dare say things like that. Why should everyone think that because he is ill he is dead. It's just nonsense.'

Her black eyes smouldered, and Nicky had scarcely the

courage to say, 'I'm glad he's not dead.'

'Of course he's not dead, and do stop using that word, I tell you!' Then Nicky saw that after all, Prissie was not angry but frightened. The red had gone from her cheeks and she was quite white. She picked up her half-finished letter and tore it into small pieces and threw it into the fire.

'There!' she said in a voice that was more bravado than courage. And Nicky knew in that moment that someone or something was dead, but he couldn't have explained what. He only knew that all at once he was very frightened, too.

To Brigit the dark hours of the morning were endless. Fergus had gone and she again was forced to lie helpless and useless, with nothing to do but worry.

What had made Guy do this crazy thing? He hadn't worried too much about the blackmailing letter. She was sure of that. At that time he had been obsessed with Prissie. At that time—— Why, it was only two days ago. It seemed like an age. Prissie had been making her pretty green dinner dress and Guy had had an unfamiliar look of happiness and optimism. Then all at once he had disappeared, and Prissie had been as genuinely bewildered as everyone else. So the reason for his disappearance and now for his attempt at suicide had surely been due to nothing Prissie had done. He had not been aware of her secret interest in Fergus—or had he stumbled on that fact suddenly? Or had he discovered that someone else was ringing her up?

But surely if any of these things were true Guy would not have given up so easily. In the past he had had more tenacity than that. He could not be so spiritless now.

Then was it the accident with the car and the blackmailing letters that were preying on his mind? Was he suddenly overcome with remorse for the old man who had died?

No, Guy did not know the meaning of the word remorse. He was a Templar. He was cold and selfish and arrogant and determined to get what he wanted. He would not have run away because of remorse or because he had discovered that Prissie was devious and false. He would have stayed and bent Prissie, at least, to his will. There was some other reason. Fergus had to discover it. Fergus with his tolerance, his humour, his laughing eyes, who was neither arrogant nor selfish nor demanding nor avaricious. Oh, why did this family of hers have to taint and smear her marriage with their sordid troubles?

Aunt Annabel brought in her morning coffee. She set the tray down by the bed, and sniffed forlornly. Her eyes were reddened, and the damp streaks of tears lay on her cheeks.

'Oh dear!' she said. 'I'm sorry to be like this. Wait till I get my cats.' She bustled out, and presently returned with the big grey Persian, Renoir, and the black kitten in her arms. 'There, my darlings!' she crooned. 'There! You shan't starve, no matter what your wicked master says.'

'What does Uncle Saunders say?' Brigit asked.

'He keeps on insisting that we are ruined, and then he sits in his study and makes long lists of figures and tears them up. And another most curious thing.'

'What is that?'

'When Lorna was dusting this morning she noticed that the Meissen vase had been shifted. You know where it stands on that little table in the drawing-room.'

'Where is it now?' Brigit inquired without a great deal of interest.

'It isn't anywhere. That's the curious thing. That burglar must have been back, but when I wanted to ring the police Saunders wouldn't allow me to. He said—he said——'

Brigit was all attention now. 'What did he say, Aunt Annabel?'

Aunt Annabel's tears were falling on Renoir's silky coat. 'He said did I want to completely ruin him? Brigit, what does he mean?'

'Aunt Annabel! Uncle Saunders hasn't been the burglar all the time?'

'That's what I've been wondering, dear. But if he's really so short of ready cash why doesn't he sell the gold plate? That's worth a fortune. And why would he take a thing like Nicky's coat. A child's coat with a fur collar. Nicky used to look so sweet in it. Oh no, if he did that he must be mad!'

'But Nurse Ellen saw the burglar that night, Aunt Annabel. He was a little man with a green scarf. She couldn't have made that up.'

Aunt Annabel regarded her sombrely.

'Unless he was really Mrs Hatchett's ghost.'

'Oh no! Uncle Saunders couldn't be using a ghost to cover his activities. That's too absurd.'

'If he is,' said Aunt Annabel, burying her face in Renoir's fur so that her voice was almost inaudible, 'we're a fine lot, aren't we. Me tampering with the Society's funds, Saunders doing petty thieving—though how can it be thieving when it's his own property—and Guy killing that poor old man, and now trying to take his life.' Her eyes, when she raised them, were full of shame. 'You're the only decent one, Brigit. How did you come to be decent?'

'You are, Aunt Annabel. You are,' Brigit whispered.

'No, I'm a weak silly old woman and I've lived too long with the Templars. If it weren't for my cats——' She dashed away her tears. 'Oh, dear, this won't do. Look at the time. Fergus should be there by now. We should get a ring from him at any time. Oh, I do hope he finds Guy is recovering.'

Even as she spoke Mrs Hatchett came bustling to the door.

'The telephone, madam,' she said. 'It's for Mrs Gaye. It's a man.'

'Fergus,' said Brigit with relief.

'No, it's not your husband, madam. It's a strange voice, sinister sort of.'

SEVENTEEN

Aunt Annabel made a move to stop Brigit picking up the telephone by her bedside, but Brigit quickly and firmly spoke into the mouthpiece.

'Yes. Who is it?'

The voice came back, thick, slow, masculine.

'Is that Mrs Gaye?'

'Yes, I am Mrs Gaye.'

There was a slight pause, and a sound of heavy breathing. Then the voice came again.

'Why haven't you been answering my letters?'

'Your letters! Your—*oh*!'

Was that a hoarse mocking chuckle that came through the receiver? Abruptly Brigit moved it away from her ear as if it would contaminate her.

'I see you know now who I am. I've been waiting for that parcel since yesterday. It's too bad it hasn't come, because now my price has gone up.'

'I shall call the police!' Brigit exclaimed involuntarily.

She was aware of Aunt Annabel giving a gasp and sitting down on the side of the bed. She must have squeezed the cats too violently, for Renoir gave a harsh protest, and the black kitten escaped from her arms and pounced playfully at the dangling telephone cord.

'I wouldn't do that,' came the slow thick voice. 'You'd be sorry. Your children might suffer.'

'My children!' Brigit's voice was no more than a horrified whisper.

'I want a hundred pounds by tomorrow morning,' said the voice inexorably. 'Wrap it up and post it the same way. If I don't get it you'd better watch your children.'

With a click sounding in her ears like doom, the receiver at the other end was replaced.

This was the worst of all. That, for the moment, was all that Brigit could think. When Aunt Annabel's frightened eyes mutely asked her what had happened she could not speak.

The black kitten, leaping with outstretched claws at the swinging telephone cord, missed it and the sharp claws caught Brigit's wrist. The sudden pain broke her icy trance. She gave a cry and began to tremble violently.

'Aunt Annabel—we must get a hundred pounds at once. You'll have to ask Uncle Saunders. Tell him it's desperately important. Tell him everything. After all, there's nothing to be gained by protecting Guy or anyone else now. Just see where it's leading us.'

Aunt Annabel gripped her wrist. 'What did that horrible man say about the children?'

'He didn't say anything, except make a threat. Oh, it's unspeakable!'

'You mean—kidnap them?' Aunt Annabel whispered.

'I suppose that's what he meant.'

'My dear, now we can't delay any longer. We must get the police. Guy will go to prison, so will I, but anything, anything is better than having the children in danger.'

Aunt Annabel's distraught state enabled Brigit to pull herself together. She spoke more calmly.

'Tell Uncle Saunders first. We must at least send that money today. When Fergus gets back——' She gave a dry despairing sob. It was no use trying to hide these things any longer. Fergus at last would have to know. She would have to risk him despising her and her family for ever. But first the children's safety had to be ensured.

She sent for Prissie and said as calmly as she could:

'It's cold out today, isn't it, Prissie? I think perhaps we'll keep the children in.'

Prissie gave her a quick glance. Her face seemed to have grown smaller and to have a pinched look. There was something of which it reminded Brigit, but for the moment she couldn't think. Her mind was hazy with apprehension and fear.

'You've let them go out on colder days than this,' Prissie said sharply.

'Have I? Then it was unwise. Nicky catches cold very easily.'

'Has something happened?' Prissie asked in a tight voice.

Brigit raised herself on her elbow. 'Why should you ask that? Did you expect something to happen?'

Prissie's eyes slid away, but not before Brigit caught a glimpse of the terror in them. If Prissie were frightened of something, too, why couldn't they talk about it? They might have been able to help each other. But it was strange the aversion Brigit felt towards doing such a thing.

'Do you expect something to happen?' she asked Prissie again.

Prissie began to make a denial, then suddenly she burst out, 'Anything could happen in this house. It has a hoodoo on it.'

'You're worrying about Guy,' Brigit said more gently.

Prissie brushed her hand across her eyes although they were quite dry.

'I didn't do anything to him!' she said. 'I only——'

'Only what?'

'Didn't stop him falling in love with me,' she muttered. 'I suppose I should have done that.'

'Then you didn't love him?'

Prissie's eyes were full of scorn. 'Of course I didn't. At least not in that way——' And then again the mysterious fear took possession of her and she reiterated, 'It isn't my fault, no matter what anyone says.'

'I don't think anyone is blaming you, Prissie, and I'm sure Guy is going to be all right. But in the meantime we'll concentrate on one thing at a time. Just keep the children indoors today. Can I trust you?'

'I'd like to know why you couldn't, Mrs Gaye,' Prissie returned stiffly, and with her small head held high with dignity she left the room.

Now her feelings were hurt, Brigit reflected. But that really didn't matter. It would mean that she would take especially good care of the children, and somehow the awful danger could be staved off until Fergus came home.

In the meantime that hundred pounds must be sent. It was like feeding a hungry monster who, if he were to remain unfed, would take revenge by devouring oneself. Or Nicky and Sarah...

Panic mounted in Brigit again. She rang the bell, and waited impatiently for someone to come. There was a long interval before anyone came at all. The house, all at once, was completely silent, as if there were no one in at all, and Brigit had a sudden nightmare vision of the children kidnapped, and everyone out looking for them, while she herself lay in bed, helpless and forgotten.

Frantically she rang the bell again, keeping her finger on it, and hearing its distant shrilling like the scream that she seemed to be holding back inside herself.

At last there was a scuffling in the passage as Renoir, the black kitten, and an aged tabby tom preceded Aunt Annabel into the room.

'What is it, dear?' Aunt Annabel asked in a high nervous voice. 'Are you ill? Has anything——'

Brigit lay back, controlling her rapid breathing.

'No, nothing else has happened. I'm sorry if I startled you. It's just about that money. Have you seen Uncle Saunders?'

Aunt Annabel came closer and it was then that Brigit saw the distraught uncomprehending look in her eyes. Her hair was fantastically wild, and within the circle of it her face seemed to have shrunk, as Prissie's had, as if they shared a mutual fear. But the thing that frightened Prissie could not be Aunt Annabel's fear, also?

'Darling, Saunders is in his study with the door locked.'

'But he would let you in, surely,' Brigit exclaimed.

'Yes, he did.' Aunt Annabel nodded her head slowly, almost vacantly. 'When I left him he was crying. Crying! Can you imagine it? That big man!'

'Not—Guy?' Brigit whispered.

'Guy!' Aunt Annabel caught a flash of contempt and scorn. 'Oh no, indeed. Saunders doesn't weep for people!'

'Money!' Brigit said intuitively.

Aunt Annabel nodded.

'He hasn't got any, he says, none at all!'

Brigit looked at her incredulously. 'But that's nonsense! Surely it's nonsense! The Templar fortune——'

'It doesn't exist, dear. Saunders has frittered it away. Mostly on the Stock Exchange, he says. But it's gone. We're paupers, he says.'

Brigit sat up vigorously. 'Oh, that's absolute rot. What about the famous gold plate?'

Renoir sprang on to the bed, and Aunt Annabel, gathering him into her arms, began to laugh in an hysterical way.

'But it isn't gold, it's faked. Long ago Uncle Saunders sold the genuine gold plate and other things of value.'

'All of them?' Brigit demanded unbelievingly.

'Most of them. There were just one or two genuine things left, like the Meissen vase and the gold angel.'

'So he pretended they were stolen!'

'You know how he has always enjoyed practical jokes,' Aunt Annabel said miserably. 'Oh, if only he had been lucky on the Stock Exchange. But he has always lost, he said. Yet he couldn't give it up. It was a disease with him. He cried on my breast,' she added, more to herself, and suddenly her face was young and gentle in a strange and touching way. It was a glimpse of the girl Aunt Annabel had been before Uncle Saunders with his noisy arrogant imperceptive ways had driven her into timidity and vagueness.

Oh, this dreadful destroying family of hers, Brigit thought desolately. She wanted to tell Aunt Annabel not to be deceived by a few weak self-pitying tears, that Uncle Saunders would soon regain his bullying autocratic ways. Instead she found herself patting the old lady's trembling hand and saying:

'You'll be happier without all that money. Really you will.'

Aunt Annabel pushed back her undisciplined hair.

'I know we will. It isn't the money that worries me. It's the'—she lowered her voice to a whisper—'criminal aspect. Saunders has deceived the insurance company. It's about that gold angel. It wasn't stolen by the burglar, you know. Saunders had it all the time. The night the burglar came he saw his opportunity and hid it and said it was stolen. So of course the insurance company is going to pay, and——'

'Yes?' said Brigit impatiently, as Aunt Annabel hesitated and looked doubtful about making her final revelation.

'That blackmailer knows,' she blurted out.

'*Our* blackmailer!' Brigit echoed, and then had an hysterical desire to laugh at her note of possessiveness.

'Yes, dear. Somehow he knows Saunders has the gold angel, and he threatens to tell the insurance company unless Saunders pays up.'

'How much this time?' Brigit asked sharply.

'It's quite absurd, of course. He wants a thousand pounds. He thinks Saunders is wealthy. Isn't it ironical? And in reality Saunders has mortgaged this house and furniture to the hilt.'

Brigit had a desire to chaff Aunt Annabel gently on her business jargon, anything to delay a few minutes her absorption of this new alarming news.

But there was no opportunity to say anything, serious or otherwise, for Prissie was at the door, a tray in her hands, a look of shocked astonishment on her face.

Her moment of awareness was quickly erased as the children followed her in.

Sarah galloped forward with her usual energy, her fair little face beaming with innocent trust. She had never heard dark dreadful words like kidnapping and blackmail. She was with her family, and perfectly safe. She smiled widely at her mother, shouting 'Me horsey horsey!' and went on her energetic way to the window where she climbed on to a chair and stood with her short fat legs firmly apart looking out into the square. Nicky followed, his hand in his pocket, his gaze abstracted.

'What have you got in your pocket, Nicky?' Brigit asked.

'Only my handkerchiefs.'

'His coloured silk ones,' Prissie explained. 'He adores them, either for their colour or their feel, I don't know which. I brought your tea, Mrs Gaye.'

It was obvious that Prissie's mind was not on what she was saying. She put the tray down, slightly slopping milk from the jug, and then looking round agitatedly for something to mop it up. The information Aunt Annabel had just imparted, and which Prissie had undoubtedly overheard, had upset her, Brigit realized. Yet why should it, for she frankly admitted that she had no emotional interest in Guy. Guy was the only means by which the Templar fortunes could concern Prissie.

'I must go back to Saunders,' Aunt Annabel murmured, gathering up Renoir and the black kitten. 'But you realize the significance of what I have been telling you, Brigit. It must have been an *inside* job!'

'Funny man! Funny man!' Sarah chanted from the window.

Nicky joined her, and looked out, the two fair heads, so like Fergus's, close together.

'Where's the funny man?' he asked in a superior voice.

Sarah pointed a chubby forefinger. Nicky gave a small cry.

'Clementine!' he ejaculated.

Prissie flew to the window and looked out. Then she lifted Nicky from the chair and set him on the floor. She turned to Brigit, shaking her head.

'It's only a street hawker,' she said. 'He's wearing a large black hat. That's the only funny thing about him. Come along, you two, you'll only worry your mother.'

'No, wait!' Brigit ordered. 'Nicky, did you see Clementine just now, truly?'

Nicky looked at her with frightened blue eyes. Then, in a disturbingly adult way, his eyelids drooped and he said airily:

'I was just pretending for Sarah. She likes pretending.'

Sarah certainly did, for she had clambered down from the chair and was galloping her noisy way round the room. Prissie grasped her hand, saying, 'Hush, darling! Hush! Such a noise. Come along with me. Come, Nicky.' And before Brigit could protest further the children were whisked out of the room.

Clementine just outside the window! And she chained to the bed as surely as if there were actual chains round her legs. Brigit, angry tears in her eyes, sat up and desperately tried to move her legs. They refused to respond.

Somewhere out there, in the mist beneath the leafless trees perhaps there was a person called Clementine, a queer faceless menacing person. Or was it just a funny little man in a large black hat innocently selling his wares? Whoever the person was, he was not for her to see. She was the pampered patient in the aristocratic Spanish bed doomed to be kept in the dark for ever.

Upstairs, Prissie peremptorily shut the children in the nursery. Nicky expected a reprimand for his unguarded mention of Clementine, and another lecture on telling lies.

But quite mildly Prissie told them to play with their toys while she wrote a letter. Half an hour later, after biting her pen more than writing words on paper, Prissie went to the telephone that had an upstairs extension outside the nursery door.

Nicky stood with his ear against the keyhole and listened shamelessly. Prissie wanted to speak to Clementine, he knew. But how could she speak on the telephone when Clementine was just outside in the square, kicking up the dead leaves and looking at the house with sharp beady eyes.

Surely enough Prissie came back and went on with her letter. Nicky, creeping silently close enough, could see the thick black writing she was making, as if she were angry with the words she was putting on paper.

> 'It's no use any more, I do love Fergus—I've lied to you about it, but now I'm telling you the truth. I know from the way he kisses me that he loves me, too. So like Phillip, who took what he wanted by force if necessary, I am going——'

The telephone rang outside. Prissie, stopping writing, listened. No one downstairs went to answer it. Finally she went to answer the insistent ringing herself.

At first her mind had not been on Fergus. It was still on the letter that she had ceased to try to compose tactfully. Rather absently she picked up the receiver and said, 'Hullo,' crisply, as Brigit would have done.

'Biddy, is that you, darling?' It was Fergus, and he had mistaken her voice. He thought he was speaking to his wife.

Without a clear idea as to why she did so Prissie said, still in an excellent imitation of Brigit's voice, 'Yes, this is me,' and Fergus went on:

'First, darling, I love you. Please will you think of that and keep it in your mind all the time.'

'Yes,' Prissie whispered, in all the voice that she could command. Her face had gone tight, her fingers gripped the receiver until the knuckles stood out as if naked of skin. Those whitened knuckles seemed to express all the anger viciously held inside her body.

'Darling, are you listening?' came Fergus's urgent voice.

'Yes, I can hear.'

'Will you remember what I said?'

'Yes, Fer—darling.'

'That's my girl. I'm afraid the news is bad. Guy died half an hour ago.'

Now there was no need to pretend shock and grief. She felt both, so keenly that her voice was almost inaudible.

'Oh, *no*, Fergus!'

'I'm afraid it's true. He never recovered consciousness.'

'But *why*!' Now she was more consciously Brigit again, and trusted that Fergus would not later wonder at the temporary strangeness of his wife's voice.

'He's left a letter. Something about that car accident, and—other things. But we won't talk of it now. I'll be home later this evening. And, darling, remember what I said. I love you.'

Prissie was silent. She was trying not to tremble. She felt as if a storm were breaking inside her, a storm of rage and pain and desolation.

'You do believe me, don't you?' came that maddening caressing voice that was not for her. Those kisses, those false false kisses!

'I did wonder—about Prissie——' she began in Brigit's hesitating uncertain voice.

'Oh, my darling, no! No! As I will explain when I get home. Don't grieve too much for Guy. I think he's happier where he is.'

And then the telephone clicked, and it was she who was bereaved. Completely and for ever.

Prissie was not used to being without some driving emotion. Only temporarily was she numbed. Then, within her small taut body, hate began to grow.

On one of her impulses, which usually had such brilliant successes, she ran downstairs and went swiftly and quietly along to Brigit's room.

The room was darkened, so that Brigit would rest. At first one could scarcely see her fair head, like a daffodil, on the pillow. Her illness had not dulled the brightness of her hair, nor indeed her eyes nor the warmth of her smile. One would have thought she would, by this time, have grown anaemic and colourless . . .

'What is it, Prissie?' came her courteous voice.

'Oh, Mrs Gaye, your husband has just telephoned.'

Brigit started up. 'Fergus?'

'Yes, he spoke to me. He said not to disturb you.'

'Not to disturb me! But——' The hurt was obvious in Brigit's voice. Nevertheless, she collected herself instantly and went on, 'What did he say, Prissie? What about Guy?'

'Guy's dead.'

Perhaps she spoke too brutally. Momentarily she felt a stirring of her own angry grief. Then, looking at Brigit's lovely ashen face, she whipped up her hatred and jealousy.

'Fergus said he would be home later, and not to worry.'

'Not to worry!' Brigit echoed in a disbelieving whisper.

Prissie came forward.

'You've had a shock, Mrs Gaye. Shall I get you a sedative?'

But Brigit shrank back against the pillow.

'No, no! Just leave me! Please leave me!'

So that was done. Prissie went slowly upstairs, fingering her locket. Now one had only to wait until Fergus came home. Then she would begin using her wiles on him. Never before had she known them to fail with a man . . . She smiled secretly to herself, regaining her confidence. Of course he would have to speak like that to his wife when he was breaking such tragic news to her. It needn't have been true. Or it needn't be true for much longer . . .

Idly Prissie's fingers pressed the catch of the locket and from habit felt for the folded paper within.

It was not there.

Prissie stood still, aghast. When had she taken it out? She hadn't. Of course she hadn't. Then who could have taken it? Who had had the opportunity?

With the blood draining out of her face and fear filling her to the exclusion even of hatred and jealousy, Prissie remembered Fergus's traitorous kiss, his fingers on her locket. She, trusting susceptible little fool that she was, had lost every sense but that of delight. And Fergus's prying fingers had found what they wanted.

Now what was she to do?

EIGHTEEN

NICKY refused to put on his coat. He said, 'But Mummy said we were not to go out today. It's too cold.'

He stood rigidly defying Prissie to attempt to force his arms into the sleeves of his new coat with the velvet collar, that he had had to wear ever since his old one had been mysteriously lost.

Prissie said in a very quiet voice that was somehow more frightening than her cross one, 'It isn't cold now. The sun is almost shining. Come along, Nicky, don't be difficult.'

It took courage to disobey this new white-faced unsmiling Prissie, but not as much as it would have taken to go out into the square where Clementine lay in wait. The thought of her malicious little face caused him to grow more resolutely stubborn.

Sarah, already in her overcoat, danced about saying, 'Come on, Nicky. Come on, Nicky,' impatiently.

Prissie silently held the coat before him, waiting for him to slip his arms in the sleeves. Nicky summoned all his courage, and struck it out of her hands on to the floor.

'I won't go,' he said.

Prissie looked at him thoughtfully for a moment. Then she said quite quietly, 'Very well. You wait here while I get my things on. Perhaps by then you will have changed your mind.'

It had never happened before in broad daylight. But it happened today just as Prissie, wearing her coat and hat and carrying a suitcase, came back. The croaking voice sounded from the wardrobe at the other side of the room.

'Are you being a naughty boy, Nicky? Didn't I tell you

what happens to naughty boys? The dark hole, Nicky. The deep dark hole...' There was a dreadful chuckle. Then, quite brightly and cheerfully, the voice went on, 'Do as Prissie tells you, Nicky, that's a good boy.'

Nicky looked dumbly at Prissie who was standing listening beside him. She nodded in agreement, and helplessly he held out his arms for the coat to be put on.

Almost at once he began to sob.

'Not to Clementine's house! Please, not to Clementine's house.'

Prissie lifted her slender black brows.

'Who is Clementine?' she asked.

Sarah, whose sympathetic nature was always affected by tears, abruptly began to sob in company with Nicky.

'Oh, goodness, you are a fine pair!' Prissie exclaimed. 'We're only going out for some fresh air. Come along, and please don't make so much noise. You'll disturb your mother and you know she will never get better if she's always being disturbed. Down the stairs as quietly as you can.'

In spite of her injunction to hurry, however, Prissie lingered on the stairs, looking at the portraits with a queer expression, almost as if she were going to cry. Then she ran her fingers over the banisters and looking at them said 'Dust!' in a disgusted voice. There were dead flowers drooping in a vase, as if no one cared how they looked. One of Aunt Annabel's cats, a thin tabby with a sad pointed face, ran in front of them. Prissie's gaze flickered from it to the dead flowers and the dust. Then it went again to the portraits. 'Liars!' she said in a clear contemptuous voice, and began to hurry the children down the stairs.

In a few moments they were out of the house and in the misty street. It was not true that the sun was beginning to shine. It was darker than ever, and Nicky was sure that Clementine was lurking behind one of the trees, although he could not see her. He was inordinately thankful when Prissie unexpectedly hailed a taxi, and pushed the two of them into it, following herself with her suitcase. At least they were safe for a while in a taxi.

But it had been too much to hope that they would not go to Clementine's house. They arrived there all too soon. But still blessedly there was no sign of Clementine. Prissie hustled them up the steep narrow stairs, and into a room that had almost no furniture in it, and was very cold. She threw off her coat and scarf, leaving them lying across a chair, and said:

'Stay here until I come back. And try not to make a noise.'

Then she went out, shutting the door, and making it click. After a moment Nicky went cautiously forward and turned the knob. It wouldn't open the door, and he knew that what he had suspected was true. The click had been the key turned in the lock. He and Sarah were in prison.

Sarah, after pottering about inquisitively, looked distressed. Her lip began to tremble.

'Go home!' she whimpered.

'We can't. We're in prison,' Nicky told her. 'The door's locked.'

Sarah's mouth hung open. She sensed both Nicky's fear and the strangeness of the room. She began to sob.

Nicky badly wanted to sob, too, but he knew that that would bring either Prissie, or, worse still, Clementine. Valiantly he tried to comfort Sarah.

'Don't cry,' he said. 'Look, I'll do you my tricks.' He whipped the coloured silk handkerchiefs from his pocket and began sliding them through his fingers. Gratifyingly, Sarah did stop sobbing to watch. Suddenly she saw the scarf Prissie had flung on the chair. It was a brilliant red one with a design of tiny white leaves. She pounced on it, and began to clumsily imitate Nicky, saying, 'Look! Me, too!'

But Nicky momentarily forgot his tricks in looking at the scarf. He had seen it before somewhere and it had frightened him. Where?

After Prissie had left her with Fergus's message Brigit was too forlorn even to weep.

So Fergus's contempt for her family had finally reached her. How could it be otherwise when he chose to give such tragic news as the death of her brother to a comparative stranger.

But of course Prissie was no stranger to him. No, indeed, he counted on Prissie for everything now, the care of his children, the nursing of his poor sick wife, the comfort and pleasure of her company during his short intervals at home.

(Oh, Fergus, my darling, couldn't you have been patient a little longer, to see if I would get well? Or even if I were well, would you still have wanted Prissie? You brought her home that day, flaunting her like a carnation in your button-hole...)

Aunt Annabel was bending over her, stroking her brow.

'Don't grieve, dear. You know Guy wouldn't want you to. After all, he chose this way——' Her voice quivered piteously. 'Look, I've brought you a little hot milk. I'm having some, too. Drink it up now, that's a good girl.'

Like a child, Brigit drank from the glass held to her lips. When she had finished Aunt Annabel gave a satisfied sigh.

'That's right, dear. There was a sedative in that. Now you will get some rest.'

Brigit started up wildly.

'But I don't want rest! Guy's dead, and there's that horrible man making threats about the children, and Nicky says Clementine is out there in the square—do look, please, Aunt Annabel—and I don't believe I'm ever going to walk again, and—and Fergus——' Brigit's voice died away in stifled sobs.

Aunt Annabel, peering through the window, said, 'I can't see anything for mist. Oh, there's a man sweeping up leaves. That's all, dear. Just a man with a barrow. So you can sleep in peace.'

'But I don't want to sleep!' Brigit protested. Nevertheless, already Aunt Annabel seemed a vague shape, with her wild white locks, like a kindly witch, and the pillow was deep, deep...

She dreamed that she was walking. It was cold and misty, and through the mist she kept seeing the lighted shop windows, little square glowing caverns of light and brilliance. Here were jewels, in all the colours of the rainbow, here were hats with pink roses as large as cabbages, here were shoes studded with brilliants, here laces and ribbons and ballerina skirts with frothing frills. One could warm one's hands at the glow of the windows. But if one could walk into the inviting doorways of the shops it would be better still. If only one's legs would move. They were so heavy, so slow, as if they were dragging through thick mud...

Brigit opened her eyes slowly to find the bedclothing disarranged and the quilt slipped to the floor. Also, her legs were aching and tingling.

Instantly, realizing what had happened, she was wide awake. In her dream she had walked, and her legs, obeying the fantasy in her mind, had disturbed the bedclothing. They had moved again!

Cautiously she tested them. They were heavy and tired, but they did move a little, didn't they? Excitedly she rang the bell and waited impatiently for someone to answer it.

It was Mrs Hatchett who came and stood within the door, rotund and comfortable.

'Can I get you anything, madam?'

'I want you to help me get out of bed,' Brigit said excitedly. 'I can walk really. I'll show you.'

Mrs Hatchett shook her head.

'Now, now, madam! Do you think you should be trying to get out of bed?'

'Of course. I've been out. I was out the other day, only no one would believe me. If you won't help me, ask my aunt to come.'

'She's lying down with a bad head, madam. And Prissie took the children out a couple of hours ago, so there's no one else to help you. If you really insist, madam, but I'm sure I don't think——'

Brigit, however, was no longer listening to Mrs Hatchett's qualms. An icy terror had seized her.

'Mrs Hatchett, what did you say about Prissie and the children? I told them not to go out. Surely she hasn't disobeyed me!'

'Well, I saw them going, madam. Nicky in his new coat, bless his heart. I thought they'd have been back by now. It's getting dark.'

'Mrs Hatchett!' Brigit was sitting up, clinging to the bedpost. 'Help me, please! Now I've got to walk somehow. Please! Because I think my children are in danger. Deadly danger! Oh, God, help me quickly. Let me get to them before anything happens.'

But it was no use. She could only stand and collapse. Again and again, with Mrs Hatchett patiently holding her upright, she tried to walk. Once she took three steps. Mrs Hatchett exclaimed in wonder and delight. 'Well now, love, so you could do it all the time. And none of us would believe you. Well now, isn't this going to be good news for your husband. Easy now. Take it quietly.'

But again her legs, weak and trembling, collapsed ignominiously beneath her. She was too anxious. The mist outside seemed to keep coming into the room, and swirling in it were shapes and sounds, the funny man Sarah had seen in the square (had he a white-and-black look?), the croaking voice from the chimney saying, *'I am you and you are me,'* and Prissie's small white three-cornered face—now she knew what it made her think of, that other face that had leaned over her in the house in Hammersmith, the face that was Prissie and yet not Prissie, the face with the brilliant taunting eyes and lank long black hair . . .

And then, strangest of all, Fergus's face swam before her. It was thin and tired, and yet it seemed to be alight with joy.

'Why, Biddy darling, you're walking!'

Why should he look so pleased that she was walking? It was much too late to be pleased. Prissie had thieved all the pleasure for herself. House, portraits, works of art, children, husband, all were Prissie's . . .

Someone was shouting something at her, trying to rouse her.

'Brigit, where did you go that day? Tell me!' Momentarily Fergus's voice was clear and urgent in her ears.

'But you wouldn't believe me,' she said in a drugged way.

'Never mind whether I believed you or not. Where did you go?'

'15 Pelham Road, Hammersmith,' she said in her far-off voice. 'Why do you want to go there?'

'Because I think Prissie might be there.'

Oh—Prissie. Always Prissie. Now she could not arouse herself to say anything more at all.

NINETEEN

OUTSIDE the door Nicky could hear the voices, Prissie's and the man's. Prissie was saying in a low angry voice:

'I tell you there was nothing between Fergus and me. I hate him! I hate him as much as I hate her. Why would I do as you told me and bring the children here if I was in love with him?'

'You wouldn't do that at first.'

'Because I was angry with you then. Guy shouldn't have died. That was your fault. You killed him.'

'He killed himself.' The man's voice was contemptuous. 'He had no guts.'

'And no money either!' Prissie began to laugh in a high-pitched way. 'The famous Templar family is bankrupt. Isn't it a joke?'

'I don't believe it,' the man said harshly.

'I'm afraid it's true. The great and mighty Saunders wouldn't shed tears over anything but lack of money.'

'It can't be true.' The man's voice had a desperate note. 'We've got the kids, haven't we? They'll pay for them.'

'With what?' Prissie asked wearily. 'Fake gold plate? I tell you I brought them here to satisfy you, and to give her the fright of her life, but after that——'

'You don't really intend to give them up. Do you?' The man's voice was both wheedling and cunning.

'Why should I? They should be mine!'

'Because they are Templars or the children of that good-looking airman?'

Prissie's voice broke on an angry sob. 'Shut up, will you? You've got them here, haven't you? That's what you wanted. You say you can get blood out of a stone. Well, try.'

'They'll find the money somewhere, for the kids,' the man said confidently.

But now Prissie was pleading with him. 'No, Jacques. Just let me take them away somewhere quietly. They should be mine. I feel as if they are. And Clementine would like it. Anyway, it's too dangerous to do anything more. Because Fergus has that letter of mine. He'll have guessed everything.'

'What do you mean?' The man's voice was alarmed.

'He stole it out of my locket—I don't know when.'

'You little fool! What did you want to carry it about with you for?'

'Because I liked having it. I liked making up stories about it. And don't you dare call me a fool! It's you who is a fool standing there wasting time talking when we should be arranging to get away. How safe do you think we are here, now she's been to this house? It'll only be until Fergus gets home and then she'll tell him——'

But at that point Nicky could contain himself no longer. Oblivious of the fact of how he frightened Sarah he began banging on the door and screaming.

'Let me out!' he called. 'Let me out! Let me out!' Then all at once he was silent, because his voice had been so much the echo of another voice, that of Nurse Ellen from the bottom of the dark hole.

But there was no hole here. It was all right! It was all right!

The door opened abruptly, and Prissie, and the small dark man with the pale face stood there.

Prissie said sharply. 'Nicky, what a noise to make. Now you've made Sarah cry, too. There's nothing to cry about. We're going for a nice ride on a train. Clementine is coming, too. I'll call her and she can come and play with you until we're ready.'

Nicky shrank back, the tears growing cold on his cheeks.

'Not Clementine!' he whispered. 'No! Please!'

'Why, how silly you are, Nicky. You must grow to love Clementine.'

Frantically Nicky thought of some way to delay this final catastrophe. His eyes chanced to rest on Prissie's locket, and he exclaimed:

'Daddy hasn't got your letter at all. I have.'

Prissie looked puzzled. 'What letter?'

'The one out of your locket. I took it and tore it up.'

Prissie's face grew still. She sank into a chair.

'Nicky! Are you telling the truth?'

Nicky nodded, frightened now, his bravado deserting him.

'I tore it into little bits. You made me sweep it up.'

'Then Fergus—doesn't know—after all.' Her voice was halting, desolate. 'I needn't have run away. I could have made him—love me——' Suddenly she sprang up, galvanized into action. 'Oh, I'm going back. He won't be home yet. Come, children, get your coats on——'

But the man's hand was gripping her wrist. His face was dark, threatening, sinister.

'Not so fast, my darling. We'll talk this over first. Shut the kids in and come downstairs.'

Before he could shut the door, however, there were racing footsteps on the stairs, a flash of tartan skirt and two thin black plaits. And there was Clementine, her triangular face full of evil glee.

'Oh, goody, I've come to play with Nicky. Aren't you pleased to see me, Nicky? Aren't you pleased?'

She was so quick, he could never escape her. Before he could even put his arms behind his back her cruel fingers had seized and pinched.

He couldn't help it. All his self-control deserted him. He shut his eyes and opened his mouth and gave a long high-pitched scream. It came to an end only for want of breath, and as its sound died from his ears he heard his father saying:

'Good heavens, Nicky, are you being murdered?'

He opened his eyes and thought it was a dream. But Sarah was rushing forward crying delightedly, 'Daddy! Daddy!' and there, surely enough, was the tall beloved form of his father, smiling reassuringly, although his blue eyes glinted with something that was not laughter.

He swung Sarah into his arms and took Nicky's hand. Then he said pleasantly:

'No one heard my knock so I just came up. I thought it sounded like trouble. Well, Prissie, so this is your aunt.'

He turned with mock politeness to the dark man, whose face had gone thin and bitter and uneasy. Prissie, the colour suddenly flaming in her cheeks, said quickly:

'This is my husband, Jacques Clare.'

Fergus gave a slight bow, but he did not hold out his hand. His eyes turned to the child with the skinny plaits and glittering black eyes and little tight malicious mouth.

'And this—allow me to guess—is Clementine?'

'My daughter,' said Prissie, putting her arm possessively round the child.

'Well, well,' said Fergus. 'The little girl who likes toads. I think, Nicky, you might have overlooked the fact that she is, presumably, a lady, and fought her. One should be taught manners young.' He turned to Prissie, still with that glint in his eye. 'I suppose you are aware, Prissie, that my wife is extremely worried about the children, especially when she asked you not to take them out. Apparently there have been mysterious threats over the telephone——'

'They were quite safe here,' Prissie broke in swiftly. 'Weren't they, Jacques? That's why I brought them.'

'Quite safe,' Jacques said suavely. 'And Clementine likes someone to play with.'

'And things, too, apparently,' Fergus said, picking up the Dresden statuette from the mantelpiece.

'I only borrowed it!' Prissie said, the colour high in her cheeks again. 'You had so many beautiful things, and Clementine——'

'Had a right to some,' said Fergus softly.

'My wife has this love for beautiful things,' the man said, suddenly obsequious. 'She did only borrow that piece for Clementine to see. Clementine hasn't had much opportunity——'

Fergus again interrupted in his pleasant voice, 'But she would have been able to get some of her own when all those letters had brought in some money.'

'Letters?' said the man in bewilderment.

'Come now, Mr Clare, don't try to be innocent. Do you deny writing blackmail letters consistently for the last week?'

'Oh, he never did anything like that!' Prissie exclaimed in a shocked voice. 'Oh, no, Fergus. I admit I borrowed the statuette, and one or two of the children's toys—they had so many—and even Nicky's old coat because he was getting a new one, and it would lengthen beautifully for Clementine. You can't blame me for wanting things for my daughter. But we did nothing else, Fergus. Nothing criminal.'

Fergus's golden eyebrows were a bland curve over his eyes. He still spoke pleasantly, though now Nicky sensed the scarcely-controlled anger beneath his politeness.

'You didn't by any chance plan to get into my house to create all the mischief you could? You didn't deliberately cause my wife to have an accident——'

Prissie sprang forward, laying her hands on Fergus's arm. Her eyes were full of shocked denial.

'Oh, Fergus! How can you believe such an awful thing!'

'You didn't make love to Guy, believing all the time that he was your legitimate brother?'

Nicky was aware of Prissie shaking her head, her face full of confusion and anger and distress. But he could concentrate no longer on Prissie's feelings for there was something in his pocket he had to show his father. It was tangled up with the coloured silk handkerchiefs. He tugged at it intently.

'You can't prove any of these outrageous accusations,' the dark-haired man was saying angrily to Fergus.

But Nicky had the thing free. He shook it out triumphantly. Now he was no longer afraid of witch dolls in cupboards or croaking voices in the night, or Clementine's malicious vengeance on him.

'Look, daddy!' he cried. 'This is the scarf that was on the stick. I saw it. Prissie had it. She was coming from behind the fence after mummy had fallen off Polly. I wanted her to play a game with it, but she wouldn't. She threw the stick away.'

'It's a lie!' Prissie was saying thickly. 'It's another of that child's monstrous lies.'

For one moment Fergus looked at her thoughtfully. It was quite extraordinary, but in that moment Prissie's youthful attractive animated face had become that of someone else. In its pinched cruel cold anger and craftiness, it was the feminine counterpart of the painted face of pirate Phillip Templar that hung on the staircase in the house in Montpelier Square.

Whatever lies her tongue might still be impelled to tell, her face at last spoke the truth.

Fergus went to the door and beckoned to someone downstairs.

'Come up, officer,' he said. 'I think you'll get a statement now.'

TWENTY

It was the voice from the chimney and the voice Nicky said he had heard in the night from the wardrobe that still puzzled Brigit. When she thought of it, with its sinister threat, she was still aware of that cold fear inside herself.

'How could that have been Prissie or this mysterious husband of hers?' she asked.

Fergus was sitting on the bed holding her hand. On the rug beside the leaping fire were the children, bathed and in their dressing-gowns, listening to the low murmur of Aunt Annabel's voice as she told them once again the simple story of the kittens who lost their mittens. Brigit wanted them there as long as possible. For this way all her family was round her, and she felt secure at last.

'It was Prissie who did that,' said Fergus. 'Her husband is a conjurer and ventriloquist. Naturally he taught a clever little thing like Prissie some of his tricks. She became remarkably adept at ventriloquism, as you and Nicky can now testify. It was a useful trick. It frightened you into thinking you were going to be a permanent cripple, which was what she wanted, and it kept Nicky quiet about things that she didn't want mentioned. The existence of Clementine, for instance. It pleased her to give her own child outings with yours, and to buy things for her, even to steal from Nicky and Sarah for her. But of course it wouldn't do for the children to talk. Sarah was too small, but Nicky, with his observant nature, was a constant threat. So when she found he was a nervous child she had a perfect way to silence him.'

'The children's voices at the house that day?' Brigit said.

'That was Clementine's birthday party. Another bit of audacity on Prissie's part. Both Nicky and Sarah were there. Jacques did conjuring tricks, and even began to teach Nicky the one with the handkerchiefs. When you went there and collapsed she and Jacques took you home in a taxi, were able to smuggle you in unnoticed, undressed you, and then cleverly left you lying on the floor so that when you inevitably told your story everyone would think it was a delusion you had, following shock from your fall out of bed. It worked very well. Too well.

'Nurse Ellen's fall, also, was engineered. Prissie had discovered the rotting board in the wardrobe and the deep drop. Instead of reporting it she decided it might be useful one day. As it was the day Nurse Ellen proposed to find out the truth about Clementine. She purposely hung the children's coats at the back of the wardrobe so that Nurse Ellen, being heavy, would step right inside, and of course the floor would collapse. She swears she didn't mean to leave Nurse Ellen down there to die, but just long enough to give her a good fright. In the same way she says she only pretended to kidnap the children to give you a fright.'

'But why did she hate me so much?' Brigit asked in bewilderment. 'Was it just jealousy? Oh, I know she had fallen in love with you, but surely this extreme vindictiveness couldn't have been just from jealousy?'

'And that,' said Fergus, 'is the germ of the story. Darling, this is going to be rather a shock for you.'

Brigit moved her legs slightly, feeling with satisfaction their obedience, and relaxed happily.

'Nothing can shock me now,' she murmured.

'Not even being told that your whole life has been a mistake? That you shouldn't have been brought up in luxury at all? That you should have been a penniless orphan fighting your own way, relying on the kindness of an old nurse who was no relation at all to see that you were clothed and fed.'

'That's Prissie's story!' Brigit ejaculated.

'Precisely.'

'I am you and you are me,' Brigit said slowly. 'That's what the voice used to say. But, Fergus, tell me, what is this? Am I Prissie?'

'Thank God, no. Prissie is the daughter of the woman you thought your mother, Marion Templar, and her husband, Gilbert Fulton. The sister of Guy, whom she let kiss and make love to her, for the purpose of worming out of him shameful secrets about the Templar family, so that her husband could practise the pleasant art of blackmail.'

'Fergus, stop this! Tell me simply the truth!'

'The truth,' said Fergus, 'unfortunately can't be proved. All Prissie had was a letter written by her old nurse on her deathbed, confessing to a mix-up of babies the night that you and Prissie were born in the same nursing-home. Two women had baby girls within an hour of one another, one woman was Marion Fulton, a daughter of the famous and wealthy Templar family, the other was a little ballet dancer whose husband was dead, and who herself died on giving birth to her baby.'

'She was my mother!' Brigit whispered intuitively. 'I know. Because Sarah dances all the time.'

'And Prissie,' said Fergus, 'if you have noticed, is remarkably like one or two of the portraits on the stairs.'

Brigit was breathing quickly, aware of a wonderful lightness of spirit, as if she had been released from something overpowering.

'But how did all this happen?'

'That, we have to take the old nurse's word for. She says that while caring for the newly-born Templar baby she dropped it. It wasn't a serious fall, but the head was bruised and bleeding. She panicked. How could she take an injured child into that beautiful autocratic frightening girl? So, on the impulse of the moment, she took in the perfect child, the baby of the dead ballet dancer. And in that moment you became Brigit Templar, and Prissie, with all the Templar greed and ruthlessness, became you. The nurse, suffering from conscience, adopted Prissie and brought her up, and until recently Prissie genuinely thought she was her aunt.'

Fergus stopped a moment to consider Brigit.

'So you see, my darling, how it hasn't been easy for either of you, born out of your true environments.'

'Fergus, do you realize!' Brigit was crying with joy. 'Oh, do you realize I'm not a Templar after all. Nicky and Sarah aren't Templars. We're nice people. Oh, Fergus!'

'It didn't matter,' said Fergus. 'I loved you either way. You know that, my little silly. And if you thought I was flirting with Prissie it was merely that I was playing the game she had played with Guy, getting close to her to find out her secrets.'

'She said everyone had a secret. Fergus, Guy knew?'

'Guy knew. He found that he had fallen in love with his own sister. Apparently Nicky had taken the letter out of Prissie's locket, and shown it to Guy, quite innocently. He just never got over the shock, poor devil.'

Brigit reflected sombrely.

'But why didn't Prissie tell us all this secret? Why work in such an underhand way?'

'Because she had no way of proving it. She had sense enough to know that an hysterical letter from an old dying woman wouldn't stand up in any court of law. So she decided that what you had was legitimately hers and she would take it from you, if she could. At that time she was genuinely an air hostess, but she deliberately got transferred to the same air line as me, and I, heaven forgive me, played into her hands right away by falling for her hints about wanting a quiet home and children to care for. So she got into our house and began playing her pranks, and her devious husband, aiding and abetting her, thought out new variations on the theme of burglary and blackmailing. Prissie discovered Uncle Saunders's hiding place for the gold angel accidentally when searching for the housekeeping money. Of course she passed that information to her husband. Guy's trouble she deduced from finding newspaper clippings about the accident in his room, and remembering the fuss over the dented mudguard on the car the day they came down to our place.'

'The husband might have been a Templar, too,' Brigit murmured. 'Oh, Fergus, thank heaven I'm free from that tainted blood. I owe that much to Prissie. I should be grateful. What will happen to her?'

'She and her husband will serve a prison sentence. Then they'll come out and think up other easy ways to make money. Having the Templar ingenuity—but that reminds me, the ingenuity has forsaken poor old Uncle Saunders. He's a tamed lion, adding up his losses. What shall we do with him and Aunt Annabel?'

'Give them a home with us, of course,' said Brigit unhesitatingly. 'And see that Aunt Annabel doesn't get into trouble with the cats' club.'

Then Fergus's arms went round her in that old close passionate way for which she had longed.

'That remark wouldn't represent proof in a court of law, but it's indisputable proof to me. You're no Templar!' After a moment he said, 'What are you thinking, my darling?'

Brigit didn't answer. She was lost in a happy dream about the girl who had loved to dance, the fair-haired girl, gentle and full of laughter, who had been her mother.

There were suddenly shrieks of laughter from the hearth-rug as the black kitten pounced after Aunt Annabel's ball of wool.

'And so that's what happened to those naughty kittens,' finished Aunt Annabel placidly. 'Brigit, dear, will there be homeless and starving cats in the country?'

'Not where we live, Aunt Annabel.'

Aunt Annabel sighed with pleasure, her wispy hair taking on the shine of a halo in the firelight.

'It must be heaven.'

Fergus looked into Brigit's eyes.

'It is heaven,' he said.

WAITING FOR WILLA

Reality proves stranger than fiction as a girl novelist embarks on adventure in Sweden

The letter was postmarked Stockholm. Just a pleasant little note from Grace's cousin Willa about nothing in particular. Except for the signature—*Wilhelmina.* This had been their childhood code for HELP.

Grace Asherton, attractive young novelist, was not the hysterical type. But from the moment she arrived in Stockholm and discovered her cousin had vanished, she sensed there was more to it than Willa's friends had told her.

Willa had apparently run off to marry someone named Gustav. So like Willa they told her, she is such an impulsive madcap creature. It was a lie and Grace knew it. She began to wait and ask questions. Then one night she decided to masquerade as Willa . . .

'Has both the excitement of a thriller and the interest of well-developed characters'

The Scotsman

'No one can suggest an eerie atmosphere and the sinister trifle better than Miss Dorothy Eden'

The Guardian

THE VOICE OF THE DOLLS

Dolls that speak with human voices lure Sarah to the brink of death

It was a solitary little girl, mimicking with sinister skill the voices of her dolls, that first lured Sarah into the Foster household.

Intrigued by Jennie's serious nature, she became her governess for the winter and soon found herself inextricably trapped in the stifling atmosphere of intrigue and suspicion that surrounded the family in the big Kensington house—a house already witness to one 'accidental' death, which left lingering fears and doubts among its remaining members.

But Sarah, not knowing who to trust and suppressing her mounting terror, is forced to follow the issue through to its sinister conclusion.